CZECH MATE

CZECH MATE

A Max Rydal Mystery

Elizabeth Darrell

Severn House Large Print
London & New York

This first large print edition published 2008
in Great Britain and the USA by
SEVERN HOUSE PUBLISHERS of
9-15 High Street, Sutton, Surrey, SM1 1DF.
First world regular print edition published 2007 by
Severn House Publishers, London and New York.

Copyright © 2007 by E. D. Books.

British Library Cataloguing in Publication Data

Darrell, Elizabeth
    Czech mate. - Large print ed. - (A Max Rydal mystery) (A
    Severn House British mystery)
    1. Great Britain. Army. Corps of Royal Military Police -
    Fiction 2. Great Britain. Ministry of Defence - Officials
    and employees - Fiction 3. Rydal, Max (Fictitious
    character) - Fiction 4. Detective and mystery stories
    5. Large type books
    I. Title
    823.9'14[F]

    ISBN-13: 978-0-7278-7725-3

Except where actual historical events and characters are being described
for the storyline of this novel, all situations in this publication are
fictitious and any resemblance to living persons is purely coincidental.

Printed and bound in Great Britain by
MPG Books Ltd, Bodmin, Cornwall.

Acknowledgements

My warm thanks to Colonel Stephen Boyd, Commandant of the Defence College of Police and Guarding, and members of his staff, in particular Major M. R. Downie, who generously gave me their professional advice and answered my many questions. Any errors on procedures are mine alone. I plead guilty in expectation of receiving a more lenient sentence!

ED

One

Glitzy, colourful department stores seething with shoppers clutching gift lists and spending lavishly. Outdoor markets tempting families and young people with festive decorations, nativity scenes, blown-glass baubles, candles, carved wood nutcrackers, gingerbread men, hot chestnuts or potato skins, and mugs of steaming punch. Coloured lanterns bobbing in the breeze around the skating-rink where the young and not-so-young circle to the music of a hurdy-gurdy. The run up to Christmas in Germany.

At the British base fifteen kilometres from the town the usual round of events was underway. Dinner parties, cocktails, discos, knockout darts and football matches; a 'Mastermind' quiz for the more intellectual; bring-and-buy sales of home-made cakes, puddings, pies and mincemeat; bingo and tombola; fancy-dress parties for the children of the two regiments and several small detachments stationed there.

Kevin McRitchie had not wanted to attend the party. Even less had he wanted to wear fancy dress. At thirteen he regarded himself

7

too old for this kind of stupidity, although one or two others of his age were there. His birthday five days ago had made him a teenager, and his sights were set on strobe lights, amplifiers, eager fans and alcopops. He was determined to make a breakthrough by the end of the year and approach a recording company.

He was only there at the Recreation Centre because his father had insisted that he chaperone his young sisters. The final straw had been when Shona and Julie fought like cat and dog because each had suddenly wanted to wear the Sugar Plum Fairy costume. Their father had made them toss for it and promised the loser a present to compensate. Shona was flaunting her success and Julie, in a chicken outfit, was behaving abominably. Kevin felt like shaking them both, but that would be reported and lead to a thump around the ear.

He escaped for a while to have a surreptitious cigarette. He was working up to smoking pot as soon as he got the chance. That would be really cool. The first floor toilets were empty which suited him fine. Opening a small ventilator he lit up, shivering from the draught and from the gratification of defying his father's strict rules. Snowflakes were now drifting past the window; large, serious ones. The kind that settled and stayed. If they continued all night his father would insist on family fun with the girls, which would leave him alone in the house tomorrow. Hooray!

The smoke in his throat set him coughing, which meant he did not hear the stealthy footfall behind him. The blow to his head knocked him to the floor.

At the furthest boundary, well away from the beating heart of the military establishment, a number of men and women in coveralls were trying to create order from chaos. 26 Section Special Investigation Branch, Royal Military Police, was moving into new headquarters; namely two disused stores blocks renovated and adapted to police requirements. The Redcaps had arrived to find the constructors still working on the toilets and detention rooms, and the heating system not yet up and running. Snow had begun falling, the barometer showed minus six Centigrade, and tempers were getting frayed.

Max Rydal, Officer Commanding but not a man to use rank to avoid hard work, was hefting technical equipment and boxed documents from trucks to offices with his personnel. The bitter wind made minus six seem more like minus sixteen, but there was scant relief within the building. The un-heated interior exuded the damp chill of new bricks and mortar, barely dried paint and the fustiness of standard-issue carpeting that had been stored for a long period.

The convoy of trucks and assorted smaller

vehicles had set out at first light and it was now late evening. Portaloos and a drinks machine had been set up for them and Max had twice sent his staff in batches for hot meals, but he knew he must now call a halt. Boxes were being dropped, people were stumbling into items left carelessly on the floor, the F-word was echoing from the stark walls. Time to go home.

Max sighed with weariness. Home for them all was also new and strewn with boxes and holdalls. The unmarried ones had been given rooms in accommodation blocks on the base, where they knew from experience they would be cold-shouldered, resented and regarded with hostility by those around them. The Royal Military Police was the most unloved corps in the British Army until, of course, a lost child was returned to distraught parents, a rapist was caught and punished, an abused wife was rescued from a violent husband, or an advancing armoured column in a war zone used the safe route earlier reconnoitred and cleared of hazards by the RMP. Then, the Redcaps were the heroes of the day.

No married quarters being presently available, the new arrivals were being temporarily housed on a small estate several kilometres from the main gate. The German residents did not welcome British soldiers and their families any more than the British wanted to live cheek by jowl with them. It was supposed to be a short-term arrangement, but no one believed the rumour that 26 Section would eventually have its own mess and living quarters. The latest cuts in defence spending made nonsense of that hope. Max had had no option but to secure a room in the nearest Officers' Mess to the new headquarters. It was an arrangement he was unhappy with. Living amid the members of a large regiment was akin to being a cuckoo in someone's nest. Add the fact that he was generally regarded as a policeman, who knew little about *real* soldiering, and the cuckoo theory was greatly strengthened.

Leaving his office and locking the door behind him, Max set about sending everyone off into the snowy night with thanks for their efforts and offering them a late start in the morning. Then he crossed to his second in command, Sergeant-Major Black, who was checking the internal security before they left.

'Any word from Klaus Krenkel on our missing truck, Tom?'

'Zilch. It's Saturday night. All his guys are out patrolling the town, covering the trouble spots. In their view this is our baby.'

'It is, of course, but a little cooperation wouldn't hurt when it's pretty obvious the truck has been hijacked by locals who know how to shift stuff faster than it can be traced.'

'Sure it has. If Treeves was in cahoots with

11

some wheeler-dealer he'd hide his payout where he could fetch it later, concoct some lie about being jumped while checking a rattle in the engine, and make bloody certain we'd find him swiftly.'

'He'd also have gone all out to ensure he was the last in the convoy. The other drivers insist it was the luck of the draw. No, I don't believe this was an inside job. It's been obvious for some weeks we were preparing to move out lock, stock and barrel. The local sharp boys spotted that and awaited their chance. Our equipment could be on sale in Holland tomorrow.'

Tom perched on the edge of a desk, arms folded. 'They'd have to swap vehicles before the border. That leaves a vast area to search for Treeves and the truck, possibly no longer together. Hicks and Styles drove back over the first part of our route; Stubble and Meacher took the rest. Found no sign of a truck heading off the road into the trees. You know those narrow tracks running through the forest, just wide enough for a tractor? Could conceivably get a truck far enough along one to conceal it.'

'We'll probably have to write off the equipment, maybe the truck, but Treeves' fate has to be our priority. I doubt he's been killed, but he could die of hypothermia if they've left him badly disabled in an isolated spot.'

'He'll make every effort to hole up somewhere to gain protection from the cold,' Tom reasoned. 'I'll send fresh patrols out at first light, but if it snows all night any tracks will be totally obscured.'

'I'll get a helicopter up as soon as the weather clears,' said Max with a nod. 'If he can, Treeves will endeavour to light a fire. The pilot might not be able to spot a truck in the trees, but he'd see smoke.' He headed for the door. 'Come on. It's so bloody cold in here, if we stay much longer I'll take apart some of these chairs and light a fire myself.'

Tom followed, taking his car keys from his pocket. 'Nora called me ten minutes ago to say she has a hot meal waiting. How about you?'

'Ham rolls and a cup of soup in my room. In the old days when mess staff were soldiers it was possible to book a late dinner. Now the catering is done by civilians they pack up on the dot.'

Tom entered the security code now they were outside. 'You should find someone who'll cook for you whatever time you get in.'

'I did,' came the brief reply.

Knowing he was treading on eggshells, Tom said, 'After three years it's time to move on, isn't it?'

'My prime concern is to get this place organized and operational.' Max headed for his car. 'Buzz me if there should be news of Treeves. Goodnight, Tom.'

'Goodnight, sir.'

Tom headed across the base to the main gate and a small house a short distance beyond it. Nora and the girls had moved in a month ago while he had been engaged in the gargantuan task of packing up a well-established headquarters and continuing to investigate several cases at a critical stage. Each time they had to move house Tom gave thanks for a wife who could make what could be a traumatic period into one of relative ease. Their daughters Maggie, Gina and Beth were growing up fast and could be a handful, but Nora still held their respect and friendship so managed to keep control.

Nora was also adept at making bridal and evening gowns of the most intricate design – a sideline she enjoyed immensely. The house was frequently decked with satin, lace and tiny handcrafted rosebuds. The girls revelled in it. Tom would have welcomed some torn shorts, rugby shirts and studded boots around the place to offset the female predominance.

Being the only male in a house with four women sometimes drove him to his private alcove where he kept his collection of model steam engines. At present, they would still be in their boxes: Nora refused to handle them. He would have to find the best place in this new house to display them; a bolt-hole for when giggles and gushing over weird-looking youths or stick-thin models became too much for him.

Fat chance of sorting out his engines yet! Not when the last truck in their convoy had failed to arrive. It was a damnable problem at a time like this. Apart from the driver's possible fate, the loss of expensive technical equipment could seriously hinder their on-going cases. Christmas festivities were certain to breed trouble – they always had in the past – and with workmen still completing the construction of detention cells and interview rooms there would be little hope of spending much time at home until the new year.

Welcome warmth greeted him on entering a house he had so far only inhabited during a snatched weekend fourteen days ago. A lump formed in his throat on seeing the difference Nora had wrought in that time. She was one in a million.

'Hi, stranger,' she greeted, coming from the sitting-room. 'Good thing I got rid of lover boy ten minutes ago.' Pulling gently from his fierce embrace, she smiled up at him. 'I think I'll give him the push. You're far better at the rough stuff.'

He kissed her again. 'God, I've missed you. I just told Max three years are long enough to grieve, but I know I'd never stop if I ever lost you.'

'They were only together two years, Tom, and Susan really had got herself a lover,' she pointed out. Linking her arm through his she led him towards the kitchen. 'When you grow maudlin it's because you're hungry.

Eat first, shower later. There's stew with dumplings and a plum tart.'

'Gee, the woman cooks as well as turning basic rented houses into homes,' he joked in an effort to lighten up as he washed his hands at the sink, then flopped on a chair before the table. 'It's amazingly quiet. Where's the brood?'

'At a fancy-dress party.'

'Already? They've only been here four weeks.'

Nora ladled stew on two plates and added vegetables. 'Our girls have had to be able to adjust quickly, you know that. The party's for all the younger kids on the base. The teens get a disco next Saturday.' She sat opposite him and poured wine. 'I made very basic outfits for them. Maggie's gone as a shepherdess, Gina as a ghost and Beth wanted to be a Roman centurion.'

Tom grinned, already relaxing. 'Are there any sheets left on the beds?'

Before she could reply, his mobile rang. He reached for it hoping there was news that Treeves had turned up in a reasonable state.

'Dad, come at once!' The voice of their eldest daughter held a touch of hysteria. 'Kevin McRitchie's been found in the toilet with his head covered in blood. They've sent for an ambulance, but we need *you*. He's been murdered!'

When Tom and Nora arrived at the Recreation Centre there was mini chaos.

Parents were driving in from parties, restaurants, street markets or their own fireside to comfort their children. They were being checked by a brawny military policeman by the double doors, where an ambulance was drawn up. Several Redcaps were searching the immediate surrounding area with flashlights.

Leaving Nora to find their girls, Tom mounted the stairs leading to the toilets. The narrow space between cubicles and urinals was crowded. Two paramedics and the Duty Medical Officer squatted beside a small figure on the tiled floor. Behind them an RMP sergeant stood observing the scene. In the corridor were two men Tom knew: Padre Robinson and Sergeant-Major Fellowes. They were talking quietly to a stocky, black-haired man and a woman in tears. Presumably, the McRitchie parents.

The hovering odours of disinfectant, urine and stale vomit added further unpleasantness to the bizarre sight of a lad dressed as a knight in black armour sprawling beneath the urinals, with a bloodied head. Tom crossed to the police sergeant whom he knew well.

'My eldest called me on her mobile. Said a boy had been killed. Is he dead, George?'

'No, sir, but he has serious head wounds. The lads who found him were shocked by all the blood and ran down to Sar'nt-Major Fellowes – he's one of the party organizers –

crying out that Kevin had been murdered. Mr Fellowes came up here, sussed out the truth and called an ambulance, then us. I have men out looking for anyone secretly watching the activity here. Soon as they stabilize the victim he'll be taken to the *Krankenhaus*. Then we can isolate this whole area.'

'You said serious head wounds?'

George Maddox pointed to a small club beside the injured boy. Tom recognized it as the kind usually hanging beside fire alarms with which to smash the glass in an emergency. 'He was coshed with that. It came from this corridor.'

'Taken by an adult rather than another child?'

'Too soon to be certain, sir. Easy enough for a thuggish kid to fell a small boy like the victim, even one in this age group.'

Tom nodded. Viciousness was manifesting in younger and younger children with appalling frequency. 'Any other activities on here tonight?'

'No. That means the bar was closed, which rules out some aggressive, rat-arsed assailant who came up here for a piss. We searched the entire building when we arrived. No one lurking or hiding. We're having to let the kids go home, but we'll take statements from the organizers and helpers tonight. They're waiting in the main hall.'

At that point the paramedics prepared to

18

leave with their stretcher. There was general movement to clear a way for them. It was then that Tom recognized Charles Clarkson, the doctor SIB had crossed swords with on a case back in April. He gave Tom a frowning nod in response to his greeting.

'You're mighty quick off the mark, Mr Black.'

Stiffening at the underlying suggestion that he was some kind of ambulance-chaser, Tom said, 'My three girls are here for the party. The eldest called asking us to collect them. They're upset.'

'Understandable. My boys found Kevin and raised the alarm.' He managed a semi-apologetic smile. 'It looked worse than it is. They all see so much violence on TV, kids see drama everywhere. Goodnight.' He clattered down the stairs leaving the two police officers with raised eyebrows. Clarkson's brusque manner was well known, but he was a first rate doctor.

Sergeant Maddox said, 'I guess we'll be handing this one on to you, sir.'

Tom gave a sour smile. 'A gift to welcome us to our new headquarters.'

Weary and aching after his heavy day he went down to the hall where the party had been held. The floor was strewn with paper plates and cups, coloured streamers, paper hats, squashed biscuits and sponge cake, overturned chairs and burst balloons. Here and there lay a forgotten fairy wand, a space

19

gun, a wooden sword, a paste tiara and one pair of tiny pink ballet shoes.

'*Dad!*' A shepherdess, a ghost and a Roman centurion ran to him, followed by Nora.

'There's nothing to worry about,' he told them comfortingly. 'Kevin has gone to hospital. He's going to be OK.'

Eight-year-old Beth, the most clingy of the trio, buried her face in his waist. 'The Clarkson boys said he was all bloody and *dead*.'

Tom put his arm around her. 'Major Clarkson has just told me Kevin was merely unconscious. He's a doctor, his boys aren't.' Glancing at Maggie, who looked very pale, he said, 'You were right to call me. Well done, sweetheart.'

'Are you going to find out who did it and why?' asked Gina, the practical one.

'Right now I'm going to leave Sergeant Maddox and his men to do the essential work, while I go home and wolf down the lovely dinner I left uneaten on the kitchen table. Come on!'

Nora shepherded the girls to the kitchen for warm drinks while Tom telephoned Max to give him a run-down of the situation. By that time Maggie, Gina and Beth were happy to go to bed. Thinking longingly of his meal and a quiet time with Nora before they went to bed together for the first time in two weeks, Tom kissed his daughters and gave each a reassuring hug.

Beth looked up at him tearfully. 'I wish I'd

never gone to that horrid party.'

'I know, pet, but it's all over now.'

'They were about to start the parade to decide who should win the prizes for the best costumes when those stupid Clarkson boys rushed in and told awful lies. Now I'll never know if I won, will I?'

Tom glanced across at Nora. The resilience of youth!

Max slept badly, then woke initially unable to work out where he was. The clock radio beside the bed showed 06:45. It was still dark outside the window. He sat up and disentangled his legs from the duvet he had grappled with during the night. There had been a double bed in his room at Frau Hahn's rambling house, so the duvet had rarely ended on the floor. Last night he had once even landed there himself. Single beds were not designed for large, restless men like him.

He made a mug of tea when he really wanted coffee, but the tea bags were in sight. The coffee could be anywhere. Sitting in a chair beside the standard table-cum-desk, Max sipped moodily from the mug, regretting the loss of his delightful quarters in a country setting. Living in-mess he found it difficult really to relax, be his own person. He seemed still to be on duty there.

His thoughts moved to professional problems. A stolen truck laden with valuable equipment had to be traced, but the search for the driver had greater priority. He padded to the window to push back the regulation pattern curtains. Snow had banked up during the night and it was still falling. He hoped Treeves was surviving it.

Letting the curtain fall, Max made more tea and drank it while gazing without seeing at the boxes and holdalls surrounding him. His concentration had moved to what Tom Black had reported to him last night. A serious attack on a boy at a Christmas party. Cases concerning minors were invariably tricky. Parents could be defensive, aggressive, outraged during questioning; the kids' testimony was often unreliable due to fear, bravado, insolence or pure drama.

They would all have to be approached today. Being Sunday it would mean tackling them at home. Easier if they were at school. Teachers acted as appropriate and *impartial* adults during questioning. The investigation was likely to run over into tomorrow, however. With Christmas so near and snow on the ground, families could be out shopping or tobogganing today.

The digital figures on his clock now showed 07:30. Would breakfast be available yet on a Sunday? Max's stomach was telling him fuel in the form of hot food was urgently needed, so he showered and dressed warmly for a demanding day. He hoped to God engineers would turn out to get the heating system going in the semi-organized new headquarters.

They had not when Max arrived to find most of his team ready for a briefing, in spite of the lie-in offered last night. Word of the assault on Kevin McRitchie had circulated.

'One of the advantages or disadvantages of living cheek by jowl with our prospective clients,' said Phil Piercey dryly. 'Depends how you view it.'

Max grinned. 'I've a pretty good idea how you view it, Sergeant, and thank you all for sacrificing your extra time in bed. I apologize for the temperature in here. I'll chase up the guys meant to be installing the heating and threaten them with a night in the cells, unless! However, most of you will be out taking statements on the McRitchie case. Those few remaining here to coordinate info on our stolen truck and the fate of its driver will have the sole use of two space heaters I've ordered to be delivered pronto.

'I've been advised that an air search will be mounted as soon as the weather permits, but the Met boys are shaking their heads and muttering so I'm not hopeful. I think we must accept that our equipment is by now irretrievable, so the focus is on tracing Lance-Corporal Treeves. Teams will shortly set out to once more cover the route taken yesterday but, without air reconnaissance, the chances of finding a hidden vehicle, much less its driver, are pretty slim. All that can be done will be done, in conjunction with the *Polizei*, who might have more resources now Saturday night excesses are over.'

Connie Bush, looking as fresh and alert as if she had not toiled so hard yesterday, raised a point. 'We can't completely rule out the possibility that Treeves did a runner with our equipment.'

Tom Black answered in agreement, adding, 'The Dutch police are looking out for him, and we'll bring in Interpol if necessary. Let's turn to this assault on the boy at the party.'

After outlining what he had seen and heard last night, Tom went on to state that he had questioned his own daughters. They had not noticed anything suspicious prior to the attack. No serious aggro between any of the children – particularly the boys – except that Kevin had a bit of a slanging match with his young sisters who were refusing to speak to each other or form partners in the games and competitions.

'Seems the girls squabbled over their costumes before they left for the party and Kevin was annoyed by their behaviour. He also resented having to be there to keep an eye on them because he exceeded the upper age limit by one week. He thought he should instead have been allowed to attend the teens' disco this Saturday.'

'It's a difficult age,' said Heather Johnson,

who had two young brothers.

'I spoke to Sergeant Maddox an hour ago. He promised to send through to us the statements they took last night from the helpers and organizers. He had a very brief word with the parents and was told by Corporal McRitchie that young Kevin is starting to find his feet, answer back, flout the rules. A rebel in the making?

'There are a number of possible motives for an attack of this kind. We have first to whittle down which is the most likely. My eldest girl described Kevin as smaller than many of his classmates, with big eyes more like a girl's. He's middling bright but hopeless at sport. The perfect target for bullies, you'd think, but he holds his own because he's a whizz on the guitar and can strut his stuff like the top pop idols. So Maggie says.' He surveyed the team. 'Input?'

'Macho schoolmate, captain of every sports team and half as big again as our Kev discovers his hot girlfriend prefers a weedy warbler to a beefy scrum half. Giving the opposition a good hiding at a tinies' party would add to his humiliation,' suggested Piercey.

'Wrong kind of weapon for that premise, I'd have thought,' Heather reminded him tartly. 'A classmate is more likely to use a knife or give him a violent kicking.'

Derek Beeny, Piercey's friend and frequent partner, offered another slant. 'A lad like

25

that would catch the eye of paedophiles. The sexy pop performances would rack up the attraction. Maybe he's been propositioned. Several times by the same guy. Frustration could mount to instigate a savage attack. And as Phil said, dealing out the punishment at a party for small kids would add spice to the deed.'

Connie Bush said thoughtfully, 'What if one, or both, of his parents has had a serious set-to with someone on the base? I met Greg McRitchie several years ago when he gave evidence in a case. He's a solidly built, aggressive type you'd think twice about tangling with, so why not get back at him through his puny son? Hit the easier target.'

Olly Simpson elaborated on that. 'It'll be worth looking at the McRitchies' neighbours. If Kevin's a rising pop star and starting to flout the rules, could be he's driving them spare with a surfeit of rock, pop, rap, hip-hop, whatever's his scene. Full blast, hour after hour, antisocial noise can drive the most placid folk to retaliate with aggression.'

Silence fell. Tom broke it. 'I've heard no mention of a deranged intruder.' Still silence. 'OK, it's an outside possibility, but we have to check it out.'

Staff Sergeant Pete Melly volunteered to liaise with George Maddox on that, and Olly Simpson was detailed to chase up anything of relevance on Kevin's musical activity.

Leaving Sergeants Roy Jakes and Bob Prentiss to consolidate the search for Lance-Corporal Treeves, the remainder went about the time-consuming business of tracking down and questioning the children who had attended the party. Bringing up their home addresses on the screen, they swiftly divided the list into areas each would cover and set off in vehicles with chains on the wheels.

Max went first to the local *Krankenhaus* where, according to the early morning report along with copies of last night's statements from George Maddox, Kevin McRitchie was still in intensive care but medically stable. No one was prepared yet to offer an opinion on the effects of the head injury, but that was understandable. The hospital had a good reputation; the staff were renowned for their success rate. The McRitchie boy would have the very best care.

Sunday morning church bells were summoning the faithful along the route, where good Germans were answering the call dressed in padded coats, thick boots and fur hats. People familiar with bitter winter temperatures dressed to combat them. Children in chunky anoraks, woollen hats, scarves, and boots covered in cartoon characters walked sedately hand in hand behind their parents, on their best behaviour.

Max studied them, wondering what it was like to have children. Small offshoots of oneself. He had been tossing that thought around a lot lately. Did it mean he had worked through the grief for his lost son still in Susan's womb in death? Certainly, the invidious doubt about who had actually fathered the boy had been ruthlessly crushed in the past few months. Closure, the Americans called it. What name had they for the curious aftermath?

The hospital was hushed. Many of the departments closed at weekends. Treatment in hiatus? Max's boots left wet prints on the floor of several immaculate corridors. He imagined a plump *Frau* hurrying after him with a mop. A nurse approached and smiled at him. He smiled back, and the thought jumped into his mind that the new location might have some advantages, after all. Only fifteen kilometres from the town where attractive women must abound. And a new year was in sight. Time for a fresh start?

Just inside the IC Wing Max showed his identification to a male nurse who made signs of barring his entry, then asked after Kevin's progress. Satisfactory. The usual hospital language. Given permission to go to the patient, Max walked past beds surrounded by machines, tubes, drips and hoists to reach one in the far corner. A slender brown-haired woman in a crumpled grey and turquoise tracksuit lolled in a chair with her eyes fixed on the small figure whose head was swathed in bandages. She seemed unaware of another presence until Max spoke.

'Mrs McRitchie? Captain Rydal, SIB. We're investigating the attack on your son. I'd like to talk to you about it.'

Dark eyes gazed up at him as if she had not understood his words, so he squatted beside her and tried again.

'Your husband is a serving British soldier, and the attack on Kevin took place on a military base, so the case has to be handled by the Military Police. Could we, perhaps, find the coffee shop and talk there for a short time? Kevin is asleep. He won't miss you, and you look as though some coffee would be welcome.'

Max stood and held out his hand. Still as if in a trance, Mavis McRitchie took it and allowed him to help her from the chair. Even then he had to coax her away from her son. Telling the nurse where she would be if wanted, Max then took her elbow and led her to the lift that would take them to the ground floor coffee shop.

It was not open. At weekends there were no outpatient appointments, and official visiting hours were some time away. The nurse who had smiled at Max passed by in the reverse direction and hesitated before approaching them to say they were much too early for coffee and snacks. Max explained who he was and the situation regarding his companion, who had been all night beside her injured son. Studying Max and apparently liking what she saw, the nurse then said she would take them to the staff canteen and arrange for them to have something to eat and drink without questions asked.

Settled in the corner with large cups of coffee and a plate holding two soft rolls filled with ham and cheese, Max had to remind himself he was on duty and reluctantly parted from the nurse with only a warm smile of thanks. He sat for a while letting Mrs McRitchie nervously sip her hot drink with both hands holding the cup. She ignored the plate he pushed towards her.

'You'll feel better if you eat,' he said quietly. 'Have you been with Kevin from the moment he was brought in?' She nodded. 'How about your husband?'

She shot a curious look across the table at him. 'He had to see to Shona and Julie, of course.'

'Your daughters?' She nodded again. 'I understood a friend was looking after them.'

'Last night, yes. Greg went to collect them and give them their breakfast. He knows what they like to have on Sundays. Porridge, teddy bear biscuits and toasted marshmallows.' She gave a wan smile. 'He said it's important for them to carry on as usual, not to be alarmed by what happened. The way we go on now will make all the difference to how last night affects them in later life. Girls aren't as tough as boys. If a big drama is made of what happened to Kevin fear could lie dormant until they're young women, then come to the surface to make them unstable and neurotic. He won't have their lives blighted by this.'

Max had to struggle not to ask *What about his son's life?*, but he already sensed a possibility not put forward by the team an hour ago. Child abuse was frequently perpetrated by parents. Fathers more often than mothers. He began to probe the family's relationships.

'I believe you and your husband took Kevin and your daughters to the party, telling him he must keep an eye on them until you picked them up at nine thirty.'

'Yes.'

'Then what did you do?'

'We played badminton like every Saturday. Never miss.'

'I see. Keen on the game, are you?'

'Greg is. He's a brilliant player.' Again the wan smile. 'I sometimes make up a set with three other duffers.'

Max was starting to get a picture he had come across more times than he cared to remember. 'So you have a sitter for the girls every Saturday?'

'Oh, no. Greg won't have sitters. You hear dreadful stories about kids being hurt by them; shaken to death when they cry a lot. No, they come to the club with us. To watch Dadda play. They love their dad.' Her fingers aimlessly pushed the plate of rolls about the table, her concentration on it while she spoke. 'Weekends are their special times. Breakfast in bed on Saturday as an advance reward for tidying their room. Then off to town for lunch at a pizza place and to buy their presents.'

She then glanced up at Max. 'Greg likes to supervise how they spend their pocket money. Won't have them buying rubbish. Checks toys to make sure they bear the seal of safety and that they're from reputable European or American manufacturers. Anything made in the Far East is taboo. Well, you hear such awful stories about kids swallowing eyes that fall out of dolls, or being injured by sharp points projecting through soft toys, don't you?'

'It's wise to be careful,' Max agreed. 'So family Saturdays end with badminton. Do the girls play?'

'They're *far* too young,' she said almost admonishingly. 'Do you know it's easier to injure yourself during games and sports than most other activities? Greg doesn't want anything happening to his babies while their bones are still growing.'

The unwelcome picture was growing clearer by the minute to Max. 'How about Kevin? He's old enough to play, surely.'

'He prefers to stay at home with his music.' Her voice grew softer, warmer. 'Can't think who he gets his talent from. Not me, that's for sure. I'm not clever at anything.'

'From his father?' Max suggested, recognizing a battered wife. Battered by words, not fists, but almost as degrading.

'That's a laugh,' she retorted, suddenly animated. 'He can't even accept that his only son's passion is twanging a guitar and *caterwauling*.' She concentrated again on fiddling with the plate. 'There was even a time when he suspected Kevin wasn't his.'

Sensing that shock was driving her to unburden her inner feelings to a man who seemed interested in what she had to say, Max allowed a brief silence before asking, 'Has he cause to doubt it?'

She slowly shook her head. 'It was always Greg from our schooldays. He knew that. Kevin was born nine months after our wedding. Greg was that proud and excited he borrowed from a mate one of those vans with loudspeakers and drove around calling out, "I've got a son. I've got a son." Real daft he was in those days.'

Max knew the type. To sire a male child was a macho achievement for such men. 'And when your daughters were born?'

Her nervous fingers now set to work on one of the rolls, pulling tiny pieces from it to drop on the plate. 'We'd been trying for five years for another one. Greg couldn't understand it after being so quick off the mark first time. He grew very moody. Sent me to the doctor for tests, but he said we were just too anxious. When Shona appeared Greg was so disappointed he went on a bender. Julie came a year later. That's when he decided three kids were enough.'

A large woman in an overall appeared beside the table to ask if they had finished their snack. Max asked for two more coffees and smiled inwardly at her expression of disgust at the mutilation of the ham and cheese rolls by people who had no real right to be in the staff canteen. They got their coffees, however.

'So how long was it before your husband recovered from the disappointment of having two girls, Mrs McRitchie?'

She sipped the hot drink as if she had asbestos lips, gazing at the region of Max's chest with a glazed look in her eyes. When he was on the point of repeating the question, she raised them to meet his.

'Those first years he took Kevin everywhere. Footie matches, swimming – Kev could swim before he was two, you know – excursions to museums where they keep old steam engines or aircraft through the ages. They saw the lions at Longleat and the tigers at Marwell. Greg had a mate in tanks who wangled a ride for them. Strictly against the rules, but...' She sipped more coffee, then put the cup in the saucer with energy. 'Every weekend they were out flying kites or model gliders; sailing toy boats on the lake; trekking over the moor; camping in the woods.'

Poor kid, thought Max. Manhood being forced on him in hefty doses. He waited to hear what he knew must come.

'The dog was the last straw.'

'Yes?'

Her eyes grew glassy with unshed tears. 'Little Kev showed no interest in old trains and planes; lions and tigers frightened the life out of him. He was sick and screamed in the tank. He cried to go home in the tent in the woods, and point blank refused to fly a kite. Sat down and sulked. Then Greg brought home this dog whose owner was going overseas. A German Shepherd. Kevin took one look and ran to hide behind me, shaking like a leaf. That was the moment Greg lost all interest in him,' she added in a faraway kind of voice. 'Funny, isn't it, to think a dog could do that?'

Two

Tom was sitting with Jack Fellowes, running through the statement given to Sergeant Maddox last night, when his mobile rang. Nodding an apology, Tom rose from the chair beside which was a small table bearing coffee and a mince pie brought by Sheila Fellowes, and walked through to the hall.

'Tom Black,' he said briskly, hoping for news of Lance-Corporal Treeves.

'I think you should get around to the McRitchie quarter, talk to the father,' said Max. 'There's a definite problem with his attitude to the boy which needs probing further.'

Gazing at the cream-emulsioned wall often found in this type of accommodation, Tom murmured, 'He looked genuinely shattered last night.'

'Because of the effect the drama might have on his two small daughters. He's abandoned wife and injured son to make sure *they* are given their favourite Sunday breakfast. Told Mrs McRitchie there was no way he would let what happened ruin *their* lives. Don't say it! It was also my first thought.'

Tom whistled softly. 'Kevin not man

enough for him?'

'Got it in one. Sees it as some kind of slur on his own virility. Recognize the type?'

'Dangerous.'

'He's presently at home with the objects of his excessive affection. Good time to catch him ... and, Tom, he spent last evening playing badminton but unless he can produce witnesses who will vow he was in plain sight the whole time, he has to be a suspect.'

'My big problem is that whoever attacked the boy had no way of knowing when he would use the toilets, or even if he would that evening.'

'Unless Kevin had arranged to meet someone there at a specific time. The doc says there are no signs the boy's been using drugs, but he could have been supplying, Tom.'

'Jack Fellowes has just told me he thinks Kevin went up there for a smoke. There was a box of matches and a pack containing three cigarettes on the sill beneath the open ventilator. There was also a smouldering stub on the floor when Jack arrived.'

Max chuckled. 'My mind goes into overdrive on teens today. Of course, smoke a surreptitious fag then flush the stub down the pan. Did it all the time at school. How about you?'

'Back of the bike shed, me. Any info on the extent of the injury?'

'Doc says the blow wouldn't normally do

more than heavily stun the recipient. Kevin happens to have a thin skull, hence the excessive damage.'

'So it could have been intended as a warning. That fits with Beeny's theory of frustrated sexual advances. By his father?'

'I doubt it, but his obsession with the two girls could well be unhealthy. I'm off to talk to the Clarkson boys. The hospital will contact us when the patient is fit to answer questions. They say probably not until tonight or the morning, and his recollection could be extremely vague. Call me after you've interviewed McRitchie.' Short pause. 'Finish the mince pie before you go.'

Tom smiled as the line went dead. Mince pies were a major hazard of Christmas investigations. He returned and settled in his chair to recap on their earlier conversation.

'So there were the Padre's new wife, Lieutenant Farmer, Sapper Rowe and two of the tinies' mums helping you with the kids. They were all present from start to finish and no one else came for a short while, then left.'

'That's right,' Jack Fellowes confirmed. 'Could have done with a couple more volunteers – that age group can be demons to control – but everyone's got so much on at this time of year. Lieutenant Farmer holds dance classes at the Centre on the first and third Saturday each month, so some of the girls know her well. She also has an advanced first aid certificate. Useful when kids are running and jumping about in large numbers. There's always several who trip and fall, others who eat too much and regurgitate shortly afterwards.'

Tom pulled a face. 'Tell me about it.'

'The Padre's wife was asked if she would come to judge the costumes and hand out the prizes – one for each age group and one for the most original in any group – but we were about to start the parade when Kevin was discovered.'

'So Mrs Robinson had only just arrived at that point?'

'No. When she agreed to do the honours she said she'd come at the start and help in any way she could.' Fellowes raised his brows. 'Between you and me, Tom, she was bugger-all use except for serving dollops of trifle and smiling the entire evening.'

Tom nodded. 'I met her very briefly a month or so back. I knew the first Mrs Robinson quite well and liked her. Brisk woman who fought her illness with great courage right to the last days. This one seems a bit otherworldly, less fit to be a padre's wife.'

'She might settle to it in time. They've only been married six months. First husband was a bank manager.'

'Switched from saving pounds to saving souls.' Finishing his coffee and resolutely ignoring the mince pie, Tom asked, 'How about Sapper Rowe? I've not come across him at all.'

'A good lad. Clever with his hands. The eldest of five, so he's good with tinies. He set up all the apparatus for the team competitions. You know the kind of thing – scrambling through hoops, putting boxes within boxes, bouncing balls into buckets. He really got them all going, raised their competitive spirits.'

'Christ, he'll have the PC brigade after him if they hear,' put in Tom dryly. 'These days they all have to win equally.'

Fellowes shook his head. 'These are army kids. They know all about being the best.'

Tom referred to the printed statement made to George Maddox. 'You've provided the names of the two mothers who were helpers. One of my team will talk to them but, from your recollection, you noticed nothing or anyone suspicious up till the time Kevin was discovered.'

'Nothing, Tom, but I was pretty well occupied. No time even to visit the bog until I went up there to find the boy. Mind you, there was a steady stream of kids up and down to the toilets all evening. If Kevin was attacked by an intruder any one of them could have been the victim.' He looked unhappy. 'Nasty business. Parents will be edgy until you get who did it.'

Tom got to his feet. 'Your two are back at uni, so no need to worry about them.'

'Don't you believe it. The older they get the bigger the problems,' he said with a smile that belied his words. 'But they're good lads.'

Sheila Fellowes walked in at that point. 'Oh, are you going, Tom? You haven't eaten your mince pie.'

'Had an urgent call from the boss. Have to be elsewhere, I'm afraid,' he replied smoothly, and escaped into the snow.

The McRitchie house was on the end of a block of four in a mini village of married quarters built decades ago and badly in need of renovation. Many families were too uncaring to add personal touches, and regarded their quarter as simply somewhere to sleep, eat and slouch on the sofa to watch TV for hour after hour.

It was instantly apparent to Tom that Mavis McRitchie was a home-maker. The room was bright with framed posters of country or coastal scenes glowing with colour, and the cushions wore handmade red, green and white patchwork covers that matched the tablecloth arranged diagonally beneath a bowl of gilded fir cones. Sitting on what looked like a patchwork throw across the settee were two dark-haired girls dressed in scarlet leggings with blue and white hand-knitted tunics.

'We were having our usual Sunday question and answer session,' Greg McRitchie explained as he ushered Tom in. 'We always enjoy it, don't we, sweethearts?'

Two heads nodded; two sullen expressions appeared as brown eyes stared at Tom who

41

had intruded into their family activity. With no more than a year between them, Tom put them at around Beth's age. She was mercurial, with swiftly changing moods, but he had never seen such aggression in her eyes as there was being directed at him from Shona and Julie McRitchie.

'I've come at the right time, then,' he said encouragingly, 'because I need to ask some questions to which I hope you'll give some important answers.'

'We only play the game with Dadda,' said one with finality.

'Yes,' agreed the other in the same tone.

Their father hastened to soothe them. 'Mr Black means that he wants to ask *me* a few things. Nothing to do with our game. That's our *special* fun. Go up to your room and make a list of what you want to buy at the market this afternoon, while I talk to Mr Black.'

They rose as one and headed for the stairs, ignoring the visitor.

'Hey, haven't you forgotten something?' asked Greg in teasing manner, and they turned back to run to him and kiss his cheek. 'That's better. Off you go. Only one Twix bar each, mind, or you'll have no room for your dinner at Maxie's.'

Tom watched all this with mounting disquiet. How long before this insidious petting developed a sexual aspect? He made a mental note to speak to someone in welfare

42

about his concern. He also determined to question the girls about last night's party in the presence of their teacher tomorrow, although he realized he was unlikely to get useful answers from them. A session with young Kevin would surely yield more about the routine in this family.

Corporal McRitchie turned to Tom still wearing a disturbingly fond smile. 'Light of my life, those two, sir.'

'How about your son?'

The smile vanished. 'I gave my every off duty minute to teach him how to make a success in life, to make something of himself. Wish I'd had a father prepared to provide the wonderful opportunities that boy was offered.' He scowled. 'Total waste of effort. He's weak and spineless. Can't even catch a ball cleanly if you throw one to him. Know what, sir? When I brought a dog home, he cried and ran to hide behind his mother's skirts. No guts at all!'

'Yet last night you charged him with the responsibility of looking after his sisters.'

'And he even failed at that! Off on his own, *smoking*! He knows that's strictly against the rules.'

'Which rules, Corporal?'

'Mine, sir, for my family.' His eyes lit with fervour. 'An army is successful because there's discipline, rules that must be obeyed so each individual soldier knows exactly what he and his fellows have to do. Reduce that system to an individual regiment, then to a battalion, a company, a platoon. It works in every case. Adapt that principle to a family and it can't fail to be successful, too. You've just seen my two little charmers. Good as gold and happy as the day is long.' The fervour faded. 'Kevin has never understood the need for rules and has now begun openly to defy them.'

Disliking the man more by the minute, Tom said, 'Evidence of guts that should surely please you. Now, I need a rundown of your son's main activities outside school, his interests and the names of his principal friends.'

'The answer to the first two is the same. He fancies himself a future star of the pop scene. He plucks his guitar, prances around and jabbers like all the big names now. That's *all* he does. Even his mother can't get him interested in anything else. His only friends are Johnny King, Malc Carpenter and Callum Peters. They call themselves a group.' McRitchie's swarthy face screwed up in disgust. 'Swinga Kat! They've even had it printed on their T-shirts.'

Reflecting that his girls would probably call that a pretty cool name for a group, Tom asked if Kevin and his mates ever played in public.

'At the Youth Club, sir. They tried to get a gig in town but were told they're too young. Too bloody pathetic, more like!'

Tom let that pass. The man could be right. 'Does Kevin know any of the younger musicians in the regimental band, particularly those who play in the splinter group performing at discos?'

'Shouldn't wonder at it. That's all he thinks about.'

'How about squaddies? Is he friendly with any seventeen- or eighteen-year-old lads?'

'Doubt it. He rubbishes the army, so he'd have nothing in common with squaddies. Why d'you ask?'

The sound of squealing and running feet overhead took McRitchie's attention. 'So is that it, sir?'

'For now, Corporal, but isn't there something you want to ask me?'

'Like what, sir?'

'Like who could have made such a brutal attack on your son.'

'Some weirdo who wandered in to use the bog and got angry when he found a kid there having a smoke. It's the only explanation.'

'No, Corporal, there are a hell of a lot of possible explanations and, as you appear to have little concern over why Kevin should be the target of a vicious assault, I shall have to ask others to provide me with the answers that'll lead us to catch the perpetrator.'

Tom drove away curiously loath to leave those two young girls with their father. He wondered just what questions and answers comprised the game they only played with

'Dadda'. Was it the overture to something criminal? Was the next stage the one where the girls were encouraged to show him their special places while he showed them his? As the father of three daughters Tom held strong views on the rape and sexual abuse of girls. He had even grown slightly wary of horseplay with Maggie, whose breasts and hips had rounded to budding womanhood in the last twelve months. Pubescent daughters were complex. Sons would be easier to handle.

On that thought he questioned himself harshly. If he had a son would he need the boy to be tough, rough and all-out male? If the lad ran in fright from a dog would it disappoint and disgust him? If a son's sole interest was to grow a long pony-tail, dress in skintight spangled satin and wail into a microphone in smokey dives would he feel the way Greg McRitchie felt?

To banish the uncomfortable suspicion that it might be all too likely, Tom restored his equilibrium with the certainty that, whatever the situation, if young Master Black were ever attacked *his* father would hunt down the person responsible with rage in his heart.

Unsettled by his train of thought, Tom had just decided to go home for soup, a sandwich and Nora's uncomplicated philosophies when his mobile rang. He pulled up beside the gymnasium to answer.

'Tom Black.'

'Jakes here, sir. Lance-Corporal Treeves has surfaced.'

'Alive?'

'And kicking. With a tale and a half to tell.'

'I'll be there in ten.'

So much for his plan to offset the unease prompted by the McRitchie interview! He made a three-point turn in driving snow and headed back across the base to their chilly new premises.

Sergeant Roy Jakes was eating a Mars bar with relish when Tom entered the large main office. 'If that's a substitute for lunch you'll be dozy by mid-afternoon,' he observed, sitting beside the desk where Jakes manned his computer.

'Bob went over to the NAAFI, brought back fish and chips half an hour ago,' came the reassuring reply that set Tom wanting some.

'Give me the stuff on Treeves. Who sent it in?'

'You're not going to believe it, sir.'

'Try me.'

Jakes crushed the chocolate wrapper in his large hand and tossed it in the nearby bin. 'A certain Herr Haufmann returned with his wife early this morning from an emergency visit to his infirm mother, and discovered an army truck parked well down his driveway out of sight of the road. The cab was empty, as was the interior. Or so he thought, until he spotted in the half-light a bundle in the corner that looked like a roll of carpet.'

'Our man Treeves?'

'Inside a sleeping-bag stuffed inside the roll of our carpet. Haufmann initially thought he had a body on his hands, but his wife is a doctor and knew better. She helped Haufmann take him in their house and set about reviving Treeves while her husband called the *Polizei*.' Jakes grinned. 'They passed the buck very swiftly to us.'

Tom grunted. 'They're very punctilious when they want out of a tricky problem involving one of ours.'

'They'll soon be back in the thick of it if what Treeves claims is true,' put in Sergeant Bob Prentiss.

'So he's back in the land of the aware?'

Bob nodded. 'We initially attempted to get an ambulance to pick him up, but they're only turning out for emergencies. The Haufmanns found Treeves' explanation hard to accept, so he gave them our number to verify his story. We confirmed the fact that one of our trucks was missing with its driver, and described Treeves as well as giving the reg. number of the vehicle. They then allowed their unwelcome guest to speak to us.'

'Go ahead and amaze me,' Tom invited.

Roy Jakes referred to his print-out of the conversation. 'Two men on a motorbike overtook the truck on a long, acute bend which hid the rest of the convoy from view.

48

The bike cut in and skidded, causing Treeves to brake sharply and slew across the road. A guy in a balaclava brandishing a gun appeared from nowhere to climb in the cab and demand the keys. He tossed them to the pillion rider who got behind the wheel, made a three-point turn, and headed back a couple of miles before turning right on to a forest track just wide enough to accommodate the vehicle.'

He glanced up at Tom. 'Treeves reckons these men knew the forest well. They drove through it like old hands at the game.'

'I suppose they both had their faces covered.'

Jakes nodded. 'No hope of future identification.'

'And Treeves was held at gunpoint throughout?'

'So he says.'

'Go on,' said Tom, thinking it sounded like the screenplay of a cheap thriller.

'They broke from the forest as darkness fell. Treeves says he didn't recognize the road they then travelled for two or three hours before entering a long, tree-lined drive that suggested the approach to a large house. They halted before there was any sign of lights ahead. Treeves then realized there was another truck backing up to his.'

'That's where the stuff was transferred. I guess three men could do it without much trouble. Did they disable their prisoner then?'

'When they were ready to drive off. In the darkness he didn't see the blow coming. Next thing he knew he was lying on a sofa with two irate Germans bending over him.'

Tom sighed. 'Everything points to the hijackers being a local trio. They knew we were on the move yesterday, they knew the forest tracks well, and it's likely they also knew the Haufmann place has a long approach hidden from the road. Ideal for their purpose.' Giving a twisted smile, he said, 'We'll pass the buck back to Krenkel as fast as his guys passed it to us. They can check the whereabouts yesterday of their known gangs with contacts over the border.'

'This was a gang with very kind hearts,' put in Prentiss with an angelic expression. 'They brought along a lovely padded sleeping-bag so their victim would be snug and warm until he recovered.'

'And they ensured they wouldn't split his skull by coshing him with a sock filled with sand,' added Jakes.

Tom frowned. 'Say that again?'

'Herr Haufmann found it in the truck beside Treeves. A socking great sock filled with grit.'

The Medical Officer's sons had contrasting personalities. Ten-year-old James Clarkson was forthright and assured to the brink of arrogance, like his father. His brother

Daniel, younger by two years, seemed more deeply affected by last night's drama. He sat quietly, allowing James to answer Max's questions. Mrs Clarkson had taken their teenage daughters to a small Christmas market specializing in hand-crafted tree decorations. The Major sat in on the interview but refrained from interrupting, which somewhat surprised Max.

After breaking the ice with general questions about the party, which of their friends were there and what costumes they wore, Max asked, 'Do you remember seeing anyone on the steps or in the corridor when you went up to the toilet?'

'No,' James answered firmly.

'Not even a distant glimpse?'

'No.'

'How about footsteps, the sound of someone who was maybe out of sight?'

'No, nothing.'

'Did you notice at what point Kevin left the main hall, how long before you did, for instance?'

'We were involved in team competitions most of the time.'

'Or eating pizzas and stuff,' put in Daniel.

Max paused a moment, assessing them before asking carefully, 'Was there any reason why you went upstairs together, apart from the obvious one?'

The boys exchanged glances with their father, then James said quietly, 'Dan's a bit nervous of empty corridors. They can look a bit creepy at night. Good thing we were together to find what we did. We thought he was dead. All that blood!'

'Kevin is going to be fine. I've just seen him in the hospital ward. There was blood because he unfortunately fell on his face, cutting his lip and causing a heavy nose bleed.' Max then broached the crux of his questioning. 'We think whoever attacked Kevin only meant to frighten him. Now, you both go to school with Kevin. He'll be in a more senior class, but you'll know him well enough to be able to tell me if he's fallen out badly with any other boy. I don't mean a short difference of opinion, more a long-term serious hostility.'

Four dark eyes just gazed back at him, so he elaborated. 'Has there been trouble over a girlfriend, for instance? Or a dispute over ownership of something reasonably valuable? Mobile phone, iPod?'

Still no response. 'You can't think of anyone at school who would do that to Kevin as a warning to give up his claim to something?'

James tried to be helpful. 'You mean had Kev stolen something and refused to give it back?'

Max smiled to soften the moment. 'I'm sure Kevin wouldn't do that. I just want to find out if anyone at school constantly picks on him. A bully. Leader of a tough group, perhaps.'

'That wouldn't happen,' James replied with certainty. 'Kev has cred. He's leader of Swinga Kat.'

Max tried to understand that, then asked, 'Would you please explain?'

'He's the lead guitar and vocalist of the group.' Sensing that he was dealing with an old, out-of-touch person here, the boy explained further. 'Kevin's formed a group with his mates. It's called Swinga Kat. Most of us think they're pretty cool. Even the toughies.' He frowned. 'I really don't think anyone at school would want to hurt him that way.'

Max changed direction. 'When you both discovered Kevin you ran immediately to tell Sergeant-Major Fellowes. Did you happen to notice if all the other helpers were still in the main hall?'

'Not really,' said James frankly. 'We were upset. We thought he was dead.'

'Yes, of course. You must feel better now you know Kevin will soon be up and about again.' Max stood. 'Thank you, boys. You've been very helpful.'

Major Clarkson rose to show him out and closed the door leading from the sitting-room to the hall so they could speak privately. 'Are you seriously considering an assault by another boy?'

Max turned to him, resenting the scepticism in the doctor's tone. 'We have to con-

53

sider every possibility. The weapon could easily be wielded by a lad nearing his teens.'

Clarkson held open the door. 'I thought you'd know knives are the must-have weapons for schoolboys.'

Max would not let that pass. 'On the last investigation during which our paths crossed, you accused me of telling you how to do your job and assured me you wouldn't dream of telling me how to do mine.'

Clarkson almost smiled, but not quite. 'Point taken. I'll be in touch if my boys recall anything useful later.'

Max was halfway down the path when a high voice called to him. Young Daniel stood in the doorway pressing against his father's side.

'I've just thought,' he said. 'There *could* have been someone there. A lady could have hidden in their toilets next door, and we wouldn't ever go in there to notice her.'

Smiling at the boy, Max said, 'I think you've just earned some cred yourself, Daniel. That's a very astute observation.'

Deciding to have lunch, Max called Tom from his car before heading for the Mess. When Tom picked up he asked, 'Finished with McRitchie?'

'Not by a long chalk. He's off my list of suspects for the assault, but I don't like his attitude with those girls. Or his callousness towards what happened to his son. I'm at Headquarters, by the way. Treeves has turned up alive and well.'

'He's there being questioned?'

'No, sir. He was dumped at the property of an international financial adviser whose wife is a doctor. They found him in the truck early this morning and took him in. He called in from there. I've contacted our boys near the border. They'll pick him up and hand him over to Stubble and Meacher when they manage to push through to them. Driving conditions are very hazardous, so they might have to delay their return until the blizzard dies down.'

'What's the story, Tom?'

'Of the cock and bull variety judging by what Treeves told Sergeant Jakes. Without a doubt our stuff's in Holland now, and if Treeves wasn't involved I'm a Dutchman's uncle.'

'Have you contacted Krenkel?'

'Just about to, but we can't take it far until we have Treeves here and get a full statement. Any useful info from the Clarkson boys?'

'Only that Kevin is popular with his peers. We're unlikely to be looking for a school bully on this. I'm more inclined to pursue Beeny's frustrated sex offender theory. The location of the assault lends strength to that, and one could say the weapon has phallic symbolism.'

'On that, sir, if our two assault cases hadn't occurred miles apart on the same night, I'd say there's a nutter running around with phallic symbols as weapons. Treeves claims he was knocked cold by a sand-filled sock.'

'Strange coincidence! Maybe they're the latest must-haves. Remind me to tell Major Clarkson. I'm going to grab some lunch before I come over. I want the statements given by the adults attending last night checked over. We should look into their backgrounds.'

'Some of the team have called in to say they've gone as far as they can on questioning the kids, so they're coming in.'

'Good. They can work on it. Then we'll consolidate info collected so far and explore the most likely avenues. My guts are hinting that the McRitchie case will prove more complex than it appears.'

'Just what we need in the run up to Christmas.'

'It was ever thus in this job, Tom.' He hesitated, then asked, 'Have you ever heard of something called Swinga Kat?'

'Of course. Listen to it all the time. It's a pretty cool pop group.'

Aware of the amusement in his tone, Max said, 'And you're a pretty cool liar, Sar'nt-Major.'

Lunch took the traditional Sunday form expected by British officers. Having been deprived of a late dinner last night, Max decided he deserved the luxury of doing it full justice. The tale of Treeves and the sand-filled sock could wait an extra half an hour.

Gazing through the windows at the madly swirling snow while he enjoyed his soup, Max reflected on Daniel Clarkson's afterthought. Anyone could have hidden in the women's toilet on hearing the brothers approach, then left when they ran for help. An adult male assailant would not have Daniel's scruples about entering a forbidden place. But why leave the weapon there to be tested for fingerprints that would incriminate?

'Hallo. You're our new mess member, aren't you?'

Max came to from his thoughts to see a young, curvaceous redhead smiling down at him. Her uniform bore two pips on each shoulder and the scarlet duty officer's lanyard. He half rose, but she waggled well-manicured fingers to dissuade him and took the seat facing him.

'Mind if I join you and get acquainted? I'm Lucy Farmer.'

'Max Rydal ... and please do,' he replied, wondering at the stroke of luck that sent to him the subaltern who had helped at the party. Pity she was a possible suspect. She was very easy on the eye.

'You're with SIB, aren't you? We've never had a detective among us before.'

She had an upper class accent and frank green eyes that reflected her smile. Unfortunately, her overture strengthened his feeling of being on duty even when off duty, living in-mess as he was now obliged to do.

'I don't detect during meals.' He tried to inject warm humour into the words, but apparently failed.

'Oh dear, did I sound like a police groupie?'

Her alluring chuckle coaxed a smile from him then. 'A police groupie! Good God, are there such creatures?'

'Bound to be. Detecting has been glamorized by Inspectors Morse, Frost and Barnaby on TV.'

Max's roast beef and her soup were brought at that point, causing a conversational hiatus. When the steward departed, Lucy looked at Max eagerly.

'I suppose you'll want my observations on last night's ghastly end to the kids' party.'

'Not over the lunch table.'

She pulled a face but still managed to look attractive. 'Boobed again! Sorry.'

'If you're not yet acquainted with Ben Steele of the Cumberland Rifles, I must introduce you,' Max said dryly, starting on his beef.

'Explain, please.'

'He took too keen an interest in a case we investigated back in April.'

'I was in the UK then. Is that your tactful way of saying he meddled?'

'So how long have you been here in Germany?' he responded pointedly.

'OK, I give in,' she said with another chuckle, 'but you will want to hear my account of last night, won't you?'

'Someone will contact you officially later today. Will this be your first experience of a German Christmas, Lucy?'

'Oh no!' She finally tasted her soup. 'My older sister is a ballerina with a touring company based in Brussels. They sometimes stage *The Nutcracker* here during the festive period. The parents and I twice came over to see her dance, then went on to ski.'

'What does a ballerina think of your chosen career?' he asked with real interest.

'Oh, we both consider the other one crazy. She shudders at the thought of my wearing army boots and participating in mock battles, but I tell you, what her profession does to her feet and body is far worse than the most gruelling exercise has done to mine. She's twenty-five, but her bones and muscles have suffered the wear and tear of someone twice that age.' She shrugged. 'She simply lives to dance.'

'Do you live for the army?'

She gave a bright smile. 'I'm much more down to earth. My interests are many and varied.'

'Two being skiing and watching TV detectives.'

Her smile widened. 'You're nice. I was so afraid you'd be grim and judgemental. Look, Max, these days it's possible for women to do almost anything they choose. It's all out there, and I mean to take up every opportunity that offers itself.'

The lunch hour passed very swiftly as Max listened to her enthusiastic opinions on any subject he raised, and was not a little charmed by her. By the time they parted he knew there was one of the adults present at the party whose background now did not need to be checked. Not really detecting over the lunch table, was it? Just making friends with another mess member.

Three

The heating system had been completed, but could not operate because the motors had frozen solid, so they all clustered beside the two space heaters to report on interviews conducted that day. Nothing useful had been gleaned from the children, which was much as they had expected. No one had seen a stranger lurking in the corridors, and they had gone up to the toilets in pairs or groups if not accompanied by one of the adults. Children afraid of the dark or deserted places found long, empty corridors scary.

Tactful questioning about the adult helpers had produced no hint of suspicion. They all liked Miss Farmer and Sapper Rowe. They were fun and had joined in the games. Little had been said about Mrs Robinson except that she was 'sort of smiley but too old for a party'. Clearly, the forty-two-year-old second wife of the Padre was not a hit with the tinies.

Jack Fellowes was known and loved by the younger children on the base as an uncle figure who always participated in their social and sporting activities; someone to be turned to when problems arose in the confidence that he would make everything come right. Their faith had been dented over Kevin McRitchie. Several had actually said they were upset that Uncle Jack had not picked Kevin up and made him better.

On the subject of Kevin himself, the general feedback strengthened Max and Tom's received information that he was admired for his guitar playing. Even the youngest partygoers were enthusiastic.

Summing up after hearing these reports, Max said, 'So we have a boy of just thirteen who's interested in pop music and little else. Small for his age and strongly averse to what we would call macho activities. Openly despised by his father for having no guts, I suspect he has a close relationship with his mother. She's certainly the parent who's concerned and standing by him now.' He studied his team still wearing their coats and scarves. 'On the surface Kevin McRitchie is a prime target for school bullies, but he's saved by his musical skill. Even regarded with awe by a number of schoolmates. So I think we can dismiss the theory of an attack by a minor, for the moment.'

Tom nodded at Olly Simpson. 'Did you get anything from McRitchie's neighbours on noise provocation?'

The lanky sergeant wagged his head. 'I spoke to the families on each side. They both said McRitchie refuses to let his son practise at home. Kevin joins one of the other three in the group. I managed to speak to the Kings and the Carpenters. They live in the semis on the western border of the base. Not adjacent, but very near. They said they get the occasional complaint when the boys rehearse, but it's never vicious. They usually tell their sons to give it a rest if it goes on too long.'

'So we can probably discount a neighbour driven berserk by loud pop night after night?'

'I should think so, sir. Interestingly, Sergeants King and Carpenter seemed very tolerant of what their boys were doing. Even supported their ambition to fix a gig in town. Reg King is his regiment's champion boxer, Jim Carpenter is a former inter-services silver medal miler. They don't appear to feel emasculated by their sons' musical obsession.'

'My money's on Kevin's dad,' said Piercey, rubbing his hands together for warmth. 'He knew where the lad was last night. Probably also knew he would be set to have a crafty smoke. A man like McRitchie's likely to let fly because his rules are being broken.'

'I checked with the people at the Badminton Club,' put in Heather Johnson, always happy to rubbish Piercey's notions. 'Three of them vouched for Greg McRitchie's presence the entire evening, even in the toilet. Seems they relieve themselves in quartet at the end of a match.' She could not resist adding slyly, 'None of them spotted him sneaking an additional phallic symbol in his shorts.'

Tom took control swiftly. 'I judged McRitchie more likely to be goaded into giving the boy a hearty cuff at home. He's not interested enough in his son to plan the assault at the party.'

Max added to that. 'Mrs McRitchie made it plain to me that her husband has virtually abandoned Kevin to dote on the two girls he can control absolutely. No, he's not our man.'

Staff Sergeant Melly picked up on that. 'It's unlikely to be an unknown intruder. I checked at both gates. Plenty of people leaving the base. Saturday night exodus! Only two actually *entered* before nine. Colonel and Mrs Trelawney, of the Cumberland Rifles, returning from a cocktail party given by a local dignatory.'

Piercey made a point with slight sarcasm. 'An intruder bent on mischief is hardly likely to enter by the main gate and sign in. Have Sergeant Maddox's boys checked the perimeter wire?'

'*Yes*,' said Melly with such aggression it put an end to that subject.

'Which narrows the field to personnel on-base at the time the assault took place,' Tom said decisively. 'By eliminating all who checked out for the evening we can narrow it further.'

Derek Beeny spoke for the first time. 'So far we've not unearthed a motive for the attack. Why Kevin? He's popular with his peers, doesn't annoy the neighbours. He's hardly likely to have the necessary nous to become a pusher and tangle with an outside supplier. Can we be certain Kevin was the intended victim rather than a random one?'

'We don't know enough about him to answer that yet,' said Connie Bush. 'Although he spends most of his free time with the King, Carpenter and Peters boys he has to meet with other people. He tried to fix a gig in town. That means he made contacts there, for a start.'

'But we've agreed it had to be an inside job,' protested Staff Melly.

'We're running before we can walk,' said Tom firmly. 'With everything operating normally tomorrow we can interview those not available today, and Kevin should be fit for questioning. That'll give us a great deal more input.'

'I did manage to talk to the two mums who helped at the party,' Connie Bush added belatedly. 'A pair of rather dopey women who each think their own child is the sun, moon and stars. Kept using the phrase "my darling little pet". Neither of them would be aware of anyone else's child, much less hit it with a handy club.'

'And I was made aware of something

worth following up,' put in Olly Simpson. 'Sorry, sir, it slipped my mind. Must be the low temperature in here.'

Tom let that pass. Civilians would have walked away from a workplace as cold as this. Soldiers had to tough it out. 'Yes, Sergeant?'

'The Carpenter boy, Malcolm, said Kevin sometimes met up with Musician Clegg, a drummer in the Cumberland Rifles band who's also in the splinter group that plays for discos on the base.'

'Ah,' breathed Tom. 'I tried to get that kind of info from McRitchie to possibly support Beeny's theory of revenge for advances spurned. I'll follow that up in the morning.'

Max got to his feet. 'Now to Lance-Corporal Treeves, I think we all agree with Mr Black that his story is of the cock and bull variety. The *Polizei* have been alerted, but until we get the driver here for a full account they won't pull out all the stops on it. Right now, I'd like some personal info on the adults at the party. Shouldn't take long, then we'll all go home before we freeze to death. Great effort under difficult conditions today. Well done!'

The day ended in frustration. The duo attempting to collect Treeves were unable to reach the RMP Headquarters where he was being held. They had to put up for the night in a wayside inn where their uniforms guaranteed a reception almost as cold as the temperature outside.

Max set out to drive to the hospital on learning that Kevin could now be questioned, but drifts made the road impassable five kilometres out from the base. He was not altogether sorry to turn back. It was better than being stranded at the hospital all night. The usual human dislike of such places was exacerbated in him by memories of identifying Susan's broken pregnant body three years ago. Whenever his job demanded visits to wards or mortuaries, he made them as brief as possible.

Tom entered his new temporary home with a sense of relief. A loving family welcome, centrally heated warmth and a steak and mushroom pie almost ready to eat. He was a lucky man.

It was good to sit down together for the meal, even if his daughters talked non-stop about clothes and someone called Helmut Weber, a former ice hockey star now a fashion model who apparently turned women into crazed idolators. The man had certainly done that to three females named Black. Thankfully, there was still one who was sane enough to appreciate the bird in her hand.

They played board games until, one by one, the girls went up to bed. As Tom stretched contentedly on the settee, Nora came with a beer for him.

'There's only enough wine for one glass,' she said sitting beside him with it in her hand, 'and I didn't think we should open another bottle tonight.'

'No, we'll need them for when the social round gets fully underway.'

She cast him a wry glance. 'You might even be here for some of it.'

'If only everyone observed the goodwill to all mankind mantra, I'd be here for all of it every year.'

'How's Kevin McRitchie?' she asked after sipping her wine.

'Recovering. I guess his mother's still with him. Max said the road's blocked, so she'll stay another night there, at least.'

'How about the two little girls?'

'Oh, they'll be happy as the day is long with *Dadda*.'

Nora looked at him quizzically. 'There was a hidden agenda in that comment.'

'I found that set-up slightly nauseating. They all seemed too *fond*. But Connie Bush interviewed two mothers today who also drooled over their perfect little darlings, so perhaps I'm the weird one.' He studied her. 'Do the girls think me cold and uncaring, love?'

'Hey, what's all this?' she demanded, setting the wine glass back on the table before them.

He sighed. 'I don't know. I just thought ... You know how much I love them, but I don't think they're the most perfect children ever born. Should I?'

'No, love, because we're not the perfect parents either.' She laid a hand on his arm. 'It's not like you to get broody over nonsense like that.'

He then told her about McRitchie's inflexible attitude to the son he was unable to mould to his ideal. 'I despised him for it, yet I couldn't help wondering if I'd be the same in his place.'

She smiled broadly. 'No, because I'd never let it happen. That boy's mother is halfway to blame for allowing a sensitive, timid child to be forced into activities totally unsuited to his temperament at such a tender age. You're hot on sexual abuse, Tom. That's a case of character abuse. It often happens, but can't be stopped because it isn't a perceived crime. Poor kid! Small wonder he finds escape in his kind of music. That's his comfort, his solace, the one thing in life he feels safe with.' She frowned. 'Shouldn't be surprised if he finds it difficult to have relationships when he matures. He might suspect women will let him down the way his mother has, and men will want to dominate him.'

'As to that, Derek Beeny has a theory that Kevin might have repelled paedophile advances once too often. It seems the most plausible motive for the attack so far.'

'Mmm, that's a possibility. Remember there are also a lot of frustrated lonely wives on a base this size. Husbands are often away on duty, or out with their mates doing man things. Many are forced to fantasize.'

'Like Helmut Weber who turns sensible daughters into gushing ninnies?'

She smiled. 'He *is* quite a hunk. Yes, like him. Other frustrated women get the reverse urge. They want to be in control, to dominate. They see a vulnerable young lad entering puberty and yearn to initiate him, hold him in thrall. You should look very carefully among the females as well as the males connected with this case. You know the old adage about a woman scorned.'

The blizzard had blown itself out leaving a bright, calm morning. Snowploughs had cleared roads around the base so military routine could resume after the weekend break. Having little faith in new heating systems with frozen motors, Connie Bush was glad to be driving to interview Mrs Robinson in what should be a warm, comfortable home. She had not met the Padre's second wife. Her only guidance on what to expect was that she was 'very smiley but too old for a party'.

It was a good description. Connie had frequently found children were very observant witnesses. Estelle Robinson wore a grey tweed pleated skirt and a wine-coloured jumper with a single strand of pearls more suited to a much older woman. She *was* very smiley, which contrasted curiously with her cool, commanding manner.

Leading the way to a sitting-room where a log fire burned, she told Connie the coffee was ready and waiting. 'I knew any police person was certain to arrive exactly on time.' Smiling broadly, she pointed to an armchair near the window. 'Sit there!'

Obeying the order, Connie surveyed the contents of the room with a professional eye. Prim. There was no other word for it. A few inoffensive ornaments – nothing even bordering on statuettes of naked women – and the framed prints of country scenes were innocent of any suggestion of naughty goings-on in the hay. So it was the home of a man of the cloth and his lady, but Connie had a few times encountered Justin Robinson, an ideal soldiers' churchman ready to enjoy a drink and a blue joke with his flock. What had drawn him to this lacklustre woman?

He came in as Estelle handed Connie coffee in a plain white cup and saucer with a matching plate bearing a mince pie, a tall man with laughing eyes and crinkly greying hair.

'Hallo!' he said heartily. 'It's Sergeant Bush, if I remember correctly. How are you?'

'I'm very well, sir. It's nice to see you again, even if we only meet when something unpleasant has happened.'

'Yes. Well, sadly, our work leads us into it. I'm fortunate to have the upside as well. Weddings, christenings, baptisms, all the up-

lifting singing of hymns.' He laughed bois-
terously as he sat to accept coffee and pie
from his wife. 'You get your kicks from
collaring the villains, I suppose. Have a go at
that mince pie. My wife makes the best I've
ever tasted, and I've eaten a good number
during my parochial visits. Go on, try it!
There are plenty more in the kitchen.'

Connie sipped her coffee knowing she
would have to eat and exclaim over it before
she departed, but delaying the moment
would save her from another.

'I intended to drive over to see young
Kevin, but the road won't be open until this
afternoon,' the Padre said through a mouth-
ful of pastry and mincemeat. 'The two girls
are at school today and their mother should
be back at home for them when they return.
A nasty shock for the family. At yesterday's
services Estelle and I were made aware of
the concern felt by other childen at the
party. An attack of that ferocity on a younger
child could have proved fatal.'

'Indeed it could,' his wife agreed, 'although
I told you, dear, that an adult accompanied
the little ones when they needed to go up to
the toilets.'

Now they had reached the crux of the
matter, Connie embarked on her questions.
'Did you take any up there, Mrs Robinson?'

The smile appeared again and remained
fixed regardless of her words. 'I was kept
busy in the main hall. No opportunity to

sneak away like that. So many demands from children wanting the assurance and comfort of an older woman, especially over torn costumes, tummy ache or coming last in the games. I was kept on my toes all evening.'

Knowing this to be no more than self-important imagination, Connie asked, 'So you had no opportunity to take note of when Kevin slipped away?'

'My dear, there were two hundred children at the party. There was a constant stream going up and down the outside stairs. Impossible to remember one boy.'

'But he went up there alone, so could have easily been noticed. The Medical Officer's sons discovered Kevin when they slipped up there together before the parade was about to start, because the younger boy was afraid he wouldn't be able to wait until it was over. The attack must have occurred shortly before that.'

'Then I certainly wouldn't have noticed anything. I was to act as judge and present the prizes, so I was totally occupied with the importance of that duty.' The smile never wavered. 'More coffee?'

Connie allowed her cup to be refilled and tried to analyse her reaction to her hostess's bouncy brightness. Was it hiding more complex feelings, or had Estelle Robinson seen too many old black and white films depicting vicar's wives as cheery scatterbrains and adopted that image on her marriage?

73

'During your hectic duties on Saturday night you would surely have been aware of any serious squabbles between the children. Especially the older boys.'

Mrs Robinson slid another mince pie to sit beside the untouched one on Connie's plate, and smiled. 'The evening was full of squabbles, my dear. To ask such a question shows you've had little experience of children en masse. When they're overly excited and competitive they're like small demons ready to poke each other's eyes out, if necessary. Girls can be as venomous as boys. They pinch, scratch and kick, whereas boys use fists and any handy weapon. Young humans are like young animals. They obey basic, inborn instincts that only maturity teaches them to subdue and control. Whoever attacked that boy will now be suffering from belated guilt which will very soon drive him to confess and expect forgiveness as usual.' The smile broadened. 'Wait a few days and you'll have the culprit. No need for all these questions.'

Justin Robinson rose to pour more coffee in his cup and to select another golden pie. 'My wife taught psychology to college students for fifteen years, Sergeant. She understands the human psyche very well.'

Leaving the house ten minutes later with two mince pies carefully wrapped in a paper napkin, Connie reflected that the Padre's wife understood *her* psyche not one whit. Far

74

from being impressed by the woman's superior knowledge of human behaviour, Connie had found her irritating, smug and patronizing. Unfortunately, police professionalism and the fact that she was in the home of a major and his lady prevented her from doing what her psyche had urged. Her only opportunity to satisfy that urge was a rubbish bin at the end of the road into which the perfect mince pies went with great force.

Phil Piercey tracked Sapper Rowe down on the eastern side of the base, where he was with a team clearing snow and ice from security lights and cameras surrounding the armoury. Squaring with the lance-corporal in charge, Piercey invited Rowe to sit in the comparative warmth of his car while they talked. Large but compact, with brown hair and alert brown eyes, the young RE seemed concerned by Piercey's arrival.

'I told the Redcap all I could remember about that business on Saturday night,' he said immediately. 'I haven't thought of anything else, although I've been over it in my mind several times.'

'We've taken over the case and I need some answers. Get in my car, please.'

'I had nothing to do with hitting that boy,' he protested, standing firm in snow that almost topped his boots.

'The car!' ordered Piercey, who occasionally enjoyed putting the frights on cocky nineteen year olds. Alan Rowe had been alibied by every other adult at the party, who said he had been occupied with the games and competitions the whole time. As all detectives knew, in any large group activity it is impossible for participants to be absolutely certain of the unbroken presence of every person around them. Someone slips outside momentarily, goes to the toilet, fetches something from another room unnoticed.

'Right then,' Piercey began when they were settled in the warm vehicle. 'In your statement you claim to have seen nothing unusual, no strangers hanging around, no aggro between the kids and Kevin McRitchie. Is that correct?'

'Of course. I wouldn't have said it else.'

'You also stated that you don't know Kevin, couldn't describe him.'

Rowe nodded. 'There were a couple of hundred kids there. I had to ask their names for the score-cards, because I don't know any of them. I don't go to the married quarters.'

'Is that so? Mr Fellowes claims you're very good with the tinies and they like you. How come if you never go near them?'

The other man shrugged. 'I've two younger brothers and two sisters. I'm used to sorting them out; understand little kids. I used to babysit them before I joined.'

'Babysit for any on the base, do you?'

Rowe glared at Piercey. 'That's against the

rules.'

'No moonlighting, then?'

'What is this, Sergeant? I thought you wanted to talk about Saturday night.'

'Do you go to discos, Rowe?'

'Like everyone,' he replied edgily.

'Ever heard a group called Swinga Kat?'

Rowe frowned. 'The schoolkids? They guested once or twice at the Recreation Centre. They're quite good for their age.'

'Then you do know Kevin McRitchie and could perfectly well describe him. He leads that group.'

'The scrawny kid on guitar?' His surprise was genuine.

'Why say you don't know him?'

'I don't. I saw him on the stage for about half an hour once or twice, that's all. No idea of his name. Unless he had a guitar in his hand I wouldn't know him from any other kid. He would have been in some sort of costume on Saturday, anyway.'

Piercey fixed Rowe with the steady gaze he used to unsettle those he questioned, and said nothing.

'Look, Sergeant, I don't even remember writing his name down for any of the competitions or games.'

'He didn't participate. Thought it too childish for a boy just passed thirteen.' He switched the line of questioning. 'Did you go up to the toilet or take a group of boys there during the evening?'

'I'm not stupid,' Rowe said forcefully. 'The women took that on, and I used the one at the back of the storeroom. I had the key because I put all the equipment there overnight.'

Piercey seized on that. 'Where was the key overnight?'

'In Headquarter Company office, where it always is.'

Piercey smiled. 'Unusual for a young lad like you to give up a Saturday night to entertain tinies, when your mates were surely all in town having a good time. What did your girl think about losing out to a kids' party?'

'She's on UK leave right now. Back just before Christmas.'

'Serious, is it?'

'What's that got to do with the attack on that boy?' Rowe asked, reddening with a mix of anger and embarrassment.

'Nothing,' lied Piercey, fairly certain now that Rowe was not homosexual. 'Just interested.'

'Is that all?'

'Just one more question. During the party was the storeroom unlocked?'

'Of course. I had to change the equipment over at the end of each game.'

'So anyone could have gone through there and out again by the loading door at the back.'

'I suppose, but...'

'Thank you, that's all.'

Piercey drove off filled with satisfaction. Someone at the Recreation Centre on Saturday had gone through the storeroom, circled the building and entered by the front door, to climb the stairs, snatch the club provided to smash the glass of the fire alarm and clout Kevin with it. A swift return by the same route before absence had been noticed. Yes, it had definitely been an inside job, and he had just sussed out how it had been executed.

Heather Johnson was waiting outside Lucy Farmer's office when the subaltern returned from giving a lecture. Heather had called in at the Section's new headquarters after lunch and before driving to Hedley Company's offices. The heating system was at last sluggishly underway, but it was still much warmer here. She decided there was no need to hurry the coming interview. Although it was merely to get confirmation of what Lieutenant Farmer had said immediately after the attack on Kevin, Heather was sure she could spin it out a bit.

The disadvantage of previously having their headquarters equidistant between the two bases they served was that they only knew the personnel they had dealt with on cases. Now they were living on one of the large military establishments they would soon be familiar with many more. Lucy

Farmer was unknown to Heather. She hoped the officer would not be as supercilious as one or two women she had come across.

In fact, Heather was filled with envy on meeting the tall, graceful redhead who had every attribute for a career as an actress or model. Whatever was this beautiful young woman doing dressed in khaki and heavy boots, giving lectures on how to disarm booby trap mines? She herself was short, inclined to be top heavy, and with hair the colour of peanut butter, and she could only dream of looking like Lucy Farmer. To add salt to the wound, the subaltern had the brand of unaffected cordiality people of her class often extended to whoever they met.

'Come in, Sergeant Johnson. Take a seat,' Lucy said with a smile as she reached her office along the corridor. 'Lovely weather for skiing. Not so good for working.' Becomingly flushed from the outside temperature, she placed the files she carried on a side-table and sat behind her desk. 'Captain Rydal indicated that someone would come to corroborate what I told the Redcap corporal on Saturday evening.'

'We've taken over the case, ma'am, so there are a few points we need to clarify.'

They ran through the statement far too quickly for Heather. Ten minutes only had passed. Lieutenant Farmer was fast talking and very assured. In possession of Phil

Piercey's input, which he had delighted in telling in tones of one-upmanship, Heather began her questions.

'You helped to organize the pairs or teams for the competitions or games set up by Sapper Rowe. Were you involved in creating the equipment for them?'

'Not precisely. I scrounged materials he couldn't get by his own methods. He's a marvel not only with his hands, but with ideas for games. When he leaves the Army he could start up a business along those lines. We'd had several committee meetings in the two weeks prior to the party, and Sapper Rowe mentioned what he would need.'

'Who sat on the committee, ma'am?'

'Sar'nt-Major Fellowes, Sapper Rowe and myself.' She grinned. 'Rather a fancy tag for what were really informal discussions. With such a large number of children it's terribly important to be completely organized and to allocate tasks in advance. Mr Fellowes is an old hand at tinies' parties and controlled things admirably. All I contributed to the meetings was my knowledge of what girls were capable of doing in teams alongside boys.' She leaned forward with her elbows on her desk and her chin in her clasped hands. 'I'm sure you'll agree it would be bad to have boys winning all the time because they're stronger ... and don't hesitate to cheat,' she added with a chuckle.

'Even when they become big boys,' added

Heather, charmed in spite of herself.

'*Especially* when they're big boys! Luckily, we got the balance about right on Saturday.'

'And you just helped generally there?'

'A number of girls know me from the dance classes I give, so Mr Fellowes thought it a good idea for me to go along. "To supply the female influence",' she added in an ultra posh tone.

'But there were two mothers and Mrs Robinson on hand.'

'Ye-es.' She pursed her lips. 'Frankly, Sergeant, the mums only looked after their own offspring and gossiped. Mrs Padre seemed out of her depth until she began doling out trifle.'

'She didn't help with the competitions?'

Lucy Farmer shook her head. 'I sorted the teams and got them underway. Sapper Rowe judged the winners, wrote down their names for the list of prizes.' She leaned back in her chair. 'That was another small bit of advance assistance I gave. Mr Fellowes bought the boys' prizes and I got the girls'. Just little things like bracelets, teddy pencil cases. Nothing too elaborate because they all had a present to take home. They had to be delivered yesterday in the blizzard. Due to what happened to Kevin we had to leave the parcels in the storeroom after the party.'

Heather's thoughts pulled up sharply. 'You had access to the storeroom?'

'Had to have. Sapper Rowe left all his

equipment there on Friday night, and we had to go in and out at the party changing it for each game. The presents were in boxes ready to be given out as the kids left. I guess there's one waiting at home for Kevin. Poor boy won't want any reminders of the party.'

'One last question. Can you think of any reason why he was attacked?'

'Apart from some maniac on the loose? Or drugged to the hilt and on the rampage? No, Sergeant. Although Corporal McRitchie is in Hedley Company I know him only as a competent NCO. I've not yet encountered his wife, and I wouldn't know which of those kids at the party were his. I've only been at the base a few months. No time to get to know any families and their backgrounds.'

'Aside from the girls who attend your dance classes. And the parents who deliver and collect them.'

Cordiality was suddenly eclipsed by cool wariness as she rose. 'Yes, aside from them. Good luck with tracking down the bastard who harmed young Kevin, Sergeant.'

Heather reached her car faintly smiling. Not so perfect, after all. Was there something going on between Lucy Farmer and someone's dad? It seemed more likely than a lesbian fancy for one of the girls at her dance classes.

Tom entered the smaller of the two buildings housing the regimental band of the Royal

Cumberland Rifles. Several classrooms and offices then led to a row of small practice rooms, from which came a medley of musical phrases played on various instruments. Bandmaster Captain Booth was in his office speaking excellent German over the phone. He waved at a chair when he saw Tom in the doorway, and pulled a scribble pad forward in order to write down the information being given. That signalled the end of the call. Replacing the receiver, Christopher Booth nodded at Tom.

'Give me a few moments, Mr Black, and I'll be with you.'

They had met once before when money had started going missing from bandsmen's lockers. Tom had liked this stocky, humorous Yorkshireman who inspired his musicians to give their best; a man who had been genuinely hurt by what he felt was a betrayal of the family-style bond he had created between them.

His note-taking finished, the Bandmaster looked up with a smile. 'December's always a hectic month for us. The lads and lassies rarely have a chance to get up to Christmas mischief like most young soldiers on the base. They have to work so others can enjoy themselves. I've just finished finalizing details of the annual concert we do in conjunction with the local massed choirs. Nothing highbrow. First half folk songs and opera choruses. Second half carols. And a couple of my own festive compositions. That's the price they pay for our participation,' he added with a laugh. 'What can I do for you? Not thinking of joining us, are you?'

Tom grinned. 'The music master at my school once claimed I'm tone deaf. I'd like a word with Musician Clegg, sir.'

A frown. 'Done nothing wrong, has he?'

'Not that I know of. I just want some info on a young lad he knows who was assaulted on Saturday night. We've not yet been able to question the boy, so anything your drummer can tell me will be useful.'

Captain Booth got to his feet and came around the desk. 'He also plays trumpet and xylophone. Gifted young man. About to take his first exam on the French horn. He's in room four.' As they walked the corridor, Tom's companion said, 'I can vouch for Clegg's whereabouts on Saturday night. We were returning from Holland after a marching up and down parade at one of their lively open-air festivals.' He laughed heartily. 'Hardy people! All there in their national costumes, dancing and singing amid stalls selling cheeses, sausage, sweetmeats, liqueurs, toys and all manner of breads. Never mind the temperature!' He reached a door bearing a large 'four' and began to open it. 'Due to the snow we weren't back here until two in the morning. He's not a suspect.'

'No, sir,' agreed Tom, mentally taking

Clegg's name from his list.

On seeing Tony Clegg Tom regretted that certain alibi. Small-boned, milk blond with blue eyes surprisingly framed by dark lashes, he could have fitted Beeny's theory of sexual advances spurned by Kevin. Lowering the French horn, Clegg stood to attention in respect for the Bandmaster. He looked with interest at the big, dark-haired man in civilian clothes, until told Tom's identity. Then Clegg appeared worried.

'I'm investigating a serious assault on Kevin McRitchie,' Tom told him in neutral tones. 'You're his friend. I'd like you to tell me a little about him. What kind of boy is he?' Tom waved a hand. 'Relax! You're not on parade.'

'I'm not exactly his friend, sir,' Clegg explained. 'I play with the band's rhythm section at discos. Kevin's formed a group with three mates. They're not bad, so we gave them a go a couple of times during our breaks.'

'I heard that you meet up with him sometimes.'

Clegg shook his head. 'Not really, sir. He hangs around here after school waiting for me to leave. He's had no training, just picked it up himself, but he wants guidance on how to learn more. He wants to really *understand* music the way we do. I told him to find a teacher and have lessons, but his father's against it.' Carefully placing the horn on its stand beside him, Clegg said, 'I feel sorry for him. He's not like the usual kid his age who thinks he's on the brink of stardom. He so much wants to make music his career.'

Clegg turned to Captain Booth. 'He asked me to persuade you to hear him and give advice, sir. I told him I couldn't do that. He got very upset. Started talking about getting away, going on the road, finding someone who'd take him seriously. I thought it was just talk.' His gaze swung back to Tom. 'Has someone beaten him up?'

'Not in the sense you mean, Clegg. He hasn't done anything silly along the lines he threatened. Have you any knowledge of other friends he might have? Among the squaddies, for instance? Has he approached anyone else on the base he believes might help him?'

'Sorry, sir, I really know nothing about him apart from what I've said. I did suggest that he enlists as soon as he's old enough and applies to join a band. He said he hates the army.'

Tom sighed. 'He never spoke to you about his home life?'

'Only that his father won't let him practise at home and regards playing music as a pastime for males with no bottle.' He grim-aced.at the Bandmaster. '*His* words, sir.'

Captain Booth laughed. 'No one who saw us parading through the edams and dirndls in the snow on Saturday would deny we have bottle, Clegg. And if that lad's parent was familiar with the hours we put in during an average month, he'd eat his words.'

Back in their chilly premises the team went over the facts they had gleaned that day. 'We have two options,' Tom declared. 'The first is that the attack was mounted by one of the adults at the party, and we know it was possible to reach the toilets via the unlocked storeroom. The two mums did nothing but gossip and see to their own offspring. Mrs Robinson merely helped with the food and sat around smiling. She apparently predicts that we just have to wait for the culprit to come to us driven by remorse.

'The other adults present were Lieutenant Farmer and Sapper Rowe, who were working their socks off all evening organizing the games. They did have easy access to the storeroom, but Sarn't-Major Fellowes states that they were stacking equipment away there in preparation for the fancy-dress parade at the time we believe Kevin was attacked.

'So, we're left with the other option, that someone came to the Recreation Centre that night and waited for the victim. That poses further questions. Was Kevin the intended target, or would any lone child have been assaulted? A random assailant picking on a random victim will be a bastard to investigate, given the number on this base. If the target *was* Kevin, we then have to determine if the boy had a prearranged meeting with a person he knew. If so, it's most likely to have been connected with drugs or sex, given the venue.

'I'm inclined to believe he was the target, but we can't advance on that until we have a motive. Once that is established, the identity of the perpetrator should become obvious. Get to work on the motive.' He produced a faint smile. 'I have little faith in remorse sending the guilty party to us, despite the lady psychologist's conviction.'

Four

Max's usual low spirits on entering a hospital lifted slightly on discovering Kevin McRitchie was now in a children's ward. It was bright with wall paintings and multicoloured bedcovers and, although the unmistakable hospital smell was in the air, the patients were not elderly, defeated and dying.

A nurse explained that Mrs McRitchie had gone to have something to eat before arranging to go home. 'We had some persons staying all night because of snow. They sleep on chairs in the entrance place. Not good, but they have no place to go in the storm.'

'It took many by surprise,' Max agreed. 'How is Kevin?'

'Hurting. Unhappy. Does not like to be here.'

'But is he rational?' Seeing her problem with that word, he tried again. 'Does he understand what people say to him?'

'Yes, yes, but he cares not to talk. You will discover.'

Max discovered. Head bandaged, arms lying outside the blue and white cover, Kevin gave no reply to Max's greeting apart from a sullen glare. The boy remained silent throughout enquiries about his general well-being, and when Max said that any information he could give about what happened on Saturday night would be vitally important, Kevin turned his face away and closed his eyes.

After a short pause, Max said conversationally, 'Johnny, Malc and Callum are very upset. They say Swinga Kat can't function without you.'

The face came round then, eyes opening wide to show Max why men might have an unhealthy interest in this slender boy. He pushed on now he had the lad's attention. 'Your friends are all going to the teens' disco on Saturday. A good chance to play, I would have thought, but they said you weren't planning to attend.'

'Said I was too young, didn't they?'

'Who?'

Sullen silence again.

'Thirteen is a tricky age for us all, Kevin. There are so many things we want to do, yet we're still regarded as a child. My mother died when I was six. My father was in the army, so I attended boarding-school in England. For the long holidays I'd fly to wherever he was stationed. Sometimes it was a long-haul flight, maybe with one or two connections. I did that from the age of ten, which I thought made me a sophisticated man of the world.' He smiled. 'Not so. I was

91

caught smoking by the headmaster when I was your age, and punished because he said I was too young to indulge in adult pastimes.'

Seeing a softening in the drawn features, Max kept smiling. 'I actually didn't like the taste of tobacco, but I did it to prove something.' He sobered to say quietly, 'Is that why you went up to the toilets on the night of the party?'

It seemed the chummy approach would not work, then Kevin muttered, 'I did it to show what I thought of his pathetic rules. And I deserved a reward for having to look after *them*.'

'Them?'

'The brats.'

Possibly an apt description of Shona and Julie, thought Max recalling Tom's report on the family set-up. 'I don't have young sisters, but I'm sure I'd resent having to go to their party instead of the one my mates were attending. Did they give you grief over it?'

He shook his head. 'They know what it's like for me.'

'So you maybe arranged to meet them for a smoke and a yarn to offset the chore of babysitting.'

'Couldn't, could I? Didn't know if I'd be able to sneak away. Anyway, they had other things on. Saturday night! *Course*, they had.'

Max shifted on the hard chair. 'Saturday night is when your parents play badminton,

92

and the girls go to watch. You get the evening to yourself every week. What do you do?'

'Rehearse, watch pop videos to get the movements, like, grab a pizza and make plans.'

'For Swinga Kat?'

'Yeah, what else?'

Now they were discussing his great passion, Kevin had dropped his guard. Max advanced further. 'Have you ever tried places in town where they might give you an audition?'

Some of the light in his large eyes died. 'Waste of time, wasn't it? We even gave them a video. Had it filmed in a proper studio, nothing amateur. Didn't take it out of the box, did they?'

'The story of every budding performer's life,' Max said with sympathy. 'It takes years or an enormous stroke of luck to make it in any of the arts. The studio that filmed your video,' he continued casually, 'concentrate on musicians, do they?'

'It was just a small place. Couldn't afford a top recording studio. They make all kinds of audition tapes. They've got all the gear. Background scenes, costumes, furniture, stuff like that. Comes out on the video like you're in Vegas, or LA. Or anywhere in the world. We chose New York. Looked like we were really there. It was great!'

Max had a good idea of the kind of videos mostly made in such a studio, and pursued that line. 'Didn't they give you any tips on who you could approach?'

'They were really impressed by our performance, especially my versatility on guitar,' he explained with the guilelessness of youth. 'Gunther, the owner of the studio, offered to introduce me to a guy he knows who's interested in talented young musicians. Lives in a big house near the border that has an acoustically balanced studio with amplifiers and strobe lighting.' Kevin frowned. 'I've been trying to suss out how to work it. Gunther's willing to drive me out there, but I'd have to pretend I was overnighting with someone *they* couldn't check with.'

Something to persuade Klaus Krenkel to follow up, Max decided, but not a likely lead to the assault on Saturday night. Time to get back to that now he had the boy's cooperation.

'Kevin, what happened while you were having your defiant smoke in the gents?'

Vitality drained from the young face. 'I was looking out at the snow falling. Then I woke up here. I don't understand what's going on.'

'Someone hit you hard enough to knock you out. Surely that's been explained to you.'

He broke eye contact. 'I thought they were making it up.'

'Why?'

'Because ... who'd do that?'

'That's what I'm determined to find out. Has anyone been bullying or threatening

94

you? Or can you think why someone you know, even someone you like, might decide to hurt you to make a point? Whoever attacked you committed a serious offence. My job is to ensure they are punished accordingly.'

No response.

'I know it's difficult to speak about personal things, to talk about private concerns you're uncomfortable with, but I always found it easier to unburden myself to a stranger than to parents and family when I was your age. Mums and dads make such a song and dance over everything, don't they? You and I can speak man to man here without anyone overhearing.' He waited, then asked gently, 'How about it?'

The large eyes swivelled to a point over Max's shoulder, and they darkened with feeling. 'I'm tired. I want to sleep now.'

Mavis McRitchie appeared beside Max, saying urgently, 'Don't go to sleep, Kev. Mummy's back. She has things to tell you.' Bending over the bed she seized his hand and shook it. 'Kev, don't tease! I know you're not asleep, darling.'

Max could not have been there for all the notice she took of him, and the determined hand agitating brought results. Kevin's eyes opened, but Max knew the moment of trust had been lost and, for now, would not be recaptured. After a conventional word with the woman he had breakfasted with yesterday, he took his leave. During the difficult drive back to base, he took advantage of one of the lengthy delays to call up Tom.

'We haven't had a breakthrough yet, sir. Plenty of input, but none of it adds up without a known motive. Any luck with the boy?'

'It was hard going, but I learned two things. He hasn't a clue why he was attacked, or who might want to hurt him. And he heartily dislikes his mother. I feel sorry for the lad. He's despised by his father, ousted by his sisters, and babied by her. You're concerned about McRitchie's fondness for the girls, I'm suspicious about his wife's smother love for her pubescent son. If that boy had been drugged, shot or cut with a knife I'd wonder if it was self-inflicted. As it is, he couldn't have knocked himself out that way, and it strikes me we should find witnesses to Mavis McRitchie's unbroken presence at the Badminton Club on Saturday. She told me she occasionally makes up a set with "three other duffers" so she would not have been on court continuously.'

'Mmm, Nora said we should look carefully at the women in this case, who might have been repulsed in their desire to initiate a cock virgin.'

Max smiled. 'Your wife should join our team. I've told you that before. I'm likely to take some time getting back. The traffic's snarled up all the way, and there's black ice forming. I'll see you in the morning for a briefing. Maybe we'll all have a fresh view of it after an early night.'

'Righto, sir. Oh, Treeves is being brought in. Should arrive around midnight. What d'you want done with him?'

The cars ahead began moving slowly, so Max put his in gear and followed. 'Tell them to take him direct to the Medical Centre, ostensibly for observation following an assault. None of us is going to sit up half the night waiting to interview him. We'll do that in the morning.'

Tom welcomed the new short drive home. Road conditions were worsening as night fell. He called up the Redcaps bringing Treeves in and passed on Max's directive, but they had doubts about completing their journey by midnight. Tom privately sympathized. It was an unenviable duty.

Garaging his car, he walked to the front door aware of the slippery crust on the snow. Was this the prelude to a Siberian-style winter, he wondered moodily. It would make investigations doubly difficult. Their area of duty covered a second base now twice as distant.

His mood lightened on entering the hall and smelling lamb hotpot. His nose was familiar with all Nora's recipes and this was one of his favourites. He counted himself lucky she was not a woman who loved to spend hours and large sums on 'creating' dishes that looked on the plate more like a piece of abstract art than a meal. He liked the things his mother used to make and still did. What she called good, plain, healthy food. Nora now cooked it for him.

In the sitting-room were his wife, three daughters and a blond youth of around fifteen, all engaged around the coffee-table in unwrapping Christmas tree baubles. The boy got to his feet swiftly and stood almost to attention, gazing at Tom with a hint of uncertainty in his blue eyes.

'Hi, Dad. Hi, Dad. Hi, Dad,' came the usual triple greeting, but Maggie was on her feet to gently push the boy forward. 'This is Hans Graumann. He lives across the road.'

'Good ee-ven-ing, sir,' said the boy thickly, still at attention.

Tom glanced quickly at Nora, who smiled an urgent message. 'Maggie slipped on the ice on her way from the school bus. Hans helped her up and brought her to the door. We invited him in for tea and cake.'

Silence.

'Hans's father is the manager of an insurance company,' Maggie said, giving the boy a glance rife with something Tom read clearly. 'He's learning English, so I said I'd help him with that if he'll help me with German.' When Tom still said nothing, she gave a nervous giggle. 'Hans, not his father.'

Nora came from the table, saying, 'I'll leave you all to finish that. Take care. Some of those baubles are so ancient they'll fall

98

apart with rough handling.' She smiled at the boy. 'Thank you for your help, Hans.'

Tom followed her from the room to a kitchen redolent with the aroma of lamb hotpot. There she rounded on him. 'The cat's got your tongue, has it?'

'Now hold on a minute. I've just got home after a hard day.'

Her eyes flashed. 'Don't give me that corny old line, Tom.'

He took a deep breath. 'I usually give you a kiss ... and get one in return. What happened to that?'

'I'm waiting to hear.'

'I'm waiting to hear why that boy's in there with Maggie. She's only twelve, for God's sake!'

'She'll be a teenager next month. "That boy" helped her up when she fell, and escorted her home. How many his age would do that? We've taught our children good manners, so she naturally asked him in to meet me. His mother works, so we gave him tea and cake rather than let him go home to an empty house.'

'He'll be used to that.'

'No doubt, but today he had a pleasant reward for a good deed.' She fixed him with a gleaming eye. 'Tom, they mix with boys every day. At school, at the Youth Club, on outings, at parties. They have lives outside those brief times you manage to join us, you know.'

'Don't start sniping,' he retorted. 'I saw the way she looked at him, even if you didn't.'

'I saw. She's never encountered male gallantry, so let her revel in it for a while. She's unlikely to experience it all that often in today's world.'

His curious sense of anger intensified. 'She's a *child*, Nora.'

'But a biological woman from several months ago, and starting to experience emotions that are difficult to understand and deal with. Good God, you heard her raving about Helmut Weber, and you've seen the posters on her bedroom wall of heart-throbs in revealing togas or brief loincloths.'

'That's different, they're fantasy men.'

'Fantasy is no longer enough for her, Tom.' Leaning against the worktop, she folded her arms and smiled. 'They're only unwrapping baubles in that room. I don't think they're having sex.'

Her ridicule fanned his anger. 'He's German!'

'And we're living in his country.'

'That blond hair, blue eyes, the metaphorical clicking of heels. The pure Aryan!'

'Whose father is in insurance and his mother serves in the local babywear shop! Hans Graumann isn't reviving Hitler Youth, but you know who is. You've come across them in town often enough, picking fights with our squaddies. Shaven heads, earrings, tattoos, spiked boots and flick knives.'

'All the more reason why we should protect our girls from nationalism in any form.'

'I do. You are forced to trust me on that as with every other aspect of rearing them largely single-handed.'

This reminder of the demands of his job that took so much of his time irked him further, but her next comment blew his fuse.

'Face it, love, you're suffering from paternal jealousy.'

It cut into him like a knife. He could not believe she had said it. 'That's ... that's *unforgiveable!*'

On the brink of a rare first-class row, Nora hastened to defuse the atmosphere by crossing to take his hands in an urgent clasp.

'Calm down! I didn't mean what you think. You're so hot on child abuse you misinterpreted my words.' Her eyes appealed for his understanding. 'Every natural father has the undeniable instinct to protect and defend his daughters.' She produced a faint smile. 'It's a man thing, love. For the first years of their lives *he's* their hero. Suddenly, other males start to attract and almost imperceptibly coax them away. That natural protective instinct sees these males as contenders unworthy of the role they're trying to usurp. Paternal jealousy is universally common. It's a fact of life and has nothing to do with perversion, you goof! Better get used to it. We've two more growing up fast.' She kissed him, smiling into his eyes. 'The plus side is that dads come into their own again when granddaughters appear, and daughters never entirely lose that belief in them as someone special.'

The anger began to drain from him. He stroked her hand. 'Sorry, love. Shouldn't have taken it out on you. I've had a gutful of parents and their kids over the last few days. McRitchie has an *un*natural instinct concerning his girls, believe me. Now Max has indicated the wife shows excessive fondness towards young Kevin, which echoed your comment about frustrated women yearning to initiate cock virgins. Perversion was heavily on my mind, I'm afraid.'

Nora kissed him again, more lingeringly. 'I prefer it straight, just the way you do it.'

The inevitable multiple accident delayed Max by more than an hour, so dinner was about to be served when he reached his room. He was ready for a meal and showered swiftly before searching for a clean shirt in baggage he had not yet unpacked. Perhaps it was because it would suggest he was going to stay put, when he fully intended to find more amenable quarters.

Having time for that would be difficult. The McRitchie case was tricky, and there was Treeves to deal with. Max now had little doubt the man was involved in the theft; proving it would be difficult. All too often SIB knew who was guilty but could not produce strong enough evidence to mount a case. When they could, the decision to prosecute lay with the offender's commanding officer. Military Police personnel knew all too well how loath these men were to make things official in the courts, preferring, whenever possible, to deal with it less publicly and so protect the reputation of the regiment.

His reflective mood was jolted on discovering a large number of men and women gathered in the ante-room. Bright conversation, laughter, an air of cameraderie more usually found on obligatory dining-in nights were exactly what he did not want right now. Having had no time really to get to know anyone he felt very much the cuckoo in this merry nest. Tempted to turn around and seek a meal elsewhere, regardless of the snow, Max was prevented from leaving by Lucy Farmer who greeted him effusively.

'Hi there! How are you on traffic control? This lot need to be channelled into lanes leading to the food. I'm ravenous, are you?'

'What's the occasion?' he asked, ignoring her flippancy. Maybe she really was a police groupie.

'*This* isn't the occasion, that comes later in the week. Best togs and deeply intellectual conversation. Tonight's just an informal welcome to the eggheads.'

'Eggheads?'

She patted his arm sympathetically. 'You

wouldn't know, of course. Too busy detecting. For the next ten days the annual inter-services chess championship is being held here on the base.' She adopted a grave expression. 'It's all deadly serious. Service honour is at stake in addition to personal esteem. Players frequently take hours over each move.' She then laughed. 'Can you think of any other game played so slowly? I prefer sport with furious action. How about you? You look the athletic type.'

Max shook his head. 'My father is an outstanding all-round sportsman. I'm merely a competent rugby player and oarsman, I fear.' Appreciative of her attractiveness in a figure-hugging pale blue sweater and skirt, he wished she were less shallow. 'I'll steer clear of the eggheads. Chess, like all sedentary games, has never held any interest for me.'

Putting her head on one side and studying him in a very frank manner, she said, 'I think you'd be good at chess. Your mind is geared to fathoming solutions from miscellaneous facts. Have you discovered yet who attacked young Kevin?'

Max was spared a reply by an eager, fresh-faced young man who dragged Lucy off through the press of people moving to the dining-room. Max held back, still vaguely inclined to eat elsewhere.

'Steering clear of the deadly serious chess players?' asked a voice tinged with amusement from beside him.

She was tall and dark-haired, with eyes so deeply brown they seemed almost black against her pale skin. The red-haired Lucy Farmer was glowingly attractive, but this woman's understated sensuality robbed Max of words.

'I plead guilty to eavesdropping on your conversation. Quite a feat in this hubbub, but you made such an arresting couple I was unashamedly inquisitive.' She offered her hand. 'Livya Cordwell. One of the eggheads.'

Her handshake was firm, her gaze was steady. Those things usually told Max a lot about people, but all he could think of now was how nearly he had missed this moment by going elsewhere for his dinner.

'Your head isn't in the least like an egg,' he said, then cursed the banality of his words.

She laughed. 'That's the strangest compliment I've ever received. Rugby player and oarsman, but what else do you do and who are you?'

How he wished he had inherited his father's abundant ease with women. 'I'm Max Rydal. SIB.'

'Ah, that explains the comment about fathoming solutions from miscellaneous facts. She's right, you'd probably make a good chess player.'

Fighting to recapture his equilibrium, Max demurred. 'You have total control over the pieces on a chess board. We deal with humans who make their own moves, frequently turning our conclusions into a dog's dinner.'

'But you forget we have an opponent who forces us into moves that make a dog's dinner of *our* stratagems. We don't have total control, you know.' She nodded in the direction of the dining-room. 'Shall we continue this while we eat?'

Max followed her unable to take his eyes from her curves enhanced by her tightly belted amber wool dress. The evening had grown unexpectedly exciting. They found two seats together at the end of a table. Unfortunately, they were opposite two men involved in the championship. They knew Livya Cordwell and embarked on anecdotes of previous such occasions. This at least enabled Max to collect his thoughts. It was a long time since he had been so dumbstruck on meeting a woman. Well ... since first meeting Susan.

Livya soon adroitly ended the focus on chess and concentrated on Max. He then took the opportunity to find out more about her.

'Are you with a regiment or corps? You didn't say when you introduced yourself.'

She smiled. 'I was too busy being a bighead about being an egghead, wasn't I? I'm with Intelligence.'

His interest multiplied. 'So we have a link. We rely on info from you to get to the bottom of some of the cases we investigate.'

'I'm more concerned with internal security, Max.' She studied him closely. 'Are you in any way related to Brigadier Andrew Rydal? I can see a faint resemblance.'

'You know my father?' he asked, unhappy about the comparison she was certain to make.

'Not well. Our paths have crossed once or twice. He's very charming.'

Max moved from that subject quickly. 'Is your name a shortened version of Olivia?'

'No. My mother is from the Czech Republic. She had a close friend with that name. It ends with ya and is pronounced Liv-yah.' She smiled. 'I have numerous Czech relations whom I adore and visit often.'

'You're bilingual?'

'With a smattering of German and Polish.'

He was now getting a good idea of how she knew his father, and in which department in Intelligence she worked. Her Slavic connections would be useful to them. That bloodline also explained her dark attractiveness and the lilt in her voice.

Hardly aware of what he was eating, or of the activity around him, Max heard that she had been taught to play chess at the age of eight by her Czech grandfather, and had taken part in two previous inter-services championships. She had been a finalist last year, and beaten by an RAF corporal.

'Bob Hollins is a genius,' she said with

fervour. 'No one's beaten him for five years. I'd love to be the one who breaks his record.'

'I'll break his neck for you, if it'll help.'

She let her hand rest lightly on his for a moment in acknowledgement of his humorous offer. 'I want to outfox him the hard way. I'm extremely competitive.'

'So when do you fire the first shot?' he asked, wishing he had taken up chess years ago.

'Tomorrow. The pressure is on for the army to win this year.'

'I'll be following progress with interest. Should I fly flags on my car as they do during the World Cup?'

Her laughter enchanted him further. 'Black background with an egghead rampant?'

The evening flew past until they realized everyone had gone. It was then that Max had another reason for cursing his need to live in-mess. Officers were not expected to entertain members of the opposite sex in their rooms. It sometimes happened, of course, but was deeply frowned on and always prompted a reprimand from the commanding officer. If it continued, one of the officers was posted elsewhere. What they did in private hirings was their own responsibility, unless it was adultery with another serving person. Max had handled such cases in the past. He now experienced the other side of the coin and understood the temptation.

They said goodnight and parted. Max's

only consolation was that Livya would be there for ten days. A lot could happen in that time. Sleep did not come but, for once, he had no wish to induce it by listening to his CDs of mandolins or Paraguayan harps. He lay thinking of her and making plans for furthering their friendship.

Well into the early hours he drifted off, to be woken shortly afterwards by his mobile ringing. The clock showed four a.m. He grunted his name, still half-asleep.

'Sorry to disturb you, sir,' said Tom. 'I've had a call from Corporal Meacher. They've just arrived at the Medical Centre with Lance-Corporal Treeves. They believed him to be asleep in the back of the vehicle, but they couldn't wake him. The Duty Doctor has just confirmed that he's dead.'

Five

The next three days led them no further forward to answers to vital questions. The pathologist had not yet discovered why Lance-Corporal Treeves had not survived the journey back to base. The Military Police at the post near the border, who had collected the driver from the home of the Haufmanns, confirmed that they had organized an immediate medical examination in view of his alleged assault. The doctor had declared him fit to travel.

The RMP Corporals Meacher and Stubble had been questioned about the hazardous road journey. Shocked by the death, both had claimed Treeves was fairly communicative until midnight, when they stopped at an all-night café for a hot drink and a sandwich. They then believed he had fallen asleep. Most likely he had, but somewhere along the way his heart had stopped beating. A quiet, peaceful, instant death. The question was why?

The corporals said they had all had salami sandwiches, and tea from the same urn. They had all taken sugar from the container on the table. Even so, the *Polizei* investigated the café premises and checked the food suppliers they used. A German policeman, along with a sergeant from the RMP post, interviewed the Haufmanns. In particular the wife. She gave her medical opinion that the English soldier had been bewildered, hungry, thirsty and anxious to get back to his own people, but otherwise was none the worse for his ordeal. She told her questioners that she and her husband found his story hard to believe. How many gangs of thieves carried with them sleeping-bags for the comfort of their victims? But for the warmth of it the soldier would surely have suffered from hypothermia – perhaps would have died.

Throughout the investigation that fact was the huge flaw in Treeves' story. It strongly suggested that he had been party to the theft, which cast doubts on his partners-in-crime being held responsible for his death. Klaus Krenkel, commanding the area police who often worked with their military counterparts, thought the theft had probably been carried out by a gang of immigrants who had been monitoring 26 Section's preparations to move premises.

The Redcaps knew there were many illegal immigrants who were forced to turn to crime in order to live. The sleeping-bag could be explained by the belief that murder, especially of a soldier, was a crime too far for them. If Treeves had been involved there was now no case against him to pursue, and the *Polizei* were searching for the stolen equipment. In the uniformed branch of the RMP there was some sniggering over the fact that the Special *Investigation* Branch had lost their property and had no idea where it was.

Departmental rivalry was the least of the Section's worries. Forensics had failed to get any good fingerprints from the club because one of the paramedics had first trodden on it, then tossed it free of the space around their patient. Similarly, with footprints. So many small feet had scurried across those tiles that evening it was impossible to lift anything from the mess.

After again questioning the adults present at the party, who repeated their belief that everyone was there the whole time, the team had to conclude that Kevin's attacker had entered and left the building unseen. This faced them with the prospect of checking the movements of all who had remained on-base that night.

At the Thursday morning briefing Max deferred that for one day, insisting that the key to cracking the case lay with pinpointing a motive.

'Before I'll accept that this was a chance assault by someone entering the Recreation Centre with an overpowering need to bash someone for the fun of it, I need to be absolutely sure there's no other explanation. Sergeant Johnson, you said you have young brothers.'

'That's right, sir. Thirteen and fifteen.'

'I want you to visit Kevin. With your experience of male teenagers maybe you'll coax more from him than I did. Sergeant Bush, interview Mrs McRitchie at her home. Dig deeper into her relationship with her son. And with her husband. That's a very complex family group.'

Connie Bush smiled. 'Perhaps we should get the Padre's wife to psychoanalyse them.'

Piercey chuckled. 'We've only to wait and she'll spirit the guilty party to our door any day now.'

'I hope she will. I sincerely hope she will,' said Max. 'In case she doesn't, we'll continue investigating and you can go with Sergeant Beeny to interview more penetratingly the three lads who form Swinga Kat with Kevin. My guts tell me someone had a motive for punishing that particular boy. It's out there. Go and find it.'

As they dispersed, slipping their arms in the sleeves of topcoats, Max turned to Tom. 'I agree with your suggestion that it's worth checking with Greg McRitchie's platoon, and with his fellow NCOs. He's an aggressive, macho type. Excellent qualities in combat, provided they're kept under control, but in day-to-day dealings they can create resentment fierce enough to inspire revenge.

To hurt him through the boy is the easy option.'

'Particularly if it's not known that he cares nothing for his son.' Tom nodded. 'I don't accept the random attack theory either, but my problem is still the timing. Unless chummy waited up on the first floor on the off chance of Kevin visiting the bog, and un-accompanied, it has to have been an arrang-ed rendezvous. Is that boy truly amnesiac about that evening, or is he hiding some-thing?'

'Let's hope Heather gets the answer today. We can't rule out the possibility that Kevin was handling drugs, which would satisfy the notion of a rendezvous. There's no evidence the boy is a user, but I'm off to visit the studio where Swinga Kat made a video. It sounds a very dodgy place where legit busi-ness is only a fraction of what they're up to. Kevin is fervent enough about making his mark in the pop world, he's liable to agree to do anything in return for the promise of musical promotion. He's the perfect agent for a dealer wanting to start up on an army base where his own entry is prohibited.'

'Mmm,' said Tom non-committally.

'Yes, I know it's a long shot, especially when there are places enough out there where troops can buy stuff, but a dealer with a contact on the inside is one jump ahead.'

'But a young boy?'

'Who wouldn't be risking half as much as a

soldier, and who would supply his mates. Catch 'em young.' He gave a faint smile. 'One of my wilder ideas, I admit, but worth following. There's the additional question of the dependant son of a serving soldier being coaxed into spending a night at the home of a supposed talent scout with a special interest in youths.'

'*That* I do believe needs our investigation.' Tom's voice hardened. 'Neither parent is likely to protect that lad.'

Shrugging on his topcoat, Max asked casually, 'Did you know there's a cut-throat chess championship being fought out here over the next week or so?'

'I heard rumours. Last year Camberley, year before Cyprus. Nice little jolly for those who get their kicks from board games. I'd spell it b-o-r-e-d, but each to his own.'

'They're not all intense eggheads.'

Tom cast him a speculative glance. 'Is that a fact?' When Max failed to rise to that, he said, 'Like any other grand sporting contest, it's spawned ambitious amateurs. I'm reliably told by my offspring that everyone's playing it now.' He buttoned his padded coat, scowling. 'Maggie's getting "expert tuition" from a German boy who lives over the road. She says he's the local junior champ at the game. I've advised Nora to keep an eye on what game it is. They're spending a lot of time together and I can't believe they're playing chess for all of it.'

Max chuckled. 'Come on, Tom, remember what you got up to in your teens.'

'I do. That's the root of my concern.'

Heather Johnson was not a lover of snow. It looked very pretty before it turned to slush, but she felt it could only be gushed over from inside a cosy house, looking from a window at a snow-draped garden sparkling in sunshine, knowing she had not to drive anywhere. Her journey to the hospital was cold and demanding. She then spent an age finding a parking place where she was unlikely to be blocked in by a thoughtless or distraught driver.

The children's ward was bright with colour, and members of staff were engaged in hanging sparkling silhouettes of bells and angels on the walls. At home in England there would be friezes of frosted snowflakes to create the atmosphere of Christmas. Here, they had enough outside.

Kevin McRitchie was stretched listlessly in a chair at the end of the ward, where smaller children were playing with books and toys. Heather approached him and smiled.

'Hallo, Kevin. My name's Heather. I'm with SIB. Captain Rydal's caught up with something today, so he asked me to see how you're getting on.' He showed little interest, so she said, 'When my brother Keith was in hospital he found there was little to amuse a boy of thirteen. Plenty of toys and girlie

116

dolls, but no clever gismos or space games. He likes that kind of thing. And pop, of course. He'll be green with envy when I tell him I've been talking to someone his age who leads his own group. Swinga Kat's a really cool name. Did you think that up?'

Kevin nodded, sitting straighter. 'Heard it on a cop show on telly. Guy said his office wasn't big enough to swing a cat, and I thought it sounded awesome.'

'It does.' She glanced over her shoulder. 'Where's your bed? Could we go there to talk away from the noise of these tinies?'

'If you like. They said I had to sit out today, but if you're there they won't go on at me.'

They walked together to his bed. He sat on it and Heather took the visitors' chair. 'Are they strict here? Getting on at you all the time?'

He looked mulish. 'They say I can go home before long, but I don't feel well enough.'

'That's because there's nothing to do here. Keith was the same until I took him some mags, puzzles and his Walkman. He soon felt better.' She reached in her shoulder bag. 'I managed to pick up a couple of puzzle books in the NAAFI shop. The *Musicmaker* mags were back copies I guessed you'd already read, but I thought you might like to borrow my Walkman and some CDs my brother gave me a couple of years ago. Old stuff by today's scene, but stuff that's stayed the course. Pop classics, I guess.'

His large eyes gazed at her in surprised wonderment, and she anticipated his next words. 'Why doesn't *she* bring me something like that?'

'Your mother?'

He nodded, concentrating on the boxed CDs and murmuring, 'Yeah, yeah,' as he read the titles.

'It's not been easy to get to and fro since you were admitted.'

'You got here,' he muttered, still studying the CDs.

'We have special vehicles for rotten weather. Besides, your mother has a lot on her plate, cooking meals and looking after your sisters, too.'

'*Them!*' His mouth twisted in contempt. 'They've got their precious dadda.'

'But he's often on duty, and they're too young to be left on their own. That, and the weather, is why your mother hasn't been to see you, I expect.'

He looked up, eyes bright with an emotion Heather could not immediately identify. 'She's been. Every day. She'll turn up any minute now, and spoil this like she did when the officer came.'

'You mean Captain Rydal?'

'Yeah. He's all right. Knows what it's all about.'

'But your mother doesn't?' Heather prayed the woman would not come just as she appeared to be gaining ground.

118

Turning a CD box over and over in restless hands, Kevin said jerkily, 'He took the brats away from her, so she tries to...'

'Yes?'

'Nothing.'

Heather was experienced enough to move on. 'What's the food like in here?'

'The pits.'

'That's what my brother said. Still, you'll be back home shortly for meals you like.'

'I don't want to go home.' It was blurted out with something approaching desperation.

'Why's that, Kevin?' she asked gently.

There were threatening tears in eyes that appealed for understanding. 'He hates me, and she just wants to cuddle me all the time. I'm too old for that now. I don't like it. My mates don't have to put up with it. I've told her, but she just cries and says she might as well be dead and out of it because no one would care.'

Deeply concerned, Heather said swiftly, 'She doesn't mean that. Mums tend to exaggerate when they're upset.'

'She means it. *She* hates me now, because I won't do what she wants.' He dropped the CD on the coverlet and gripped Heather's hand. 'Can I trust you?'

'Of course you can,' she assured him soothingly.

'Last Saturday she got upset because he was making a big deal out of dressing the

119

brats in their costumes. Then she began to fiddle with mine, pulling it straight and that.' He took a deep breath. 'She touched me ... you know. *There*. I pulled away and shouted at her. She followed me to the door, crying. I told her if she did it again I'd leave home. I went and sat in the car with the door locked, until he came out with the brats. I could see the light on in my room. She was up there touching my things.' He clenched Heather's hand as if it were a lifeline. '*She* did this to me. She hurt me because I said I'd leave. I'm not going back there. I'm *not*!'

Phil Piercey and Derek Beeny arranged with the headmaster to interview the boys separately during their mid-morning break and the period that followed. They should have played football, but the pitch was too icy and the sportmaster intended to show videos of professional championship matches. Swinga Kat musicians could afford to miss some of that.

Johnny King, thickset with heavy features, resembled his heavyweight boxer father in looks but not ambition. His sights were set on beating the hell out of drums instead. He appeared pugnacious enough when summoned, however.

'I don't know any more now than last Sunday,' he stated, standing feet apart, arms folded, ignoring the invitation to sit.

'Neither do we,' said Piercey crisply, 'but

we're not Kevin's mates. You know him well and we think you can help us if you put your mind to it. Sit down and answer our questions ... there's a good lad.' He added the last, conscious of Jean Bakewell, school secretary, whose presence fitted the description of appropriate adult.

Johnny sat with obvious unwillingness. 'I only know Kev in the group. His drive to make it, like. He only talks music and gigs when we get together. We don't do anything else. I mean, he's brilliant on guitar, and that, but he can't tell you a thing about Beckham or Schumacher. He's never heard of Hobbits and never read Harry Potter. Fact is, I don't think he reads anything except music mags. See what I mean? He's a dead loss without a guitar in his hand.'

Beeny perched on the corner of a staff-room table to ask quietly, 'Does he ever seem hyped up when you get together?'

'You mean is he on drugs? No, he's just a nutter when it comes to Swinga Kat.' He forced a grin. 'A *nice* nutter. I mean, he's a mate, and all that.'

'But you have other mates who know about football, *Lord of the Rings* and boy wizards – mates you see when you're not playing drums?'

'Yeah, course. The group isn't all there is going.'

'Got a girlfriend, have you? asked Piercey in chummy manner.

Johnny cast a swift glance at Miss Bakewell and hedged. 'There's a group of us meet up sometimes.'

'Are Malc Carpenter and Callum Peters in that group?'

'Yeah.'

'But not Kevin McRitchie?'

'He's not into girls.'

'Oh, why's that?' asked Beeny.

'He's not gay,' came the immediate response from this sharp lad. 'Least, I don't get that he is.' He cast another glance at the woman sitting quietly to the side of the room. 'He's just—'

'Yes?'

'I ... I can't say.'

'Yes, you can,' Beeny told him encouragingly. 'This conversation is completely confidential.'

'And Miss Bakewell is very hard of hearing.' Piercey winked at the boy before turning to her. 'Isn't that right, ma'am?'

She played along. 'Sorry, I didn't quite catch that.'

Beeny moved from the table to sit on a chair next to Johnny. 'You were going to tell us why you believe Kevin's not into girls.'

Johnny appeared to be fighting a battle with his conscience, but eventually decided it was all right to speak frankly. 'Shona and Julie rule the roost in that house. What they want, they have. What they say goes. They tell tales about Kev. Things that mostly aren't true. His dad believes them and gives Kev punishments – military punishments.' He looked disgusted. 'His dad says the family's like a platoon. Has to have strict discipline.'

'How does Kevin's mum rate that idea?' asked Piercey, almost casually.

Well into letting everything out of the bag by now, Johnny said, 'She's just the reverse. Treats Kev like a baby. Still kisses him when he goes out or comes in, and insists on tucking him in when he goes to bed.' Colour flooded his face. Either embarrassment or indignation. 'He used to lock his door, but she's hidden the key. That really upset him.' Deferring to Miss Bakewell's presence, he leaned forward to whisper, 'He thinks females are the pits.'

Max drove into town where the streets had been cleared by snowploughs, and stores were being invaded by women driven by the present-buying frenzy. Toyshops, in particular, were filled almost to overflowing. Yet again Max caught himself wondering how it would be to have a child, several children, to introduce to the delight of Christmas.

He could vaguely recall his mother helping him to unwrap parcels in bright paper. The mental vision he had of her was possibly due more to photographs of a dark-haired, smiling woman with laughing blue eyes, than to his actual memories of her.

Those early Christmases had been wonderful, with his father hauling in a giant tree and mounting a stepladder to arrange coloured lights and baubles on it. There had been grandparents in carpet slippers and woollen jumpers, who had made a great fuss of him. Yet he had always wished for a brother or sister to play with.

One year he had been given a puppy, but his grandparents had had to have it back because his father had been posted to Malaya and took his family with him. Three months later, Max's mother had died of a virulent fever and he had been sent home to boarding-school. Christmas had never been a glad, warm, wonderful time again. He needed his own children to revive that loving feeling.

Almost imperceptibly, his thoughts moved on to Livya Cordwell. His hopes had been dashed on two evenings when she had failed to appear, but last night had been very successful. She had made a point of joining him on entry, and had stayed with him until the obligatory parting of the ways in the first floor corridor. The official dinner for the guests was being held tonight. Max planned to invite her to dine with him on Saturday at what he had been told was the best hotel in town. He was very, very attracted to her and those ten days were passing too swiftly.

He was having to relearn the art of courtship rather quickly. For the past three years his dealings with women had been strictly on the professional scale. The memory of Susan had always hovered on the social scene. He would never forget her, but Livya Cordwell was too vital to let slip through his fingers.

Lost in speculation, Max arrived at his destination before he was ready to abandon his pleasant thoughts. Tucked away in the sleazier area of town, the so-called studio had frosted windows bearing huge black exclamation marks on each side of a black door. Above the premises a white-fascia board bore the word RAMSCH in scarlet letters edged with black.

Max decided the owners had either a defiant sense of humour, or they were attempting to be quirkily trendy. *Ramsch* translated as rubbish, leftovers, bits and pieces. Probably a true description of the business conducted here. How had Kevin known of this place? Possibly from an advertisement in a pop magazine designed to lure such as he with the promise of fame?

Driving around the corner, Max could see the large square extension at the rear of the building. The film studio where every type of action was recorded? He parked at the end of the long, narrow street, then pulled off his tie and unbuttoned his shirt collar. Climbing from the car he replaced his polished leather boots with muddy ones, and exchanged his wool topcoat for a shabby anorak kept with the boots in the car for investigating in rough terrain. He then thought he looked more the part he prepared to play.

Crunching over the snow, Max turned the corner and pushed open the heavy black door to be met with the heady perfume of joss-sticks. The tiny reception area had scarlet walls and a desk at which sat a surprisingly classy-looking girl in her early twenties. The black velvet curtain over an archway behind her was the perfect backdrop for her blonde colouring and the ice-blue classic suit she wore.

She smiled invitingly as she assessed the tall, chunky man dressed the way many visitors to *Ramsch* were. Max had no doubts that she was as good a judge of people as himself and his team on initial contact. Her voice was low and husky as she asked how she could serve him. Wording suited to what went on here, Max thought.

He replied in English, rather brashly, that Gunther was the man who could provide the service he needed. Knew just how to handle what he had in mind, he added with a wink.

Still smiling, she got to her feet and vanished behind the velvet curtain. Guessing he was now being viewed through a hidden peephole, Max scratched his head, studied his finger nails, spat on his handkerchief and rubbed at a spot on his sleeve, looked at his watch and muttered, 'Come on. Come on.'

The girl returned and beckoned him to the nether regions – the large square area filled with cameras, some hanging from gantries, others scattered about the floor. To one side was a glass-walled cubicle containing a small desk with telephones, and a control panel with a suspended microphone.

Gunther, who came from the cubicle to meet him, was so exactly as Max expected it was as though they had met before. Stick thin and wearing black jeans with a mustard silk shirt, he had spiked gingery hair and matching designer stubble. There was no smile, no proffered hand.

'There was a recommendation to visit me?' Gunther's English was precise but expressionless.

Max thrust his hands in his pockets. 'Met this guy in a bar. Got talking, found we had similar interests. Know what I mean? Said you could fix me up.'

'He has a name, this guy?'

Max gave a conspiratorial smile. 'Fritz, wouldn't you know?'

'And you have a name?'

'George. Look, I run a nice little business in erotic videos back home, but I needed new blood. Came over to Europe looking. Found myself some new models. Two guys, three girls. All willing to do anything. Know what I mean? Immigrants who need the money. Exotic they are. Just right for my market. Problem! My studio's in London and no way can I smuggle them all over there.'

'You want to film them here?'

'Yeah. You have the props, the right set-up. Can do?'

'Of course. That is why this *Fritz* sent you here.'

'Problem! I have to go back on Sunday. Gives us just two days.'

Gunther was in business. 'If your models are good, OK, but it takes time. My studio is booked from mid-afternoon on Saturday. Tomorrow free. We do what we can. Maybe more Saturday morning. Come!'

Max followed the German to his office to discuss the number and length of the videos. Then came the demand Max had been waiting for. A large advance payment to reserve the studio for a day. In cash.

'Problem,' said Max with the right amount of regret. 'I don't carry that many euros on me, especially this time of year on crowded streets. I'll nip off and pick 'em up the easy way. Back in an hour.'

Gunther stared at him. 'The offer is open for one hour and one half. Then the studio is available for others.'

'Sure. Understood,' Max replied with a nod. 'I like a guy who runs a tight business. We'll work well together.'

They began walking back to the curtain and Max lowered his voice. 'Fritz in the bar hinted that you're also right on for supplying a man on the move a long way from his regular supplier. That right? Can you fix me up for when I come with the models tomorrow?'

There was silence until they reached the archway. Max glanced at Gunther. 'How about it?'

'I cannot help you. Try Florian at the Pink Pig.' He pushed aside the curtain. 'One hour and one half only, George.'

Max returned to his car knowing Gunther was definitely into porn, but not drugs. Florian at the Pink Pig probably held the monopoly in this town. Which knocked on the head the idea that Kevin McRitchie was being bribed into supplying as a result of the Swinga Kat video. Klaus Krenkel would be aware of what went on at *Ramsch*, but porn was usually tolerated provided it didn't involve minors or animals. Nothing about Gunther had suggested he dabbled in those areas. Another 'Florian' would run that criminal business. Even so, Max determined to drop a word in Klaus's ear about Gunther's offer to introduce Kevin to a supposed talent scout. The *Polizei* might not be aware of *that* sideline.

Tom was having a fruitless morning one way and another. The men in Greg McRitchie's platoon were tight-lipped on the subject of their corporal. Understandably. Not one was foolish enough to rubbish someone in a position to make them pay for being a blabbermouth. There was certainly no hint that he was admired as some could be, especially during active service when understanding leadership often saved lives. His fellow NCOs said, if somewhat guardedly, that he was worth his two stripes despite tending to be overly inflexible.

Lieutenant Lucy Farmer said she had been his platoon commander too short a time to know much about his personal life, but he was hot stuff on squad drilling. Also, the standard of his men's turnout and living quarters was always exemplary. He set a perfect example with his own appearance and bearing, which made him a valuable NCO.

'Maybe he's a little rigid in his attitude,' she conceded as she and Tom drank coffee in her office. 'I've not so far been in action against an enemy, but I'm sure the most successful commanders under fire are those who remember at all times that soldiers are human, not robots.'

Tom found himself being charmed by her vivid looks and outgoing personality, which brought to the surface his unshakeable belief that women should never be sent to war zones. Imagine this glowing, vital creature being peppered with bullets on some God-forsaken battlefield. No, all wrong!

In the midst of these thoughts his mobile rang. Excusing himself, he walked out along the corridor to take a call from Heather Johnson.

'Where are you?' he asked.

'At the hospital. Sir, Kevin has just indicated that his mother is too free with her loving gestures. He says she handled his penis before he left for the party on Saturday. He made his disgust apparent, probably swore at her, and said if she ever did it again he'd leave home. Seems she got wildly upset and angry because he stormed out and locked himself in the car until his father brought his sisters out.

'He's presently in a nervous state because the doctor has said he can go home before too long. It's genuine fear, sir, and I understand why. His father gives him military punishments, whatever that means, his sisters crow over him, and his mother is venting her sexual frustration on him.'

'We'll have to put Welfare on to that. All those kids are being used by their parents to satisfy some element lacking in their own lives. Now Kevin has made a definite claim of sexual abuse intervention is permissible.'

'Here's the crunch. Kevin claims his mother committed the assault on Saturday. He says it was her punishment for his threat to leave home. I asked if he actually saw her with the weapon in her hand, and he said he did. I can't credit that's the truth, sir. He could be lying due to his dread of returning to that unhappy situation at home.'

Tom sighed. 'Well, whatever, we can't question him further without a medical presence, probably a psychiatrist. See if you can

131

get the nurse to give him something calming, then head back to base.'

'One more thing, sir. I called Connie Bush, but she had missed Mrs McRitchie at the house by fifteen minutes. A neighbour said she was on her way here.'

'All the more reason for you to leave. The medical staff can deal adequately with her.'

'I told Connie Kevin has accused his mother, so she's going to talk to other women who were playing badminton on Saturday. They'll be able to say whether or not she was there the whole time. Logically, I can't see how she could get from the Badminton Club to the Recreation Centre and back in the time span, even supposing she was a mind-reader and knew Kevin would go for a smoke exactly when he did.' She lowered her voice. 'She's walking towards the ward now. Time to make myself scarce.'

Tom stood for a moment thinking about this development. The badminton courts were on the opposite side of the base to the Recreation Centre. Mavis McRitchie only occasionally participated in a game 'with three other duffers'. If Tom knew anything about keen, experienced players on a Saturday night, they would be most reluctant to surrender a court to four women who hardly knew one end of a racquet from the other. That meant Mavis might have had the opportunity to slip away unnoticed. Two problems with that. Surely Shona and Julie would miss their mother, despite watching 'Dadda' being brilliant, and rush to complain of being left unchaperoned. And, as Heather had pointed out, how would their mother have known her son would be alone in the toilet at that precise time? No, Kevin had to be lying.

He began walking back to Lucy Farmer's office, again beset by the problem of timing. The attack surely had to have been made by someone at the party, by an acquaintance Kevin had arranged to meet, by a passing user who nipped in for a quick snort or, and here was a new angle, by two squaddies who knew the bar was closed and only a tinies' party going on so planned a spot of cottaging. The team had ruled out the first theory by questioning the adults twice, so that left—

Outside the door of Lucy Farmer's office, which Tom had pulled half-closed on leaving, he was halted by her urgent words. She was speaking in an undertone, but Tom could still hear the gist of her half of a telephone call.

'Calm down, Alan! No one's *on to us*. You've just got the jitters ... Yes, you *have*. Why would anyone suspect anything? ... Rubbish! We've been very careful to cover our tracks ... No, our arrangement still stands, unless you haven't the bottle to carry it off. I've more to lose than you, don't forget

... Good, that's my boy! Ciao.'

Tom counted to ten before lightly tapping on the door and pushing it open. She was standing by the window with a mobile in her hand, and regarded him with total composure as he again apologized for having to take a call during their discussion. He then thanked her for her input on Corporal Mc-Ritchie, and said his farewell.

The snow was still crisp beneath his tread as he walked to his car and slid behind the wheel. Could that sexy redhead have been talking to the man she had worked in tandem with at the party? Sapper *Alan* Rowe? They had both had access to the storeroom and the rear loading doors, going in and out to change over equipment between games. Jack Fellowes' statement had them in there packing everything away ready for the fancy-dress parade at the time Kevin had been attacked.

Tom frowned at the windscreen. Yes, it was a possibility, if they had been in cahoots! She could have gone out by the rear door while Rowe covered for her, slipped upstairs through the front entrance, snatched the club from the wall and struck Kevin, then hidden in the adjacent women's toilet when the Clarkson boys clattered up the stairs. In the uproar following their cry of murder down in the main hall, nobody would have noticed Lucy Farmer's return to the storeroom. It all fitted very well, but what motive would she have for hurting a lad who simply dreamed of musical fame? He sighed heavily. Therein lay the crux of the case. What motive had anyone for attacking that boy?

Musician Tony Clegg was hyped to the hilt as he left the building with the Bandmaster's congratulations ringing in his ears. He had passed his first grade examinations on the French horn with distinction; both the written paper and the test pieces. Drums, trumpet, xylophone, and soon he could add the French horn to his musical expertise. Captain Booth had also told him he had been promoted. *Lance-Corporal* Clegg! He was really going places now.

Clegg loved every aspect of his life and still could hardly believe he was being paid to enjoy himself so much. Music had been his passion for as far back as he remembered. His greatest wish had been to play in a band, and he had been a star in the local youth orchestra. They were all volunteers, of course, so when Clegg left school he needed to find a job. For six months he had worked in a large DIY store, which he had hated, but his wages paid for his advanced music lessons. Then the leader of the youth orchestra arranged to take them all to a massed bands concert at the Albert Hall. The Coldstream Guards, resplendent in scarlet uniforms, had shown Clegg the exciting future he could have.

The Royal Cumberland Rifles did not command the distinction of a Guards regiment, and their bandsmen wore green rather than scarlet, but Clegg was with a military band, and he had gained a paid profession that was utterly fulfilling. A bonus was that music lessons were provided free.

So high on happiness was he that he was reluctant to go directly to his room in the noisy accommodation block. He would certainly call his parents to give them the news of his success, but he wanted to hug his excitement to himself for a while. The early evening added to his heady sense of triumph; the clear, cold sky was filled with stars, the ground was glittering with frost, the air was chill and invigorating.

He began to run, enjoying the sound of his boots crunching the crusted snow, and then he leaped in the air with arms waving, shouting 'YEE-OW!' Ahead was the Recreation Centre with the outdoor chess board alongside it. The squares were presently obliterated by snow, but the child-sized pieces were lined up on each side like frozen ranks of soldiers. Filled with exuberance, he seized the nearest queen and began a crazy dance with her, laughing and repeating the cry, 'YEE-OW!'

He was unaware of a car pulling up, and of a figure fast closing in on him.

Six

Max dressed for dinner in the uniform he wore only when the occasion demanded he must. As he knotted his tie he acknowledged that he was as excited as a youth anticipating his first date. He had definitely emerged from the bleak emotional hiatus following Susan's tragic death. Tonight would be make or break time. Livya Cordwell wore no rings, but that was no real indication of a footloose situation. If she declined his invitation to dinner it would be a bad blow. Livya had taken him by storm and time was his enemy. His father would doubtless have secured his objective by now. Max was less experienced in the seduction game.

There would be a seating plan tonight, so it was unlikely that they would be within speaking distance during the extended meal, even if they happened to be at the same table. That curtailed his opportunities severely. Her manner towards him suggested a return of interest, but that could be due to two things. The fact that he knew little or nothing about chess, which made for relaxing communion after the intensity of play during the day, or because he was Andrew Rydal's son. He could not help wondering how closely associated they had been.

Making a last check on his reflection in the long mirror, Max headed for the ground floor ante-room pushing to the back of his mind for tonight all professional problems. Before leaving his office an hour ago the latest pathologist's report had come in, stating that it was still impossible to determine the cause of Treeves' sudden death. This was bad news for Corporals Meacher and Stubble who were anxious for a conclusion that would remove any suggestion of culpability.

Then there was Kevin McRitchie's accusation against his mother that had to be followed up. Several women had attested to Mavis's unbroken presence at the Badminton Club, which supported SIB's belief that the boy had made a wild claim due to agitation over her sexual approach to him. *That* aspect had to be taken seriously and acted upon.

In addition, Tom had presented a new slant on the assault because he had overheard a telephone call from Lucy Farmer to someone called Alan. In theory, it was the most attractive lead so far, *if* the Alan was Sapper Rowe and *if* they could uncover a motive.

Max smiled as he started down the stairs. He had once quoted Scarlett O'Hara saying hopefully, 'Tomorrow is another day', and

138

Tom Black had replied, 'Yeah, but we never got to see what tomorrow brought, do we?' Right now, Max Rydal felt he could bear to wait until tomorrow came. Tonight was more vital.

The seating plan showed that Max would be next to Lucy Farmer on table two, while Captain Cordwell was to be flanked by a chess-playing squadron leader and a lieutenant of Royal Engineers on table three. Entering the ante-room, Max spotted Livya with a lively group holding drinks in one hand while simulating chess moves with the other.

As he approached she smiled warmly, which encouraged firm action. Taking her arm in a light clasp, he said to the men around her, 'Sorry, guys, Captain Cordwell is wanted for questioning.'

She was laughing as he steered her between the assembled officers to a deserted corner. 'Am I under arrest?'

'No, I'm just holding you on suspicion of being too popular with other eggheads. Am I right in thinking they were replaying all the clever moves they made today?'

'I'm afraid so. We tend to do that unless someone reminds us that there are other things in life.'

'Such as?'

'Such as talking to someone like you who knows a game is only a game. You have your feet firmly on the ground, Max.'

'Is that good ... or extremely dull?'

She looked him deep in the eyes. 'It's what you make it, don't you think?'

Feeling that it was no real answer, he asked rather bluntly, 'How well do you know my father, Livya?'

'Professionally, or personally?'

He hesitated. 'Both, I suppose.'

'We've worked together on three occasions and I have enormous respect for him. He's clever, experienced and utterly dependable. Courageous, too. On the personal side, he has great charm and knows how to use it to his advantage, but look a little deeper and you see a sad, lonely man.'

'What?' Max was startled.

'He carries a photograph of your mother wherever he goes. Although she died twenty-two years ago, I think he has never fully recovered from that loss.' She paused. 'Have you?'

He frowned, wishing he had not begun this topic. He was wasting time. 'I was only six when she died.'

Her hand rested on his sleeve with great gentleness. 'Poor little boy!'

Changing the subject swiftly, he said, 'I'm a big boy now, and I want to spend some time with you away from here. Will you have dinner with me on Saturday at a hotel in town?'

'Yes.'

Relief made him smile. 'Hoorah! A woman

who makes swift decisions.'

'No, Max, I decided two days ago to spend Saturday with you. If you hadn't asked me, I'd have asked you, but as a chess player I wanted to lure you into making the first move.'

His smile broadened. 'You're welcome to lure me into doing anything you want.'

Her dark eyes assessed him for a moment or two. 'I believe you really mean that.'

'I believe I do, too,' he agreed, sobering. 'Livya, is there anyone important in your life back in England?'

The moment of truth was lost as a bugle call announced that they should take their places at table. Tonight's host was once a distinguished cavalry regiment, which these days went into battle on wheeled tracks but retained old traditions with determination. Although this was not a VIP dinner, with regimental silver adorning the top table and all attendant ceremony, it was a guest night which called for mess dress and semi-formality. Hence the bugler to announce dinner.

The chess-playing squadron leader appeared too promptly to escort Livya to the table, leaving Max to mutter, 'Punctilious bastard!' But he was on a high, and feasted his eyes on Livya's neat curves in her regimental long dress and green monkey jacket as she walked ahead of him.

Lucy Farmer also looked disturbingly

attractive despite the clash of red hair against her scarlet jacket. She greeted Max with typical heartiness, eyeing his uniform.

'So you're a soldier tonight, not a detective. Good. I shan't have to watch my tongue.'

Max took his place beside her. 'So long as you're a soldier tonight, not a police groupie.'

She laughed, her lively eyes sending a blatant message that fell on stony ground. 'You look even more impressive in uniform. Enough to set a girl's heart beating faster.'

Shaking out his napkin, Max smiled at her. 'Careful, Lucy, or my detective half will start thinking that flattery is designed to hide the fact that you've been up to something.'

It was only momentary, yet Max saw a flash of awareness cross her face and wondered if Tom had truly discovered a significant piece of evidence. She was equal to the occasion, however.

'I'm forever *up to something*, Max. Life's too short to sit back and wait for old age. Isn't that why you're spending so much time with a certain female chess player?'

Very smart, he thought, but two can play games. 'You mean Captain Cordwell? She works with my father. He's been unwell lately and I've been unable to get over on a visit. She's revealing the facts he's hiding from me.'

'Oh, not serious, I hope?'

Unsure whether or not she believed him, Max shook his head and said lightly, 'He'll live until I take a three-day break at Christmas.'

A steward came between them to serve their starter, another to pour wine. Max took the opportunity to turn to the regimental subaltern seated on his right to ask about the list pinned up, asking for voluntteers to take part in an informal mess entertainment in the week before Christmas. He was then treated to an enthusiastic description of last year's hilarious sketches and antics performed by the more outgoing mess members. Max vowed to avoid this year's offerings like the plague.

They were well into the main course when Lucy stopped flirting with the man on her left, and the two facing her, then turned her attention back to Max.

'Are you allowed to take leave in the middle of a case?' Seeing his momentary incomprehension, she added, 'Three-day break at Christmas.'

He nodded. 'The wheels don't stop turning if I'm not there.'

She ate more carrots and lamb cutlet, then gave him a sideways glance. 'Anywhere near to discovering who assaulted young Kevin?'

'Yes,' he replied deliberately. 'The lad's memory of it is improving and he's given us a strong lead.'

'How exciting! I suppose you're not allowed to give me a clue.'

'You suppose correctly. You'll have to wait until we make an arrest, I'm afraid.'

'Soon, I hope, then you can visit your sick father with an untroubled mind.'

He recognized provocation in her attitude, but it was surely based on disbelief of his reason for interest in Livya. Lucy had betrayed no concern about the lead Kevin had given them. Yet that young woman had something to hide. His experience in dealing with people told him so. Before he could probe further, he was approached by one of the stewards who told him Sergeant-Major Black had called asking Captain Rydal to ring him at the first opportunity.

'He said it's urgent, sir.'

Max stood, offered his excuses to those around him then approached the Commanding Officer, quietly explained the situation, and asked permission to leave. Walking past table two he caught Livya's eye and attempted an optical apology. Up in his room he called Tom's mobile number. It was answered immediately.

'I've just come upon the body of a young soldier outside the Recreation Centre. A savage blow to the head. The lad's dead, sir.'

'Be there in ten,' said Max swiftly, cutting the connection and reaching for his boots and greatcoat. This was a serious development. The venue, the modus operandi and the choice of young male victim must surely link this attack with the one on Kevin McRitchie. Were they dealing with a serial offender? Would Kevin have been killed if the attacker had not been disturbed by the advent of the Clarkson boys?

As Max drove along the perimeter road, fine snow began drifting gently from a sky that had been clear and star-filled an hour or so ago. When he reached the Recreation Centre he climbed from his car and trod over the deeper snow to where Tom was in the middle of another call on his mobile. He was still wearing his dark trousers, but had replaced the tailored jacket with a padded anorak. His breath was vaporizing in the chill atmosphere as he ended the conversation. He looked unusually upset.

Max guessed why. The small body lying curled in a foetal position, on which snowflakes were silently settling, looked grotesque flanked by the large overturned figures of a red queen and black bishop. The Recreation Centre was closed and in darkness, but the security lights outside the building illuminated the scene – a pool of brilliant light piercing the hushed surrounding darkness. Had nobody witnessed the boy's last desperate moments?

'George Maddox is getting a SOCO team underway, and the Duty Doctor will be here as soon as he's dealt with a lance-corporal who slipped and cut her head.' Tom's voice grew harsher. 'He said a corpse can afford to 'wait, the girl can't.'

'Don't tell me. The Duty Doctor is Clarkson again.'

Tom's expression gave the answer.

'He's right, of course. Pity about his manner.' Max squatted beside the body. From the portion of the face half-buried in snow that was visible, Max could see he was little more than a boy. His head was bloody, his blond hair matted with it. The snow around it was red. It had been a vicious attack.

He glanced up at Tom. 'What the hell are we dealing with here?'

'I know the lad, sir,' he replied thickly. 'Musician Tony Clegg, whom Kevin pestered for guidance on how to make it in the world of pop. Clegg was apparently a hugely talented lad with a truly worthwhile life ahead. I think we have a nutter on our hands. Who else would be attacking these innocent lads?'

'Not Lieutenant Farmer. She was sitting next to me when you called.' Max straightened, pulling his greatcoat collar up to prevent snow sliding down his neck. 'And presumably not Mavis McRitchie. We *are* looking at the same perpetrator, aren't we?'

'It has to be. Clegg was struck with great force with this black chess piece. There's blood and matter on it,' Tom said. 'I guess the red queen was snatched up by Clegg to defend himself.'

Max sighed as he looked around at the

deserted white distance stretching in each direction. 'What was the boy doing here? It's completely off the route for the band offices or his quarters, and there doesn't appear to be anything going on at the Centre tonight.'

'I called the Bandmaster. No reply at home, and his mobile is switched off. Probably at some official function. He'll maybe give us a lead on why Clegg was walking here. Sir, surely this suggests the link between the two attacks is music.'

'Or repulsed sexual advances. Clegg's build is small, like Kevin's, and if music was his passion it hints at an artistic nature. Maybe a male killer was attracted to him.' The snow was falling faster now, settling like a shroud on the curled-up body. 'How come you found him, Tom? I thought you were heading home when I left the office.'

'I went,' he replied, pulling up the hood of his anorak. 'Maggie had a party invitation, so I brought her in as far as the married quarters. I drove this way back hoping I might get some inspiration in the Recreation Centre. Didn't know it was closed. I almost drove past until I noticed that one of the toppled figures looked human.' He glanced down at Clegg's frosted body. 'Poor little kid.'

Mavis McRitchie sat on the settee made bright with the patchwork throw she had sewn and listened to the happy voices upstairs. Greg was tucking Shona and Julie in their beds and helping them to choose a story for him to read before 'lights out'. It should have been a gratifying family time: a father who had been working all day, bonding with his children while the mother prepared supper for them both to share in the tranquillity following bedtime. There would be no tranquillity; there would be fireworks.

Greg had been holding down his anger for two hours, which would make its release all the more explosive. Couldn't mouth off in front of the little darlings, Mavis thought bitterly. Might scare them. Might affect them in later life. Huh, she reflected, more likely open their eyes to what 'Dadda' was truly like. *That* was what he was really avoiding.

Too agitated to take up her sewing, Mavis listened to her husband's deep voice, now and again interrupted by one of the girls asking a question about the story. They were carefully vetted before Greg would have books in the house. He would not allow anything he considered to be rubbish or a bad influence to assail his darlings' ears. They appeared to love the harmless tales he read and begged for their favourites time and again. It was another of those private things they shared, which shut Mavis out.

Hearing Greg's gentle goodnight before his heavy tread on the stairs, Mavis got to her feet and waited for what was certain to come. His face was flushed and working with anger as he crossed from the foot of the stairs to where she stood.

'You've done it again! You've bloody done it again, haven't you?' he accused in a violent undertone low enough not to reach the upper floor. 'You *know* my rules. Your duty is to be here when school's over. You're their *mother*. It's your job to keep them safe.'

She stepped back from his thrusting face and offered her defence.

'The bus from the hospital was late. There'd been a pile-up at that five-way junction. Police were still clearing the wrecks away.' She tried boldness. 'You only drive around the base. The roads outside are icy and treacherous, Greg.'

He advanced on her. 'As you're so bloody knowledgeable about the roads, you should stay off them. Three times this week you've ignored the rules.' His expression was coldly vicious as he said, 'That little wimp of yours is being cosseted and watched over twenty-four seven. Yet you go to him and abandon your two daughters, who are half his age and open to all kinds of danger. What sort of mother are you, for Christ's sake?'

Mavis sat abruptly on the settee to escape her dread of being seized and shaken – not that he had ever manhandled her – and protested vehemently. 'I didn't *abandon* them. Jean Slater knows my situation and takes the girls home with Bobby and Amanda if I'm not there on time. The girls aren't left alone.

Not in any danger.'

'Yes, they are,' he argued, thumping the arm of the settee with a clenched fist. 'Those Slater kids are wild, they run rings around their mother. And their language! Mick Slater has the foulest mouth in the platoon, and he laughs when his kids copy him. I've told you time and again I'm not having Shona and Julie mixing with the dregs on this base.' He leaned forward so abruptly, she pressed her body into the soft back of the seat. 'You're not to visit the hospital, understand?'

'He'll look for me,' she said tearfully. 'He'll be anxious.'

'Do him good to realize there are others in this family you have a duty to serve.' Greg straightened up. 'He's had things easy too long. When he gets back he'll find there's a whole new set of rules in place.'

She stared at him. 'Like what?'

'Like that guitar has been chucked out and he gets down to some real book learning, for once. Time he found out the hard way that he has to knuckle down to discipline in order to make something of his life. No son of mine will shame me by becoming a dropout.' He pointed at his wife. 'And *you* are going to stop fussing over him and start concentrating on my girls. They'll soon reach the age when they badly need a mother's guidance. Forget Kevin. *They* are the important members of this family. Time you realized that.' He turned and began walking towards the kitchen. 'Now, what's for supper ... or did you also get back too late to make any for me?'

There was a football game on TV so Greg ate his chicken and chips watching it. Mavis felt that food would choke her, but he failed to notice that she had only a cup of tea and a biscuit. She was sewing dolls' dresses for the girls' Christmas presents, so she worked on them for half an hour, then went upstairs to have a bath. The commentator's frenetic voice penetrated the floorboards as she lay in the warm water, crying.

Even when angry Greg was overpoweringly attractive. It had been like that from the first meeting. Marrying him had been an impossible dream come true. Giving him a son had been her greatest gift of love. But baby Kevin had created a division between them; the girls had completed it. Shona and Julie had robbed her of her dream lover. They now owned him. Kevin had been thrust back at her as a substitute for what she had lost. He wasn't. Nobody could replace the man who remained with her in person, but who had gone from her in spirit.

Wherever Greg had been posted, Mavis had made the temporary home bright and extremely comfortable. She cooked all the food she knew he liked. She dressed neatly and always tried to look pretty for him. She never complained when he had extra duties, or had the occasional night out with his mates. She went every Saturday to the Badminton Club, although she hated the game and was useless at it. What more could she do?

They still slept together, were intimate when he was in the mood, but it was no longer 'making love' it was purely satisfying his need. How could she get him back? How recapture the man she had fallen for so completely? Would it be possible once his darlings had married and left home? The tears flowed faster as she acknowledged that he would never let that happen. No men would be allowed near them because none would be considered good enough. Shona and Julie would be with them forever. And her unwilling substitute for her lost husband would depart and sever all contact, as soon as he could break free. Greg's new rules would hasten that moment. When that happened she might as well be dead.

Major Clarkson straightened from examining the snow-coated body and looked at Max with a frown. 'A massive blow to the head with the chess piece, as you deduced. Whoever wielded that black bishop was strong, probably an adult rather than a minor, and I'd guess the weapon was swung in a circular motion prior to hitting the victim with intent to kill. It's hard to say if the boy might have survived had he received immediate medical attention. As it is, he was lengthily exposed to this sub-zero temperature following trauma.' He tugged his coat collar closer around his neck. It was now snowing hard. 'The pathologist will give you more precise info but, from the blood loss, I'd be inclined to believe death was immediate and inevitable.' He began to move off towards his car. 'You'd better get on top of this before there's another attack; another young life snuffed out.'

Max and Tom did not need telling; two attacks on teenage boys in five days was a serious problem. This one was more difficult to follow up. The assault on Kevin Mc-Ritchie had occurred in a building filled with people, which gave SIB the opportunity to question them and collate their answers; gain leads to follow. Tony Clegg had been clubbed to death in a large open area which tonight was deserted. Yet one person had been there with him.

Leaving George Maddox and his uniformed Redcaps to reconnoitre and seal off the area, while the SOCO team searched for forensic evidence, the two detectives silently watched the body being driven away before heading back to their cars. By mutual consent they returned to Section Headquarters, where they were able to shed topcoats and make coffee to ease their inner chill while they talked.

Tom first brought up the computer details

of the dead musician. Next of kin was given as Norman Clegg, father. What a blow he would receive just two weeks before Christmas, that special family time. On the screen was confirmation of Tom's prediction of a really worthwhile life ahead for a young musician with dedication and talent. Tony appeared to have raced through each stage of his bid for qualifications.

Having downed half the mug of coffee, Max said, 'We need an in-depth interview with Kevin McRitchie. He has to know more than he's revealed so far. Accusing his mother was born of the dread of returning to the situation at home. With a psychiatrist present we *have* to get from him who he had arranged to meet in the toilets during the party. It's surely significant that Clegg was at the Recreation Centre at roughly the same time this evening.'

Propped against the edge of a desk, mug in hand, Tom looked thoughtfully at the life just ended that was mapped out on his screen. 'You think so?'

'Don't you?'

Tom glanced back at his boss. 'Let's review all that's similar in these attacks. One: the victims are young, male, small in stature with slightly effeminate features. Two: they are both heavily into music. Three: they were clubbed around the head with a weapon that happened to be handy. Four: they were both attacked at about eight p.m., in or around the Recreation Centre.'

Max leaned back in his chair. 'Get my point?'

'Let's list the inconsistencies,' Tom insisted. 'One: Kevin was assaulted when there was a high risk of someone arriving on the scene. In fact, the Clarkson boys did, and fetched help. Tony Clegg was alone in a deserted area. Two: different weapons.'

'But blows to the head in each case,' Max interposed.

'Three,' Tom continued doggedly, 'Clegg is a soldier, Kevin isn't.'

'And four, Clegg died and Kevin didn't,' Max finished with a sigh. 'What does that leave us with?'

'I'll tell you what it leaves *me* with.' Tom put his empty mug on the table behind him. 'I now believe Kevin was also meant to die. The convenient weapon was smaller and lighter than the chess piece, so it would have taken protracted cudgelling to kill. The advent of the Clarkson boys prevented that. We've been told only Kevin's thin skull resulted in so much damage.'

Max nodded. 'I also now believe it was not meant to be just a warning. That raises the question of whether the attacker will attempt to finish the job. We must persuade the hospital to hang on to him until we at least know who's behind this violence.'

Staring again at Clegg's details on the screen, Tom muttered, 'It's a real stinker. No leads whatever. Far from Mrs Robinson's advice that the culprit will turn up saying sorry, the bastard has done it again.'

'We're not dealing with a recalcitrant child, as she seems to think,' Max said wearily. 'Nor are we dealing with someone in the music business. I can't sit easy with that theory, Tom.'

'Why not? It's the one personal link we know of.'

'Coincidence! I find it difficult to believe anyone could get so steamed up over music he's prepared to kill twice.'

'People have murdered for any number of bizarre obsessions. Rare stamps, birds' eggs, prize orchids. If the yearning is great enough, killing is considered acceptable.'

'But what is this killer getting in return for taking out these lads?' Max asked pointedly. 'Kevin's merely a kid who plays a guitar quite well in a group with three pals who don't take it as seriously as he. Nothing to gain in removing him from the scene, is there? Admittedly, Clegg was a very accomplished musician but, unless he's written a brilliant symphony someone wants to claim as his own work, his death reaps no rewards. The lad didn't play the violin, so there's not even a priceless Stradivarius at stake.'

Tom stroked his chin thoughtfully. 'So let's concede there's no obvious advantage as a result of these attacks. On the assumption that the Recreation Centre was a fixed rendezvous point in both instances, we have to seriously consider drugs or sex as the motive. I personally go for the latter.'

Max nodded slowly. 'I agree. Although Clegg had the opportunity to deal in drugs by dint of the peripatetic life with the band, I don't believe the McRitchie boy had the will or interest to become embroiled. We know male coupling is practised, however much we prefer to stamp it out so, unless Kevin gives us a name, we have to suss out who's propositioning young, effeminate lads and won't take no for an answer.'

'Kevin is underage, and Clegg looked very young, so it's probably someone with paedophile tendencies. It'll be worth speaking to teachers at the school, and to those adults who run extracurricular classes or youth organizations.'

Tom broke off as his mobile rang. It was the Bandmaster, Captain Booth, responding to the message left on his answer machine. It was evident to Max from Tom's comments that the Yorkshireman was very upset by the news, and took some time giving his account of the murdered boy's prodigious talent to counter his grief. Tom ended the call by asking Christopher Booth to set in motion the business of breaking the sad news to Clegg's parents, and a request to interview the members of the band next morning.

Tom laid his mobile on the desk and explained the problem to Max. 'Bandmaster

157

said they're due to play at a winter carnival tomorrow afternoon, seventy-five Ks from here. They have to set off mid-morning after a full rehearsal.'

'Right. We'll send Beeny and Connie Bush on the bus with them. Perfect opportunity for relaxed questioning. More likely to hear confidences there than in the band's official quarters.' He then registered Tom's expression. 'There's more?'

'Might be significant,' he said with a small sigh. 'Seems Clegg had just been told he'd passed his first exam on the French horn with distinction, and also been given a lance stripe. He parted from Captain Booth in a state of euphoria.'

'So he called the killer to break the news and agreed to meet him at the Recreation Centre to celebrate? That would suggest...'

'Either he hadn't been approached for sex before, or that he was normally a willing participant and things went wrong tonight. Let's face it, the assailant hadn't taken a weapon with him. Just picked up the chess piece in sudden rage.'

Max gave him a straight look. 'Of course, we could be looking at this back to front. What if Kevin and Tony Clegg were the ones making sexual advances?'

'To the same target?'

'Why not?'

Tom frowned. 'You're suggesting the killer might have been the one saying no?'

'Very violently.'

'But if he felt so strongly about being propositioned, why did he agree to meet up with his victims?'

'Why, indeed? And that question remains equally vital whichever way around we view it.' Max got to his feet. 'Let's go home and tackle it anew in the morning. By then, Sergeant Maddox may have some forensic evidence to offer us.'

'And the pathologist may be able to tell us why Treeves died,' Tom added heavily.

'And Klaus Krenkel may have traced our missing equipment.'

'And the moon might have turned into blue cheese.'

They donned their coats in silence, each feeling the weight of problems dogging them and still seeing that small figure of a lad who had been so elated until someone had struck him down. It had stopped snowing, but a new frozen layer covered everything, including their cars. As they walked to them, Tom said, 'They're running the teens' disco on Saturday at the Recreation Centre. There should be a very evident police presence from start to finish. We can't be sure tonight's attack will be the last, and parents will see we're doing something about the situation.'

Max unlocked his door and prepared to slide behind the wheel. 'The situation is more complex than we have so far understood. My guts sense something very nasty behind the violence to those lads. I'll fix it with the hospital doctors to tackle Kevin tomorrow. He must be made to realize that he has the answers to vital questions. If we can reassure him about conditions within his family he'll be more likely to open up. Goodnight, Tom.'

'Goodnight, sir.'

There were only a few nightbirds left in the Officers' Mess when Max walked in. It was past midnight, he realized. He mounted the wide staircase, and along the corridor his thoughts were heavy. A middle-aged couple in Huddersfield were about to have their lives permanently darkened by the loss of their only child.

An envelope lay on the carpet a few feet inside the door. He picked it up and dropped it on the desk, believing it to be some communication concerning his mess membership. Maybe even an invitation to take part in the Christmas revels being arranged. He began to undress, remembering the enthusiastic description of last year's entertainment related to him at the dinner table. Not his scene, by any stretch of the imagination.

On the point of getting in bed he noticed that the envelope just bore his first name. Not what he had imagined it was, then. The page inside had a brief handwritten message: 'The next move is mine, I believe. Why not book a room at that hotel for Saturday night?'

Max sank on to his single bed assessing the import of Livya's message. The surge of excitement he felt was tempered by the knowledge that there was a strong chance he would not be free to explore her challenge.

Seven

Mornings in the Black household were always noisy and mobile. Three schoolgirls vied for the bathroom, squabbling light-heartedly over clean socks and underwear, Tom made toast while calling out regular time checks to his brood and Nora boiled or poached eggs while stirring the porridge. It was an organized type of chaos that invariably produced three clean, correctly dressed, well-fed girls in time to catch the school bus.

Today, the routine failed to work. A very heated argument between Maggie and Gina led to tears and name-calling. Nora had to intervene, leaving Tom to stir the porridge and ensure the eggs did not poach solid. They did, so extra toast had to be made and the forbidden-at-breakfast peanut butter put on the table. An olive branch was not forth-coming; Gina sat poker-faced and Maggie red-eyed while eating. Beth took advantage of her sisters' silence and launched into an account of the role she had been given in the school nativity play.

In what seemed to Tom to be a single

sentence with no punctuation whatever, she managed to convey for all of five minutes that the entire piece hinged for any hope of success on her participation. Chivvied from the table by Nora, who warned they had just five minutes to brush their teeth and collect school bags, a second quarrel broke out when Gina told Beth she was a stupid little girl who told lies about her own importance. Tom then had to play the heavy father, which sent them upstairs then down again to walk the short distance to the bus much in the manner of three aristocrats nobly facing the tumbril heading to the guillotine.

To Nora fell the brunt of discipline by dint of Tom's duties, so a rare telling-off from their father brought airs of martyrdom along with obedience. It also brought a closing of sibling ranks. Left in blessed peace in the kitchen, Tom took cheese from the fridge, pickles from the cupboard, and began to make a sandwich for himself. Daring Nora to comment, he spread pickle on a chunk of cheese and covered it with a second thick slice of buttered bread. As he took the first bite, Nora pushed a fresh cup of coffee across to him. He nodded thanks, then sighed.

'What's got into them lately?'

'It's called growing up.' She stirred her own coffee, regarding him shrewdly. 'It hasn't happened overnight. You just haven't noticed.'

Irritated by this underlying reference to what amounted to his part-time parenting, he said, 'How could I? When I come in at the end of the day they're upstairs doing homework, then giggling over fashion magazines or freaky-looking pop stars. I only see them when we're eating, or when they appear in pyjamas to say goodnight. It's you they talk to. You who understands what goes on inside their heads. This family survives perfectly well when I'm not here. I'm not really needed.'

Nora said nothing, just sipped her coffee and waited for him to continue. Tom took another bite of his sandwich, knowing he was being unreasonable. How fortunate that his family did survive in his absence on duty. Nora was the linchpin holding them together through thick and thin. He looked across at her with a rueful expression.

'You should be in our team. When you look at me that way I know the game's up. Think what effect it would have on our suspects.'

It failed to bring a smile from her. Instead, she said, 'The news of that poor lad's murder last night will be all round the school this morning. The girls will be the focus of attention because you are responsible for bringing to justice the person who killed him. Your daughters know you will. They have faith in the father who never shirks his duty, even if it means he can't be with them as much as they'd like. They *do* need you, Tom.

We all do.'

'I know, love. I talk a lot of nonsense sometimes. I'm a bit edgy this morning. Can't forget that boy's body lying in the snow curled round like a child asleep in bed. If we'd been sharper over Kevin McRitchie we could maybe have prevented his loss.'

'But there was no indication that what happened last Saturday was the first in a series of attacks, was there?' She put her hand over his lying on the table. 'It's not like you to shoulder the blame for something you couldn't know would happen.'

'It's ... I guess it's because they're so young. I can't help thinking what if it was one of our girls?'

Nora frowned. 'It's not a possibility, is it?'

'I hope to God not. The victims so far are lads.'

'You think there's a risk of another attempt?'

He sighed heavily and got to his feet. 'Two in five days. Could be a third before we get to him. Don't wait up. We'll work flat out on this until we get a result.' He bent to kiss her. 'Sorry about the grumps. Thanks for keeping the family on the rails. Where would we all be without you?'

She smiled. 'You might be lucky and never find out. I'll stick around at least until the girls leave the nest. Who knows what'll happen then? If the grumps got too frequent I could look around for a better prospect.'

★ ★ ★

Breakfast in the Officers' Mess was a self-service affair, with the exception of the hot dishes. These were served from heated containers by white-coated assistants, on request. Deciding on scrambled eggs with grilled tomatoes, Max first went to the multiple toasting machine which stood alongside several large loaves. It was busy there. He waited behind two subalterns holding thick chunks of white bread, until they were able to place them on the rotating wire shelves then move over to the hot food counter. When they had chosen and been served, their toast would be ready. At least, that was the theory. Max could not count the times he had returned with a plate of hot, tasty breakfast to find his toast burnt black, or that it had been taken by someone.

With his mind elsewhere this morning, he cut two slices from a wholemeal loaf and put them in the machine, intending to stay beside it until they reappeared in perfect eating condition.

'A man after my own heart.'

Max swung round swiftly to discover Livya beside him.

'Brown toast,' she explained with a smile. 'Men usually prefer white, and as thick as a doorstep.'

Max returned her smile, thinking how bright and fresh she looked first thing in the morning. 'The baker who supplied my

166

boarding school must have believed his bread would mostly be used as solid doughy pellets for schoolboy fights. He was right. It was totally indigestible, rubbery, tasteless and *grey*. The memory remains and I opt for brown whenever possible. Can I slice you some, or do you prefer to cut your own?'

She shook her head. 'I never refuse a gentlemanly offer. I'm not one of those tiresome women who see an insult in it.'

'An *insult*?'

'Yes, you know: you're suggesting that because I'm a woman I'm too weak and feeble to cut my own bread.'

Max laughed. 'Actually, *I've* taken great offence because you compared my preference for brown bread unfavourably with that of men who chomp white chunks as thick as doorsteps. Much more macho!'

In this light-hearted mood they collected their breakfasts and sat together at one of the tables presently unoccupied.

'I'm sorry about last night,' she said almost immediately. 'A youthful musician found dead, I heard.'

'That's right.' The brightness of her presence no longer eclipsed his dark mood.

'Set upon by a gang of squaddies?'

'Highly unlikely.'

She studied his face. 'Have I really offended you now?'

'No, no. I was enjoying your company so much I'd managed to put his murder to the

167

back of my mind, that's all.'

'And I've brought it back to the forefront.'

He gave a sad smile. 'Well, it happened and won't go away.'

'But you'd prefer not to talk about it?'

'I'd rather talk about you. And the note you pushed under my door last night.' He glanced over his shoulder. 'At any moment some of your fellow eggheads will join us and monopolize you. I doubt if I'll be here for dinner this evening, so this might be my only chance to get things straight about your suggestion.'

'Oh God, have I jumped the gun?' she asked swiftly. 'Your father told me about your wife's tragic death several years ago, said you hadn't remarried, so I thought...'

Max was instantly angry. 'My father discusses my private affairs with junior officers who only occasionally work with him? What gives him that right? He knows nothing about me. We never meet. The last time we saw each other was at Susan's funeral. We had no idea what to say to each other then, and have since merely exchanged formal Christmas cards. That's all the contact we've made for years.'

Livya faced him frankly. 'Don't malign Andrew.'

'*Andrew*?' he queried heatedly.

'That's his name.' Her voice grew crisper. 'When we were on a mission together he refused to allow me to call him Brigadier or

Sir off-duty. He's like that. Nothing in it. Just his way of relaxing. He's hot on discipline the rest of the time.'

'Really?'

'Yes, *really*.' A sudden smile broke through. 'You look very much like him right now. That same stern expression has made stouter personalities than mine go in fear of him.'

The sparkle in her eyes, the attractive figure she cut in this male-dominated room combined to disarm him. 'I can't imagine you going in fear of anyone, especially me.'

Her hand rested on his sleeve. 'So are we friends again, Max?'

'Well, when we're off-duty you can call me Max. Otherwise, it's Captain Rydal.'

His teasing tone brought a surprising confession from her. 'I'm afraid I played the innocent with you that first evening. When your father knew I was coming here he mentioned in passing that his son was serving with the relevant SIB section, so I asked him about you and promised to make contact. He doesn't blab your details to all and sundry, Max. I coaxed them out of him and had the intention of reporting back with news of you.' There was no artifice in her direct gaze. 'I wasn't expecting to be so affected by our meeting. Andrew has innate charm, but you had a greater impact on me. Hence the impetuous note under your door. I'm ... actually, I'm usually very cautious about relationships. If I've misread the signs, I'm sorry.'

Certain three men bearing breakfast plates were heading towards their table, Max spoke urgently. 'I hoped I was making the signs completely unmistakable. The impact was mutual, Livya, and your note delighted me. I'll book a table and a room for tomorrow night, then live in the hope of being free to join you.'

There was a new grimness on all their faces at the briefing. There was no doubt in anyone's mind that they were dealing with a killer who could soon strike again if not apprehended. Tom first repeated the summation of his and Max's thoughts the previous evening.

'The strong possibility of Kevin's attacker being someone attending the party now seems unlikely. We have to go with the assumption that he had arranged to meet a person he knew and trusted, at a specific time. The same applies to Tony Clegg. Of the two most likely reasons for a meeting, we feel the odds are on sex rather than drugs. Repulsed sexual advances. Just which of them was demanding and which rejecting is open to investigation. All we do know is that the third person has a hasty and violent temper. In each case he snatched up a convenient weapon, so the attacks were not premeditated but the result of sudden uncontrollable fury.'

Tom surveyed his team, still seeing that

curled body enshrouded by snow. 'We have to pull out all the stops on this. Beeny and Bush, you'll travel with the band due to play at some carnival this p.m. Find out who Clegg's friends were, whether he or any of the bandsmen are known to be gay, had he any plans for last evening. I don't need to tell you what to ask, but be certain to get some answers that'll maybe give us a lead on why he should have been battered to death.'

Roy Jakes said, 'I'll search Clegg's room, sir, and his locker or whatever he has at the band headquarters. His personal effects will have to be bagged-up, so I'll see to that, too.'

Piercey had been uncharacteristically quiet so far, but he now typically threw a spanner in the works. 'Is it so certain that the attacks were committed by the same person? Clegg was a first-rate musician who had just earned premium marks in an exam, along with promotion. Isn't it possible that he was a real smart-arse, always top of the bloody class and bragging about it? Maybe he did it once too often for one member of the band, who decided to put him out of the scene for the remainder of the Christmas concerts. Followed him, grabbed up a suitable weapon and gave him one. Then another for good measure. Didn't know his own strength. Walked off unaware Clegg was dead.'

'And guilt will send him along to us to confess, *à la* Mrs Padre?' asked Heather Johnson caustically.

'It's actually a good point,' Tom remarked thoughtfully. 'How Clegg was regarded by his fellow musicians will come out during today's questioning. But what about Kevin McRitchie's assault? No connection, Piercey?'

'I still go for that being an inside job. Someone at the party. We know it was possible to leave and return through the storeroom unnoticed. Lieutenant Farmer and Sapper Rowe had every opportunity.' He gave Tom a penetrating look. 'You overheard a furtive phone conversation between her and a man named Alan. There has to be something behind that, sir.'

'Yes.' Tom wondered if they had been too precipitate in their reasoning. Were there really two widely different attacks with several coincidental similarities? 'Have a more in-depth session with Alan Rowe. Take another look at the storeroom. Time yourself running from there to the front entrance, up to the toilet, snatching the fire alarm club and doing the deed, then returning the same way.'

'Allowing time for having to hide next door when the Clarkson boys turned up,' put in Connie Bush.

Max looked up with a frown. 'Surely that was covered earlier?'

'No, sir,' Tom told him. 'Piercey learned about the storeroom access just as Kevin accused his mother of the attack. Following up on that became our priority.' Max nodded understanding. 'Once Kevin tells us what he's been afraid to say so far, we'll have something substantial to work with.'

Max then addressed the whole team. 'I contacted the doctor handling Kevin's case half an hour ago. We had a serious conversation, ending with an invitation to ring again late this afternoon. He's worried about the boy's state of mind and wants a psychiatrist to see him before giving permission for me to visit. I explained the urgency of my request, but he was adamant. We're in the hands of medical men where that boy's concerned. I shall talk to his mother this morning. She knows more about her son than McRitchie does. She might reveal a link with Tony Clegg we're not aware of. Now, although Mr Black and I are inclined to dismiss drugs featuring in these attacks, we have to be certain. Sergeants Simpson and Prentiss will follow that up. Staff Melly will liaise with George Maddox. He should have some forensic evidence for us from last night's murder scene.' He turned towards Heather Johnson. 'Interview Kevin's classmates again, especially the Swinga Kat three. We need to eliminate for certain a musical motive for these crimes, and discover another link between Kevin and Clegg that could lead us to a third person.'

Glancing at Tom, he added, 'Mr Black has arranged to speak with the Bandmaster during this morning's rehearsal, and later with Sar'nt-Major Fellowes in the hope that they might produce a connection that isn't obvious yet. By the end of the day we should have garnered enough material between us to make considerable headway. The teens' disco is to be held tomorrow night at the Recreation Centre. There'll be a very obvious police presence. We're making that fact public. I'd like to render it unnecessary by apprehending this killer before then. There'll be a briefing here at eight hundred hours. Sergeants Bush and Beeny will have to send their reports in because they're unlikely to be back by then.'

His voice hardened. 'The disco tomorrow will bring together a number of young males in a building which is relevant to both attacks. Our murderer could be drawn there again. We *have* to prevent him eliminating another young life. Go out and find the evidence to nail the bastard!'

They all dispersed into a blue and white morning with sunshine sparkling the fresh snow from the previous night. A morning to make a person feel glad to be alive, thought Max, still buoyed up by his interchange with Livya. Strangely, it had boosted his confidence in unravelling this complexity facing him and his team. Surely by the end of the day a vital clue would have been uncovered, leading to a solution. Apart from the very real urgency of preventing further attacks, he could not deny a frankly macho wish to arrive at the hotel tomorrow evening able to claim they had the killer behind bars.

He drove to the McRitchie house deciding to say nothing about psychiatric interest in Kevin, unless he thought it necessary. He wanted primarily to assess the amount of truth in Kevin's claims of unhealthy fondness from his mother; something that made him unwilling to be sent home. Based on Tom's evidence of McRitchie's attitude towards the girls, Max thought it natural enough for the mother to concentrate on the boy. Had Kevin exaggerated? Interviewing Mavis in her home would make it easier to coax from her details she was unlikely to offer by her boy's bedside.

When Max had taken her to the hospital canteen and urged her to eat some breakfast, she had been in a dreamlike state of shock. A different woman opened the door to him. Her brown hair had taken on a shining gold colour, her pale features were covered in very obvious make-up, her fingernails were painted bright orange to match her lipstick, and those eyelashes were certainly false. She was wearing jeans and an orange polo-necked sweater, both emphasizing her lack of curves.

She smiled at Max without warmth. 'Come in. I'm doing some baking. Greg loves home cooking. It's to be a surprise. All his absolute favourites. They'll be on the table when he comes in.' She walked through to the main room, speaking over her shoulder. 'I'm going to clean the house from top to bottom, set out the best china, maybe light some candles. I got them for Christmas, but I want to make it really special for him tonight.'

This was all said in a tight, artificial voice that sounded more like a recitation to Max as he followed her to a room already bright and attractive. He wondered if she was aware who her visitor was. She turned to him with another absent smile and explained that she was going to buy flowers for the room later on.

'On your way home from the hospital?' he asked.

'I'm not going to the hospital. Do sit down. Kev is getting attention twenty-four seven. He doesn't need me. I'm going to make coffee. You'll have some with me?' She walked into the kitchen and spoke to him through the serving-hatch. 'He's had everything his own way for too long. The rules need to be changed. You can see that.'

Max sat, taking in the expert crochet work evident around the room. A natural home-maker, this woman, quite different from some near-sluts he had come across in soldiers' married quarters. There was no visual sign that three children lived there. Was it due to Mavis being outstandingly house-proud, or her husband's military routine that

Tom had been told about? Clearly a home with too many undercurrents vying for dominance.

'Here we are,' Mavis announced, still in that curious artificial tone as she entered with a tray. The best china was already out, Max guessed, looking at flower-patterned cups, saucers and plates alongside hand-embroidered napkins. He was handed coffee and a plate bearing two mince pies.

'I used my special recipe for the mincemeat. There's ale in it, and a secret ingredient nobody's allowed to know about. Greg loves it. Says even his *mother's* pies aren't a patch on mine.' She sipped her coffee, then exclaimed brightly, 'This *is* cosy, isn't it? I don't have many callers, you know. Greg says it doesn't do to be forever in and out of each other's houses. That's how germs get transferred, especially in winter. Colds and flu, you know. Can't have the girls exposed to that. Do you like the mince pies?'

They still sat on Max's plate, although he had drunk some coffee. 'Mrs McRitchie, I've called to talk to you about your son.'

'Kev's getting attention twenty-four seven. No need to be concerned about him.'

'No need at all. He's in excellent hands at the hospital. It's his friends who interest me.'

'Swinga Kat, that's what they're called. But there's going to be new rules, you know. Got to make something of himself. I've also baked Eccles cakes, and put dough to rise for a lardy cake. You can't buy them out here, and he *does* so love them.'

Was this woman slightly drunk, or was she putting on a dizzy act so that she need not answer his questions? Max put down the best china and spoke harshly. 'Mrs McRitchie, you might not have heard that last night a young bandsman was attacked and killed. He was hit around the head the way Kevin was. It's my duty to discover who took that lad's life, and I think you may be able to help me do that.'

The artificial brightness dropped away instantly. '*I* can't help you. I'm no good at things like that,' she said so softly Max could barely hear her. 'I have to look after Greg and the girls, you see. *That's* my duty, nothing else.'

'The dead boy's name was Tony Clegg. Was Kevin a friend of his? Did Tony ever come to your house?' Max waited, watching Mavis's face. '*Mrs McRitchie!*'

She glanced up to meet his eyes. Hers held a hint of bemusement. 'Nobody comes to the house. I thought I told you that. It's the germs, you see. Greg'll be mad if he knows I let you in. You won't tell him, will you? But I had to know if the pies really *are* better than his mum makes.'

Seriously concerned by this woman's behaviour, Max abandoned any hope of useful answers and got to his feet.

'Thank you for the coffee. I'll let myself

out.'

She got up quickly and followed him to the front door, asking, 'Should I buy chrysanths or roses, d'you think?'

Max turned on the doorstep feeling reluctant pity for a woman so beset by a conviction of inadequacy. She would never hit her son, but it was perfectly possible that she would seek sexual consolation from him.

'I'm sure you'll easily decide when you reach the florist and see the flowers,' he said gently, then walked out to his car.

It was only a five minute drive to the Medical Centre where, morning sick parade over, Charles Clarkson was writing up his notes. Not a man with a quick smile at the best of times, the Medical Officer looked up with a frown when he recognized Max.

'Don't tell me there's another one.'

Max took a seat facing him across his desk, trying not to rise to the insensitivity of the remark. 'I've just visited Mavis McRitchie. She appears to be going to pieces in a big way. I think you should take a look at her.'

'Give me a good reason.'

Max kept the lid on his temper as he described her bizarre manner just now, then went on to tell this brusque but clever man of the relationships in the McRitchie household. He related Kevin's accusation concerning his mother's unhealthy cosseting.

'He also accused her of attacking him last Saturday, but she has a solid alibi. We're not certain of how much truth there is in his claim that she touches him sexually, but he's so worked-up about going home they're getting a psycho to talk to him today.'

Clarkson's eyes narrowed. 'I'll talk to whoever's in charge of his case at the hospital. If I've time I'll drive across rather than telephone. More productive face to face. I'll also call on the mother afterwards. I gave her some Diazepam at the scene of the attack, to counteract the shock of seeing the state of the boy's head, and told her to come in if she needed further help. She hasn't. From what you say, I could legitimately visit to check on how she's coping with the situation. Can't do anything about your suspicions unless there's actual evidence, or someone lays a report to the effect.'

'Exactly why we haven't moved on it yet.'

Clarkson sighed. 'You've a bugger of a situation on your hands. I don't envy you. You can at least leave the McRitchie problem with me.' He gave a faint smile. 'We're on the same side, man, but catch him before he leaves another corpse for me to deal with. I have two sons in the firing line.'

Tom found Jack Fellowes in his office studying a chart on the wall. He smiled and explained his problem to someone who would understand all too well.

'Christmas and New Year leave, Tom. They all want it, of course. The minute I sort it so's we maintain acceptable strengths here, the sods come up with yarns about mother now poorly, granny's funeral, fiancée threatening to give back the ring unless he's there to meet her family coming over from New Zealand. You know.'

Tom nodded and sat beside the desk. 'Wildest one I ever heard was parents and sister lived in one of those prefabricated wooden houses, and needed him to help them move it to another location in the next village. On a sixty foot flat wagon pulled by tractors!' He laughed. 'The lad assured me the local bobby had given permission and planned to close the road during the move.'

Fellowes grinned. 'Did you send him home?'

'I thought such inventiveness deserved a reward. Bugger me, he came back with photographs of the bloody house being transported along country roads. Said the guy driving the tractor was Great Uncle George, aged eighty-seven. The village bobby must have been all of that, too, to agree to it.'

The light-hearted moment eased Tom's depression following his interview with Captain Booth. The Bandmaster was deeply upset over Tony Clegg's murder. A regimental band was a small, independent unit very much like a family, and Christopher Booth regarded himself a father figure to the young, unmarried musicians. He had been proud of the talented Clegg and clearly mourned his loss, especially in such violent manner. He gave Tom no indication that Clegg had been a braggart, or that he was homosexual. The lad had lived for his music and was, perhaps, inclined to shy from socializing as much as the others, but he was generally liked by them. They were all shocked by his death.

A young soldier brought in mugs of coffee as Jack Fellowes said, 'Terrible business last night, Tom. I knew the lad slightly. He played drums in the small group attending discos and other social events requiring the rhythm section of the band. Are you linking his death with the attack at last week's party? You know there's a teens' do tomorrow? I'm organizing it, as usual. Some parents are doubtful about letting their kids attend.'

'Understandable, but George Maddox is setting up patrols around the Centre, and if parents bring and collect their youngsters there shouldn't be any problems. Well, Jack, we have to consider a link between these two attacks, but they could just as well be unconnected. Harking back to the tinies' party, we've learned there was access to and from the storeroom. You said in your statement that Lieutenant Farmer and Sapper Rowe were in and out changing equipment and so on all evening. At the time we reckon Kevin was attacked, you stated that they were in there packing everything away ready for the fancy-dress parade.'

Fellowes' eyes narrowed as he lowered his mug to the desk on which he perched. 'You think one of them hit Kevin?'

Tom was used to this kind of reaction and ignored the question. 'Did anyone else go in there around that time?'

'Sure. Me, for one. We were all helping to clear the decks. Some of the kids wanted to join in, but I shooed them back to the hall. They dart about so fast, you can't keep your eyes on them all the time and there was stuff in there they could overturn or hurt themselves with.'

'So you were distracted by them at that vital time?'

The phone on Fellowes' desk rang. He snatched it up, listened briefly, then said, 'Yes, ma'am, that's a great help. Thank you. One point. I don't think we'll use the storeroom this time.' He flashed Tom a glance, then added, 'Too easy for them to sneak in there and get up to what teens tend to do when they get the chance.' He produced the expected chuckle. 'Exactly, ma'am. Thought we'd keep the prizes and take-home gifts in our cars until just before midnight. OK with you?' He nodded. 'That's grand.' Pause. 'The Redcaps have it in hand. No cause for anxiety.'

He rang off, then resumed his position propped against the front of his desk. 'Lieutenant Farmer.'

'I guessed. So she's helping with this week's party, too?'

'Volunteered. She runs dance classes at the Centre; knows some of the girls. They think she's the cat's meow.'

Tom thought so, also, but not in the way girls would. Even so, he found it interesting that she was so willing to devote two Saturday evenings just prior to Christmas in this way. Surely she was chased by enough unmarried sparks in the Officers' Mess to have a selection of attractive invitations to choose from. With the best will in the world Tom could not see that gorgeous redhead being of philanthropic bent. What was behind this generosity with her free time?

Tom cocked an eye at his fellow sergeant-major. 'What kind of dance classes? Kids don't need instruction in how to bounce up and down and jiggle around like cats on hot bricks.'

Jack laughed. 'Not your scene?'

'I like to hold my partner close.'

'Dirty devil!'

'What kind of classes?'

'I don't attend them, mind, but she told me they're for "self-expression in movement".'

'Bloody artistic claptrap,' exclaimed Tom with a short laugh. 'What is the lady going to do at tomorrow's affair? The only thing kids express in movement at a disco is the first signs of St Vitus' dance.'

'We're holding competitions for the best rendition of a pop song by a girl and by a boy. We've twenty entries for each of those.' He grinned. 'I'm taking earplugs, but it provides a break in the dancing every twenty minutes. Then Lieutenant Farmer suggested we get them to dress imaginatively, and she'll give a prize to the ones in the best Christmas gear.' He drank his coffee, then looked hard at Tom. 'She didn't cosh Kevin.'

'How about Alan Rowe?'

Fellowes sighed gustily. 'Look, I couldn't swear he was actually in my sight the whole time. We were organizing around two hundred excited kids. It was a party, for God's sake! I wasn't looking out for villainy. But I'd stake a year's pay on that lad being straight.'

A dark mood drove Tom home for lunch. He did not expect to eat dinner with Nora and he felt in need of her warm company before continuing with this urgent day. The natural beauty around him was in contrast to the grimness of what he was occupied with. A young man, proud and delighted with his achievements, had been brutally robbed of ever again seeing sunshine dancing on fresh snow, a giant fir tree covered in decorations that glinted and sparkled as the breeze moved its branches, lads like himself parading in uniforms like the one he cherished so highly. That thought hung in his mind as Tom drove home. Clegg's murder had upset him; a man hardened to human violence.

185

Nora was surprised to see him, and took his hands as she came from the dining-room where she had been working on an elaborate evening dress for an officer's wife. 'Hungry?'

'And wanting a quick injection of your reality.'

They held each other without speaking, until she drew away and put her palms against his cold cheeks. 'What I said this morning about looking for a better prospect was a lot of nonsense.'

'I know.'

She smiled. 'Conceited bastard!' Taking his arm she led him to the kitchen. 'I made a sausage plait for the girls' tea, but we'll have it now. Won't take long to warm it up. Get us both a lager.'

The normality of his other life eased his inner coldness, and they soon sat to eat. To Nora's quiet query on whether he wanted to talk about work, Tom shook his head.

'How's the dress turning out?'

'Something of a challenge, to be honest, love. Mrs Harper wants a half-inch vertical frill from neckline to hem to give the image of a wrap-around. I personally think it suggests an overall and takes away the elegance of the style. But she's paying me to produce what she wants, so that's what I'm doing.'

'Are you making one for yourself? For the Sergeants' Mess dance?'

She faced him frankly. 'As we're highly unlikely to attend, I'm not bothering.' When he made no comment, she said, 'We have an invitation to the Graumanns' tomorrow evening.'

'Who are they?' he asked, not interested in vague invitations they would not accept.

'The parents of your daughter's friend, Hans, who live in the house over the road from us.'

'We have to hobnob with the whole family now?' he grunted.

'Yes, Tom. It's important to Maggie.'

He frowned across the table. 'She's twelve, Nora.'

'She's an almost thirteen-year-old *person*. Things matter to her the way they matter to you. You expect the girls to understand your priorities. You must understand theirs.'

He knew she was being utterly reasonable, but a curious type of fear led him to say, 'So this meet-the-family evening is to arrange their nuptials, is it? This isn't India, it's Germany.'

'And the invitation is part of German Christmastime tradition. They keep open house for friends and neighbours,' she responded calmly. 'I heard you the other day claiming that if only people would observe the goodwill to all men maxim, you would be able to participate fully in festive fun for once. Where's *your* goodwill?'

'Crushed beneath the weight of someone's brutality to two innocent lads.' He leaned back in his chair with a sigh. 'We have to prevent it happening again. We're up to our eyes. I won't have time for this German hospitality.'

'Make time, Tom.' A suggestion of steel was now in her voice, something he had rarely heard before. 'We don't have to stay the whole evening. They know what you're engaged in and will understand your commitments, but it's important that you put in an appearance. Important to *me*.'

Wondering why Nora should choose this high-stress period to employ emotional blackmail, the unexpected confrontation was broken by the ringing of Tom's mobile. He snatched it up, tension flaring. '*Yes?*'

'Tom, here is Klaus Krenkel,' said a pleasant accented voice. 'I have news for you concerning your stolen equipment.'

It was an anticlimax, albeit a welcome one. 'Don't tell me you've found it.'

Krenkel chuckled. 'We are wonderful policemen, but not magicians. It has been sold across the border. It cannot, of course, be traced. We discovered that Herr and Frau Haufmann have for their servant a Turkish girl. She has brother and cousins who have illegal entry here. She has told them of the long, hidden way to her employers' home, where they can transfer the equipment and leave your vehicle out of sight. So they have done this.'

'She confessed?'

'Oh yes, certainly.'

Tom did not ask how they persuaded her to rat on her relatives. It was better not to.

'We now seek her kinsmen. It will be difficult. They hide away. Even she does not know where they will be on any day.'

'But if you can't trace the stolen goods you can't charge them with anything,' Tom pointed out.

'We can send them back to Turkey. That will be a good thing.'

Anticlimax was really setting in now. Krenkel's upbeat mood began to grate on Tom. So the *Polizei* had discovered who committed the crime, but had no idea where the culprits or the stolen booty were. Bully for them!

'Well, thank you for keeping us informed,' he said, trying to sound suitably grateful.

'It is important that we work always together, Tom. That is why I have called to tell you that the Haufmanns' servant is the girlfriend of your soldier, Treeves. She says they have plan this together. You should question him about that.'

Eight

Knowing dinner would most likely be soup in a cup and a ham roll, Max drove out to the hotel where he would take Livya tomorrow. He had heard good reports of the place, but had not yet seen it or sampled the food. For such an important date he wanted to satisfy himself that it was absolutely right.

He was almost sure she would prefer traditional to ultra-modern, as he did. Better not to arrive and discover it was wrong, then face the embarrassing need to find somewhere more suitable at eight p.m. on a snowy Saturday night two weeks before Christmas. Almost certainly, *Andrew* would never have subjected her to such a predicament when off-duty on a dual mission. His father had wide experience of dalliance.

Max brought his thoughts to a jarring halt. This was no dalliance. He had been overwhelmed from the moment he set eyes on Livya Cordwell. He had fun with a number of flirty girls during his oat-sowing years, but had only once before been instantly bowled over. Susan's death had left his senses in hiatus, his emotional confidence shattered.

He had deeply loved her; his trust in her had been absolute. She had betrayed both and he still did not fully comprehend why. Maybe he never would.

He was now preparing again to throw himself in at the deep end. This time there were additional hazards. In six days the chess championship would end. Livya would return to London and a different, more polished Rydal. How could he capture her serious interest in such a short time with this case on his hands? Turning his car on to the road where the hotel was located, he told himself grimly the answer to that lay in how he handled things here tomorrow. After three years of abstinence he had better remember all the old tricks ... and a few new ones she might not have come across.

He breathed a sigh of relief on first seeing the hotel. Entering it he felt a surge of excitement. Roaring log fires, velvet curtains, deep chairs and sofas in matching dark green, carved wood, discreet wall lights, large overhead chandelier glittering in the glow of firelight. It looked seductive at lunchtime. At night it would be perfect for what he had in mind.

Max ate lunch in the panelled restaurant, imagining Livya on the other side of the table, her dark hair gleaming and those lustrous eyes revealing the emotions he hoped to arouse. He then noticed two extremely elegant women at a nearby table beaming and nodding at him, and he realized he had been smiling at his thoughts. Well, he told himself, if I can attract a pair of upmarket *Frauen* without even trying, all should be well tomorrow.

His attraction rating took an immediate nosedive when his mobile rang. Smiles turned to glares so that Max felt obliged to leave his coffee to cool while he walked to the foyer to take the call.

'Thought you'd want to hear one or two items of interest,' said Charles Clarkson. 'I contacted the man dealing with Kevin McRitchie at the hospital. The boy has retreated into self-imposed silence and shows signs of retro-hysteria. Panic, in layman's terms. No visitors for twenty-four hours minimum.'

'Bugger it,' Max swore softly. 'We need to question him most urgently.'

'I called on Mrs McRitchie a while ago. She's certainly hyped-up, as you indicated, but that might not be such a bad thing. She appears to have recovered from the shock of the attack on her son and is concentrating on the rest of her family. She had decided to give the hospital a miss anyway, so was not upset by the news I gave her.'

Max was astonished. 'You didn't think she was behaving abnormally?'

'That's confidential information concerning a patient. I can't comment further.'

That was typical Clarkson-speak and Max scowled. 'As her doctor you are, of course, the best judge of her state of mind.'

'Most women behave abnormally at various times in their lives, Rydal. Don't look for criminal signs in simple human exaggeration.'

The line went dead leaving Max irritated by the man, as usual. It added to his frustration over being denied access to the lad who could surely advance this case. Unfortunately, medical authority overruled that of the police. Max could do nothing. With that line of investigation blocked he would have to find another, but where, for God's sake?

Deciding to abandon his coffee, he caught the eye of his waiter and settled his bill. Then he went to the reception desk to book a room for tomorrow night. The slim, extremely polite German explained that they were heavily booked – the time of year, sir – so all he could offer was a small double overlooking the car park.

Max had to settle for that, knowing other hotels would most probably be booked solid, too. With his earlier upbeat mood fast plunging, he turned from the desk to see Lucy Farmer standing beside the lift doors. Dressed in a long, fur-trimmed blue coat and pale suede boots she was an eye-catching sight for any man. The young one with her seemed practically mesmerized by her visual impact. Max felt he had seen the tall, dark-haired man before somewhere. His jeans, Aran sweater and sheepskin jacket marked him as

British in the indefinable way clothes do. A relative or friend of the stunning Lucy? More than a friend? They stood very close to each other and were talking earnestly, oblivious of what was going on around them.

As he watched, Lucy gripped her companion's arm as if to emphasize what she was telling him and to remove his expression of doubt. Then, abruptly, she sent him off with an imperative gesture and a dazzling smile.

Stepping into a telephone booth where she would not spot him, Max saw Lucy cross to the reception desk, hand over a room key and settle the proffered bill. The urbane receptionist smiled, nodded and pocketed the additional notes she slid across covered by her hand. It was done so smoothly Max guessed it was not the first time. So what was the young lieutenant up to with the curly haired man evidently willing to do her bidding?

Max followed her to the street, and for almost forty minutes watched her shop in the more expensive stores. Nothing incriminating in that. He returned to his car none the wiser about the unexpected encounter. Driving back to the base he reasoned that she must have a free day, or have been granted leave to meet up with a relative from the UK who was just passing through. Hence the hotel room? But why had *she* settled the bill and slipped the man a tip?

Lucy had attended the dinner last night, so

it could not be she who had occupied the hotel room. Unless she had driven out there very late. Max made a note to check on her movements at the conclusion of the dinner. There could be a simple explanation for what he had seen. Her companion had an urgent appointment to meet, a train or plane to catch, so she had undertaken to pay his hotel charges with a tip for services rendered. A girl for the night? On the surface, the hotel did not look to be the kind of establishment that had the provision of prostitutes as one of its services, but a venal, enterprising member of staff could be running it on the side.

Reaching the main gate Max impulsively turned in the direction of the hall attached to the garrison church, where the chess championship was being played out. Denied his interview with Kevin McRitchie this afternoon, and having had his anticipation of dining with Livya spoiled by Clarkson's call, he surrendered to the urge to see her. She had told him she was doing well, but the near-unbeatable RAF corporal was threatening to repeat his long-running triumph.

Max's entry disturbed the concentrated atmosphere, causing heads to turn. Max knew then that he could never become hooked on a game that demanded silence throughout. Games should be fun accompanied by vocal enjoyment, but he supposed chess addicts would claim it was an erudite mental contest not to be lumped together with the mindless snakes and ladders, dominoes and tiddlywinks. Certainly not with the barbaric rugby or soccer. *They* were games. Chess was on a higher plane altogether. He would tease Livya about it tomorrow.

She spotted him, and broke away from the circle of observers around a pair who appeared to be deep in thought as they gazed at the state of play on the board before them.

Drawing him to a far corner, Livya whispered, 'Are you here out of interest, or on business?'

He replied in an undertone, 'I came to see if you're real or a figment of my imagination.'

She smiled. 'First an egghead, now a figment. Can you stay for a while to watch?'

He smiled back. 'If I watch anything it'll be you. Those two look set to stay that way until the wind changes.'

'It's a very tense moment,' she chided. 'The next move will be crucial to the outcome.'

'Have you played today?' She looked immensely attractive in uniform. He wondered what she would wear tomorrow, which led to thoughts of how easy it would be to remove with slick expertise.

'I'm to take on the winner of this game.'

'At midnight?'

Laughter lurked in her eyes. 'What are you really doing here, Max?'

Casting a glance at the others in the room to satisfy himself they were still watching the motionless contestants, he reached for her hand and held it. 'I've just been told the only available room is small and overlooks the car park. I've reserved it, but if you'd prefer to leave after dinner we'll do that.'

Amusement still dominated as she whispered, 'Are you chickening out, Captain Rydal?'

'God, no! I'd accept the ticket kiosk *in* the car park if you'd share it with me.'

At that moment Max's mobile rang. Heads swivelled round, eyes glared, oaths spilled from the two players. Livya pushed him swiftly through the swing doors and followed, holding them steady so that they closed without a sound. The caller was Tom. Max told him he would call back in a few minutes, then made a rueful face.

'Have I committed the ultimate sin?'

'Very definitely. Mobiles are forbidden in there.' Her lips twitched. 'You'll have to sleep in the ticket kiosk while I occupy the small room. The punishment has to fit the crime.'

'If you say so, ma'am, but in my job I've learned a lot about breaking and entering. If it gets too cold in the kiosk...'

'Make that return call,' she directed, pushing him towards the outer door. '*À bientôt, mon ami.*'

As a result of Tom's report of Klaus Kren-

197

kel's information, Max then drove to the RMP station near the main gate to consult George Maddox. He could have phoned or e-mailed, but he wanted a face to face conversation.

Maddox was a highly experienced policeman. Dark-haired, sturdy and erect, with a square face that could show menace or sympathy equally swiftly. When he spotted Max he abandoned his computer and approached with an alert expression. His uniform was starched and immaculate, his boots like black mirrors.

'Afternoon, sir. I was about to send info across to you. Came in late morning.'

Max smiled. 'Anything approaching a breakthrough, Sergeant?'

'I wish! Evidence found at the scene of the second attack is negligible. A mass of prints on the weapon eliminates any hopes in that direction. Forensics are checking if there's even a partial on the chessman to match those on the weapon used on the McRitchie boy, but it's more than likely the assailant was wearing gloves in that low temperature last night. No chance of boot prints. A fresh fall of snow after the attack covered what would certainly have been Clegg's and at least one other set leading to that chessboard. Same with tyre marks. Passing traffic was light, and our vehicles plus those of the ambulance overrode any useful impressions.'

Max sighed. 'The big minus is that no one

appeared to have been in the area to see what was happening and go to the lad's aid.'

'That's right. We've appealed for people to come forward if they were near the Recreation Centre around the vital time. Trouble is, the place wasn't in use last night and it's on the far side of the base away from the NAAFI, the Sports Centre and the accommodation blocks. On a freezing evening around supper time there'd be no cause for people to be there.'

'Which strengthens the belief that Clegg had an arrangement to meet his killer,' said Max with a nod.

George Maddox waved an arm at two corporals busy at their computers. 'The lads have been checking out possible suspects, and anyone we have an eye on as possible drug pushers. They were all elsewhere and with company.' His dark eyes gazed frankly at Max. 'Clegg's clothing bore no traces of drugs and there weren't any condoms in his pockets. Same goes for the McRitchie lad.'

He walked three steps to his own desk in a corner of the small room and took up several sheets of an official report. 'Here's evidence that the attacks were made by the same person.' He read from the pages. 'Matching head hairs, dark brown with a natural kink or curl, and unusually coarse. Specimens of identical spittle on both weapons suggestive of excessive force or emotion. Dead skin samples have the same DNA.'

'It's good to have that,' Max said. 'Once we've apprehended him it'll provide strong support in the case we present. Unfortunately, unless we obtain samples of their DNA from every single person on this base, it does not take us further forward right now. The spittle is interesting. Upholds our theory that arranged meetings between the victims and the perpetrator turned unexpectedly ugly. The nearest available weapon was snatched up in uncontrollable rage. The man we want is of very unstable temperament, Sergeant.'

Maddox gave a sour smile. 'Plenty of them around here, especially on a Saturday night.'

'All set for the disco tomorrow?'

'I've had to defer leave for Sampson, Glenn and Parsons. They won't now go until Monday. Two weeks before Christmas, squaddies will be on the rampage in town this weekend. I can't afford to reduce my street patrols.' He nodded. 'The kids at the disco will be safe, sir.'

'I'm sure they will.' Max prepared to leave. 'I called in to give you some news concerning Lance-Corporal Treeves we've just had from the German guys.'

Maddox drew another sheet from the several he was holding, and grinned. 'I was keeping the good news until last. Pathology report came in an hour ago. Verdict is Treeves suffered adult Sudden Death Syndrome during that drive back here. Corporals

Stubble and Meacher are cleared of any responsibility for his demise.'

'Great!' exclaimed Max. 'That must be a huge worry removed. Uncomfortable having something like that hanging over you. Curious affliction, that. I've only ever once before come across it. A girl of two years. The parents were under suspicion and questioned remorselessly. Harrowing!'

'Indeed,' agreed the father of two children.

'We've been advised to question Treeves on the subject of his possible participation in the theft of our equipment.' He related what the Turkish girl servant had claimed. 'Treeves' complicity can never be proved or disproved now. The *Polizei* only have her word on the subject, and we must let sleeping dogs lie. Treeves' parents will remain in ignorance of the accusation, which is the only upbeat outcome of the sorry affair.'

He had been transferred to a side-room that had been occupied by a small, very sick boy. Overnight, he had vanished. Kevin was sure he had died. Lying awake in the early hours he had seen a lot of activity; people going in and out, a man in a long robe carrying a cross, a sobbing woman and a man with downbent head being led away by the priest.

That boy had died very conveniently. Being moved to a place on his own made Kevin's plan much easier. He hated being with all the tinies in a ward kitted up to

201

resemble fairyland. They cried in the night. One started, and woke everyone else. Then the rest began to holler. And they were sick and messed themselves. The place stank. There was one kid of nine and another of eleven, but they had palled up and ignored him. They only spoke German and were too young to be interesting, anyway.

Everyone around him spoke in German, of course. He knew quite a lot, but had no intention of letting on. The nurses and doctors used English when they approached him, but he had started to pretend he did not understand what they were asking. It was easy, and they had cancelled their plan to send him home. That prospect had really frightened him, because no way could he go back there after telling the policewoman his mother had bashed him on the head.

It had been a mistake to say that, but he had wanted to get back at her for treating him like her baby. And she *had* touched him. Maybe it was accidental, but if she had not insisted on fussing with his knight's costume because he was doing it to the brats, it would never have happened. No way could he go home. He was too old to be kissed goodnight and tucked into bed, because 'Dadda' was doing it to the brats. Next thing, she would be getting in there with him, because *he* was in bed with the brats.

His dumb act had prevented her coming to visit, and had stopped the Redcap officer asking awkward questions about who had attacked him. He had no idea who had, or why. All he remembered was smoking a cigarette and promising himself it would be a joint as soon as he got the chance, when something crashed against his head. It was useless to pretend he was not scared by it; worried about who could have it in for him and might try again. Another reason not to go home.

In the afternoons, the tinies were all settled for a nap and the ward was quiet. He supposed the nurses went for their lunch then. Only one stayed at the desk, and she busied herself a lot of the time in the room containing all the pills and equipment used for treatments. Today, he had waited for the right moment to slip past unnoticed. It was surprising how little attention people paid to a boy in a dressing-gown walking purposefully along corridors. Although he had never done it before, he discovered he was good at stealing.

In adult wards many of the patients sat in the day rooms at the far end with their visitors. Those too ill to get up slept through until tea was brought. At the foot of empty beds lay coats, scarves, gloves. In lockers there were purses, small piles of coins, underclothes, T-shirts, sweaters, socks and shoes. Kevin collected all he would need and, as if the gods were smiling on his endeavour, came upon a pair of winter boots temporarily discarded by a child with feet the same size as his own small ones.

Returning stealthily to his room, Kevin took one of the pillows from his bed, pulled off the cover and filled it with the clothes he had taken. Then he put the pillow on the top shelf of the cupboard containing spare bedding and medical aids like ring cushions, leg supports and back rests. Satisfied that he had done all he must, he lay on his bed to sleep. He needed to rest in readiness for what he knew would be the most difficult thing he had ever done.

There was a general air of despondency when they gathered to report their findings that day. The only significant news was the pathologist's verdict of Sudden Death Syndrome on Treeves, given with reluctance due to the lack of true medical understanding of the condition.

Roy Jakes had found nothing useful among Clegg's possessions. 'No gay or porno mags to support a sexual motive for his murder, sir. No evidence of interest in drugs. He appears to have been totally wrapped up in his music. Lived for it, I'd say, which supports the theory of a musical link between the two attacks.'

'If we're certain they are linked,' put in Piercey.

Tom said heavily, 'Today's efforts were designed to establish or disprove that. I have the reports sent in by Beeny and Bush. Their interviews with members of the band are wholly inconclusive. None showed aggro towards Clegg as a person, or as a gifted musician. No suggestion that he had rated himself better than the rest, and certainly no hints he was interested in men. They were all disturbed by his murder, unanimously mystified about why he should be a victim. We can safely rule out a motive of professional or personal jealousy by one of his fellow musicians.'

'That doesn't negate a musical link,' Jakes insisted. 'It's what singularly motivated both victims.'

Heather Johnson nodded agreement. 'I talked to Kevin's classmates, and particularly in depth with the Swinga Kat three in the class above his. They're older and more mature than the kid I interviewed in the hospital, yet they willingly acknowledged him as their inspiration and the leader of the group. Again, no hint of drugs or homosexuality, but those three reinforced what they said earlier about his mother's petting really getting to Kevin.'

'That could be exaggeration, like his claim that she clouted him around the head. We know she couldn't have done that,' said Tom.

'And she denied ever knowing Tony Clegg, which I believe,' put in Max.

Olly Simpson and Bob Prentiss reported on their investigations into the general drug and gay scenes. This had proved as fruitless as the rest.

'So we're no further forward,' concluded Tom.

'I do have one piece of interesting information.' That was Piercey, who enjoyed throwing pebbles into a still pond. 'I first went for the key to the Recreation Centre so that I could do a trial run through the storeroom, round to the front entrance, and up to the toilets.' He gave a satisfied smile. 'Key had already been collected by Sapper Rowe. Seems our friend who's good with tinies is also handy at fixing strobes and turning a basic hall into a dim and sexy pseudo disco for teens. He's volunteered to help out tomorrow.'

Max leaned forward as something clicked into place. 'What time was this, Sergeant?'

'Around ten thirty, sir. Rowe packed it in soon after. Said he had to go to town to fetch something. I then did the time check. It *is* possible for someone involved in clearing the hall ready for the fancy-dress parade to slip out through the rear door, hit Kevin, then return the same way before the parade began.' He gave another satisfied smile. 'My money's on Rowe. I checked his whereabouts last night. He claimed he was in his room working on his plans for the hall, and admits to being alone the whole time. When I questioned others in his section none could give him an alibi for the time of Clegg's murder. I'm not happy with his interest in young people. Why would a good-looking young guy like him want to spend two Saturday nights at Christmas time helping to organize kids' parties, when his mates are all in town creating double hell?'

'Because Lieutenant Farmer is doing the same,' said Tom thoughtfully. 'That phone call to "Alan" was made to him, as I suspected. Those two are in league in some way.'

'But she was sitting next to the Boss at dinner when Clegg was murdered,' Heather Johnson objected.

Max had moved to one of the computers and was bringing up on screen Sapper Rowe's details. The photograph showed the curly haired man who had been with Lucy Farmer in the hotel at lunchtime. Those two were certainly up to something, but he found it hard to believe she would condone violence and death. Saying nothing about what he had seen, Max then advised that George Maddox be asked to send one of his men who could pass as late teens, dressed in suitable gear, to keep an eye on Sapper Rowe the whole evening.

'Rowe will be the active partner if they have something planned,' he said. 'She's probably the driving force in their collusion.'

They broke off shortly after that, no one but Piercey feeling gratified after a long day of painstaking investigation. All across the base Friday evening parties were underway, but the members of 26 Section were heading for early bedtime. They were not in the mood for frivolity, hung over as they were by a black cloud of responsibility. In all their minds was the dread of another tragedy before they identified the perpetrator. The key they sought was a motive. They were all experienced enough to know they would have seen it long ago if it was a simple one. Even their boss's famous 'guts' had not done their stuff this time. He admitted being as baffled as they.

Max repeated this to Tom as they prepared to lock their new headquarters, which still were not fully organized after the move. 'Maybe we're looking at the whole business arse over apex. Are we stuck in a rut with the sex or drugs theories?'

'We've no evidence to support either,' Tom agreed, setting the alarm on the main door. 'Yet I still find it tricky to go along with murder over music. As we've said before, where's the gain?' They began walking to their cars. 'After intensive investigation we've reached stalemate.'

'Our chess competitors would call it checkmate.'

Tom eyed Max speculatively over the roof of his car. 'Growing interested?'

'In the game? No. They can sit for hours pondering their next move. I'd ask them to lend their devious skill to our complex case, but they'd still be at it at Easter.'

'By the way, sir, I meant to tell you Clegg's parents are flying in this evening. As the Bandmaster is unable to meet and take them to their hotel, Padre Robinson and his wife are standing in. A churchman is possibly better suited to the sad duty, but I'm not sure how Mrs Padre will cope with a tragic situation. The general consensus is that she wears a permanent smile.'

Max had not yet met Estelle Robinson, but he had heard about her sunny disposition. 'I'm still waiting for someone to confess and make her prophecy come true!'

'If only!'

They said goodnight and went their separate ways. Although it was past ten, Max decided to drive via the church hall in case Livya was engaged in erudite battle with the winner of the game he had disturbed. It was another clear night, with a sky full of stars and a new moon. Max recalled his mother warning not to look at a new moon through glass because it brought ill luck, and he wound his window down. Ridiculous, because he had just viewed it through his windscreen, but it was one of very few memories he had of her and the gesture seemed appropriate. The snow was firmly frozen still, the glistening white coating giving even a functional military base a kind of beauty in the pale light.

The church hall was in darkness, so he

continued to the Officers' Mess. The dining-room was deserted at that late hour, of course, but in the ante-room several eager subalterns were rehearsing their foolery for the upcoming 'entertainment'. Max hurried past and up to his room to make coffee. As he drank it, thoughts of his mother lingered, and he recalled Livya telling him something astonishing – that his father carried every-where with him her photograph. A sign of devotion Max had no knowledge of. The marriage had lasted only eight years, but his lost wife had clearly remained a cherished memory for Andrew Rydal despite the dis-creet liaisons that had cheered his later years.

Thinking of lost years and lost loves, Max impulsively picked up the telephone receiver and dialled Livya's room number. It was a while before she answered sleepily.

'Did I wake you?' he asked softly.

'Yes. Is something wrong?'

'I'm afraid so. I had this yearning to make contact and couldn't fight it.'

She gave a soft laugh. 'A big, tough police-man like you?'

'We have yearnings like everyone else.'

'Thank God for that! There's hope for tomorrow in that case.'

'Very definitely. Did you win your game?'

'No time. The one you rudely interrupted didn't end until late this evening. I play first thing tomorrow.'

'It won't go on until midnight, will it?' he asked, fearing the ruin of their plans.

She laughed again, softly and seductively. 'They need the hall for a dinner-dance. We have to vacate it by teatime.'

'Good. If I don't see you at breakfast, good luck.'

'Thanks.'

'Sorry I disturbed you.'

A short pause. 'You've done that from the moment we met. Goodnight, Max. Sleep well.'

After that declaration it was not surprising that an hour or more passed before Max sank into the depths of slumber. He was dragged up from them by a ringing in his ears. Reaching for his mobile on the bedside table, he saw that it was two a.m. He answered the call, dreading he would learn of another vicious attack.

The girls were asleep when Tom got home; Nora was still working on the evening dress. With a grimace she told him Mrs Harper had decided the vertical frill made the style too strongly resemble an overall, so wanted it removed and replaced with diamanté.

'Far more elegant than that blasted frill.'

'But a hell of a lot more work for you,' Tom complained.

'That'll be reflected in the bill I send her. I need to go to town tomorrow to buy the diamanté, so the girls and I plan on completing our Christmas shopping and having lunch at Bertrum's. Any chance of your coming with us, or even meeting us for the eats?'

He frowned. 'You girls are better on your own for shopping. No way am I prepared to sit outside changing booths with other bored males, but I might manage lunch. As of now we're clean out of ideas on this case. We've checked every possibility and got nowhere. Until we hit on a new lead we're as productive as that turkey in the deep freeze.'

Nora put aside her needles and scissors. 'How about a glass of wine?'

'Or two.' He slung an arm around her shoulders as they walked through to the kitchen. 'We'll have guys posted outside the Recreation Centre and one inside mixing with the kids during the disco tomorrow. So why do I have this sinking feeling that there's going to be another tragedy before the night's out?'

'Because you're tired and more than usually stressed-out due to the youth of the victims. One of the things I love about you is your concern for the welfare of other kids along with your own.' She poured generous amounts of red wine in two glasses and handed him one. *'Prosit!'*

They sipped, then went to the settee in the sitting-room and made themselves comfortable in their customary fashion. With her head against his shoulder, Nora said quietly, 'You haven't forgotten about the Graumanns' invitation tomorrow, have you?'

He came from thoughts of a grimmer nature. 'It's naturally on top of my list of priorities.'

There was a brief silence, then she said, 'I feel sorry for Max. He returns to a chaste room in the Mess and broods on those things you've just told me, but there's no woman to listen and sympathize. No lover to cuddle and drink a comforting glass of wine with. No children who think he's the best dad in the world and want, quite desperately, his approval of things that are important to them.'

The silence was longer this time. Tom knew exactly what she was saying and eventually responded. 'A lot of women would slang their husbands and flounce from the room, but you just remind me how lucky I am when I make cutting remarks like that.' He kissed her temple. 'Sorry, love. The way things are, there's every chance I'll be free to visit our daughter's future parents-in-law.'

Nora dug him in the ribs, knowing he was joking now. 'Give it five more years and you might very well be.'

The truth of her words about Max's aloneness stayed with Tom, and he expressed his gratitude for his own happiness with gentle lovemaking when they went to bed. She seemed happy with the low-key passion and they fell into relaxed sleep in perfect accord. When his mobile rang Tom woke instantly, fearing the worst.

'Sorry to wake you,' said Max. 'I've been informed that Kevin McRitchie has apparently run from the hospital. They've searched the premises, but he's not in the building. They had complaints of outer clothing and money missing after visiting hours this afternoon, so they believe he stole enough apparel to keep warm, and enough cash to get him well away from the area. Tom, that boy is in a state of acute distress and highly vulnerable. He has to be found before we have another death on our hands.'

Nine

Saturday dawned dull and overcast. The sky looked full of snow: the Met boys said the cold snap was unlikely to end before the middle of next week, and that was only a maybe. A day when most people would flood the street markets to shop, drink hot punch, and generally have fun promised to be a long, hard slog for SIB.

They had already been at their computers and telephones for two hours, checking with relatives and friends in the UK to discover if Kevin McRitchie had been in touch about possibly taking refuge with them. A Redcap patrol had begun cruising the streets within a twelve kilometre radius of the hospital as soon as the news came in, searching bus shelters, doorways, pedestrian underpasses and any place where a boy could hide away relatively protected from the freezing temperature until early buses began running.

Nursing staff could not pinpoint the exact time Kevin had left, which meant he might have caught the last bus to run past the hospital, but that could not be checked until staff arrived for the first shift. All-night taxi companies were questioned, but no driver had picked up a young lad wearing an assortment of odd clothes. The nearest rail station was too far distant for Kevin to have walked there, but Redcaps checked for a sighting in case he had been given a lift by a late-departing sympathetic visitor outside the hospital.

Having drawn a blank at the most likely places, SIB's fear was that the boy had been offered a ride by a cruising pervert seizing an unexpected stroke of luck. If that had happened, it was possible Kevin might not be seen again.

Knowing he could not have entered the base openly, anyone who had driven through the main gate after 23:00, which was when a nurse had last seen Kevin, apparently asleep in the side ward, was questioned and warned of the consequences of smuggling a passenger past the guards at the gate. No one had.

At first light, Johnny King, Malc Carpenter and Callum Peters of Swinga Kat were visited and asked if Kevin had contacted them about his plans. He had not. His classmates were similarly questioned, with no success. Redcaps manned the station as soon as trains began the daily timetable, hoping the lad would turn up there. Taxi companies, the bus system, police at the nearest airport were asked to contact SIB if Kevin should be sighted. Klaus Krenkel had been notified at the outset, so the *Polizei* had circulated a description of the runaway to all their officers.

Knowing they had done all they could for the moment, Max and Tom departed to freshen up and grab some breakfast. As they walked to their cars, Max said, 'They were aware of the lad's unstable state. Their lapse of responsibility towards a clearly disturbed patient should be cited when this case is eventually presented.'

'Sure it should, but I hand the bulk of responsibility to his parents,' growled Tom. 'How could any father, no matter how disappointed in his son, respond to the news with the comment, "Stupid little bugger!"? *She* burst into tears, but he made no attempt to comfort her. I perfectly understand why Kevin was desperate to escape that situation. In the old days, lads his age ran away to a brutal life at sea, but there's every kind of help for youngsters now. He was being offered it at the hospital. Why didn't he grab that lifeline?'

Max rubbed his prickly chin wearily. 'I suspect he thought falsely accusing his mother of attacking him at the party had landed him in serious trouble with us. Running must have seemed his only option.'

'So we're partly to blame?'

'Inasmuch as we were trying to find who had used violence against him. You know, Tom, whoever did caused a can of worms to be opened in the McRitchie home.'

Tom prepared to slide behind the wheel. 'When this case is tied up, it might prove to have been beneficial. That family needs sorting big time.'

'Thankfully that won't be our job. Let's get some food, feed the sluggish brain.'

A shower, a shave, a clean shirt and underwear went partway to sharpening the senses, and a large breakfast designed as sustenance for the rest of the day made Max feel a different man. Seeing Livya would provide a real boost, but that was denied him. Surely she was not already concentrating on a chess board.

Back in his office Max enjoyed another black coffee with Tom. They could only now wait for news of Kevin to come in, so they tried once more to hit on a link between his attack and Clegg's murder.

'Music and the fact they are male are the only things they have in common, on the surface,' Tom pointed out. 'So what if there's another that's not obvious?'

'Such as?'

Tom grimaced. 'That's why it's not obvious.'

'Let's say it's the Recreation Centre. One was inside it, the other was walking to it. What activities are held there that both lads might be interested in?'

Producing the handbill submitted by Jack Fellowes after the tinies' party, Tom quoted the daily programme of classes and activities. A week later it still presented no enlightenment.

'Ante-natal keep fit, Cookery for Christmas, Camera Club, Computer Training for Idiots, Creative Indoor Games, Turkish Belly Dancing, First Aid in the Home, American Line Dancing, German Language at beginner and advanced levels, Make Your Own Jewellery, and Self Expression in Movement.' He cast a glance at Max. 'That last is taught by Lieutenant Farmer.'

'She certainly expresses herself in movement very well.' Max then decided to mention her meeting with Sapper Rowe at the hotel yesterday, hoping Tom would not ask why he was there himself. 'Rowe told Piercey he had to go to town to collect something. Maybe it was for tonight's disco, which she is also helping with.'

'What was he doing in a posh hotel with her at lunch-time? Hardly a chance meeting, surely.' Tom's eyes brightened. 'Now here's an idea! She runs that arty dance class on alternate Saturday mornings, and he shows how to create indoor games on the other Saturdays. She told Heather Johnson Rowe was so ingenious he could set up in business when he leaves the army. Those two are the common link.'

'How so? Kevin and Clegg didn't attend his classes, did they?'

'No, but she and "Alan" Rowe are closely involved with the Centre, and both were in and out of the storeroom at the time Kevin was attacked.'

'So one of them could have slipped upstairs to the toilets. Lieutenant Farmer was sitting beside me when Clegg was killed, but Rowe has no firm alibi.' Max screwed up his eyes in concentration. 'What if the two victims had something going with Rowe? Because he uses the Centre a lot he's able to sign out the key with no questions asked. Piercey said he'd already taken it yesterday morning. In any case, he would have had plenty of opportunities to have the key copied to allow him entry whenever he chose. Uniform searched the building after Clegg's murder, but Rowe would have cleared the vicinity by then.'

'I can go along with that,' said Tom thoughtfully. 'But why kill Clegg out in the open?'

'The meeting didn't go as planned; Clegg walked out. Rowe followed, arguing with him. He pushes for a change of mind, full agreement. Clegg is adamant, says he wants out. Or he maybe threatens to report Rowe's activities. Rowe snatches up the first weapon to hand and silences him for good.'

'And the same with Kevin?' asked Tom, frowning as he absorbed this hypothesis.

'Yes, but the Clarkson boys interrupted that uncontrolled attack and saved Kevin's life.'

'So where does Lieutenant Farmer fit in?'

'As I said last night, I believe she would be the driving force. Rowe's the action man. I'll give her credit for not condoning violence, but she can do nothing about Rowe's ungovernable temper.'

Tom gave a long sigh. 'It's as good a theory as any, but what's their game?'

'I think you should bring Rowe in for questioning and find out. We've *got* to move on this, Tom. I know it's pure speculation, but it's all we've got right now.'

When Tom left, Max stared from the window reviewing all they had just discussed. Was Rowe the link they sought? If so, what deal had he with two lads who lived for music? Max recalled his own interview with Kevin. He had only come to life once they began to talk about Swinga Kat. How would nineteen-year-old Rowe, whose talent lay in creating competitions and games, tie in with someone six years younger and still very much a boy, who had no interest in anything save running a successful pop group?

All at once, the blood ran faster through Max's veins to spur him into action. There was one obvious place for that boy to run to. He prayed he would not arrive there too late to save Kevin.

Mavis McRitchie watched her husband button their fur-trimmed coats, as Shona and Julie talked excitedly about what they wanted to buy with their pocket money. They were more than old enough to button their own coats, yet they were happy to be treated as babies. Greg then picked up the bright, tasselled hats Mavis had knitted and fixed them lovingly on their dark, shining hair.

'By the time we get to the market you'll have changed your minds half a dozen times.'

'No, Dadda,' they chorussed.

'Yes, Dadda. I know you two all too well,' he said laughingly. 'Right, are we ready for the off?'

It burst from Mavis before she could stop it. 'Greg, you *can't*. Not today.'

He looked at her through narrowed eyes. 'Why not?'

'You know why. We have to be here in case Kev comes.'

'You'll be here.'

The two girls, in their warm clothes, moved to the front door and stood waiting. Mavis studied their bland expressions as they stared at her, and knew she had come to hate them. She moved up to Greg, who looked so handsome in the cream heavy-knit sweater she had made for him, and attempted to prevent him pulling on his padded topcoat.

'I need you here. I can't deal with this by myself. What'll I say if they bring him home? They'll ask all kinds of questions and I won't know what to answer. If I say the wrong thing it could get you in deep trouble. You know what the Redcaps are. Have it in for you before you open your mouth.'

He pushed her hands aside. 'Then don't open it. When you do, nothing worth listening to comes out.' He turned to his daughters. 'Come on, you little rogues, take your dadda to the shops and let him help you choose your presents.' At the door, he said over his shoulder, 'Time supper for six and get the badminton gear ready. I'm playing a big match tonight.'

Mavis heard their shrill laughter as they climbed in the car, and the greyness in her mind turned a shade darker. They had a limpet-like hold on him. They had lured and cajoled, petted and flattered until he discarded everything he had once loved. They manipulated him, had him performing whatever tricks they chose. They despised her, regarded her as their servant. They had worked on him so that he now thought of her that way, too. In desperation, she had sought consolation from the other family outcast, given him the love and devotion Greg no longer wanted. But her boy had turned from her in disgust, threatened to leave her. Now he had, and his disgust would become public knowledge. She did not want him back. She wanted rid of those two, as well. Things would be different then. It would be like it was before they came.

Her hands reached for the vase which held the huge arrangement of ball chrysanthemums she had bought yesterday. Her fingers gently caressed the cool incurled yellow, rust and flame petals. They were so beautiful. Next minute, she seized the tall green vase and flung her expensive token of love against the wall. She sat for a long time among broken pottery and crushed flowers wondering what else she could do to make him care again.

In the harsh greyness of mid-morning, when the bitter wind sent paper and discarded food cartons racing across icy pavements, RAMSCH looked undeniably seedy. Collecting Heather Johnson, Max had driven to town as fast as conditions allowed. Refreshing his sergeant's memory of his previous visit to the video studio, Max confessed he feared the worst.

'I strongly suspect young Kevin phoned Gunther asking him to pick him up outside the hospital, which explains the lack of sightings. I know Gunther has a booking for this afternoon – he offered me a couple of hours before noon – so it's unlikely that he's taking Kevin to the house near the border right now. There'd be no time to get back for the filming. But if he went there directly after fetching the lad, he could return this morning with ease. If that's the case, the chances of recovering Kevin before he's severely violated are slim. If it's part of a paedophile ring we may never get him back.'

'That would be a disaster,' sighed Heather. 'He's a nice kid. When I think of the understanding and encouragement my brothers get for even their wildest ideas, it makes Kevin's case all the more tragic. No matter our situation, we all need someone, don't we?'

'Mmm,' he agreed, thinking of his chances of spending tonight in the small double overlooking the car park.

He stopped right outside the black door of RAMSCH. No need for pretence this time. 'If he's here, you take him in hand. He'll be frightened, desperate, liable to make a run for it. He liked and trusted you, told you intimate secrets concerning his mother's petting. Convince him we pose no threat. Above all, assure him we don't intend to return him to his family.'

Heather smiled confidently. 'Leave it to me. I understand adolescent boys. Had lots of experience.'

Max pushed open the door and they entered the small scarlet-walled area, where the same blonde sat at the desk. Today she wore severe black and looked classier than ever. Her eyes widened at the sight of Max, then the professional smile appeared.

'George! You did not come as arranged yesterday.'

He produced his police identity, and so did Heather. 'This is an official visit. No need to announce us.'

Pushing through the black velvet curtain they entered the studio presently set up as a gymnasium, where naked actors would doubtless have sex in every possible position on the equipment. Gunther, in emerald stretch trousers and a matching silk shirt, came from his glass-walled control cubicle with eyes narrowed.

'You did not come with euros within the time I said. The studio is now booked for filming. I have no deal with you.'

Max held up his identification. 'No deal, Gunther, just a straightforward hand over. I've come for the soldier's son you collected from the hospital in the early hours this morning.'

Gunther's eyes closed to mere slits as the import of Max's identity sank in. 'There is no boy here. You have mistaken made.' His precise English began to go awry. 'I have filming here, that is all. You are please to go.'

'I'll go when you produce Kevin.' Hoping to God he was right about this, Max upped the pressure by producing his mobile. 'If he's not brought out here within five minutes, I make a call. The *Polizei* are standing by, and they'll be swarming all over this building before you know it.'

Visibly nervous, Gunther tried to brazen it out. 'I do nothing wrong here. All is over the board.'

'And a bloody sight more under it,' he snapped. 'I know about the talent scout living on the Dutch border you offered to take Kevin to meet. How many boys have you supplied him with? The local police will be *very* interested in that side of your business.' He studied his watch. 'Two minutes have already passed. Fetch that boy!'

Still Gunther made no move, and Max began to think Kevin had been taken out of reach. Then Heather began to speak in a silky tone.

'Kevin is my sister's son. Her husband is a very big man. Could easily make a meal of someone as puny as you. He has a lot of tough pals. If they should happen to learn about what you intended to do with his boy...' She let that sink in, then added, 'Ever seen what a team of angry squaddies can do to someone they don't like?' She held up her own mobile. 'I make one call, they'll be here faster than the *Polizei* and, believe me, you'd rather have German lawmen here than British soldiers bent on revenge. Well, what's it to be, Gunther?'

He held up both hands defensively. 'Please, not to call. I bring him. This is what I intend. After the filming I take him to his father. All along I intend.'

'Then why say there's no boy here?' demanded Max, glancing again at his watch. 'The five minutes are up.'

'He call me. Said to fetch him damn quick. I go to help him, that is all,' Gunther said swiftly, walking backwards in the direction of a rear door. '*He* call *me*. I do not *take* him. He said he has nowhere to go. I *help* him, that is all,' he reiterated. 'You have charge of him now. I have business in one hour.'

Max glanced at Heather. 'Go with him. I don't trust that emerald snake.'

He waited for about five minutes and was about to explore the back area when he saw, with relief, his sergeant leading Kevin forward with her arm around him. No sign of Gunther, but that did not matter. He was not the concern of the British Military Police.

The boy's face was ashen and streaked with tears. He looked pathetic in bright pink fur-lined boots, pyjama trousers, a padded coat with a company logo across the left breast, a football scarf and a scarlet pull-on knitted hat with a pompom.

'Hallo, Kevin.' Max greeted him gently and smiled. 'Johnny, Malc and Callum have been worried. They told me Swinga Kat can't function without you. During the drive back you can call them on Sergeant Johnson's mobile, if you like. Tell them you'll be in charge soon.' He laid a reassuring hand on the lad's head. 'Let's get going.'

Before starting the engine, Max called in to report that they had found Kevin, unharmed. He asked Jakes, who had fielded the call, to notify the hospital and request that the doctor dealing with the case be available when they arrived with his patient in about forty-five minutes.

Getting underway, he heard Heather, on the back seat with Kevin, telling him he was not in trouble with them for saying his mother had attacked him, because they had known all along she could not have done. She talked easily, as she probably did with her brothers, while assuring him that his theft of clothes and money could be sorted by returning what he had taken and apologizing to his doctor. Then she asked why he had sought refuge with Gunther. His reply was so quiet Max could barely hear him.

'He said he knew a man who promoted young musicians. He was sure the man would be enthusiastic about my talent.'

'Gosh, how exciting,' said Heather warmly.

'I can't go home. I just *can't*. So I thought if Gunther took me to the man, I could start working for him until I had enough money to recruit my own group. That's what I want, Heather. That's the only thing I want.'

'Of course it is. When you have a talent of any kind, you have to use it. My brother Keith's a whizz at making model aeroplanes. He wants to work for Boeing when he leaves uni. That's a few years ahead, so he's reading up as much as he can about aircraft design, and he's made friends with a former pilot who's restoring a wartime bomber at the local transport museum. Keith helps him sometimes on a Saturday. He doesn't get paid for it, but he's learning a great deal and making useful contacts for when the right time comes.'

There was a short silence, then she said quietly, 'Gunther's friend wouldn't have been able to help you, Kevin. It's difficult for foreigners to get work here unless they specialize in a field in which there's a national shortage of experts. I reckon the music scene is just as difficult to break into in Germany as it is elsewhere. You're also under age. D'you know what I reckon is the best thing you can do?'

'What?' It was faint, but interested.

'Johnny, Malc and Callum are dead keen on building up Swinga Kat. You're talented enough to do that, make it good enough to do gigs for the younger kids on the base. Why don't you talk to Sar'nt-Major Fellowes. See if he'd help with it? Add your share of the entrance fee to your pocket money, and see about having music lessons. I might be able to help you sort that out.'

'Would you?'

'I'll ask around. But, Kevin, first of all we have to let the doctors at the hospital sort out your problems. Once they've done that we can get started on those plans. No, don't put on that face. Until they know why you don't want to go home, they can't help to make things easier for you there. Isn't that common sense?'

A moment or two of silence, then, 'I s'pose so.'

'You'll talk to them, let them help you?'

He must have nodded, because Max heard her say, 'Great!'

'Will you come and visit?'

'Sure I will. I'll bring Johnny, Malc and Callum, too.'

A long pause. 'Your Keith's lucky. My sisters are right little bitches. I *hate* them.'

Tom first drove to the Recreation Centre, where Alan Rowe should be giving instruction on how to create ingenious indoor games. A notice on the door advised that all regular classes had been suspended until the second week of January to allow for special Christmas and New Year events to be held. The building was locked. A telephone call to Jack Fellowes revealed that preparations for the disco had been completed yesterday. He and the other helpers would be there at 19:00 to add the final touches. He did not know the present whereabouts of Alan Rowe.

The young Sapper was not in his room; his neighbours said he went to town. On his tod, as usual. They believed he visited a bird. Why else would he go at every opportunity and refuse their company? Piercey had reported Rowe as having said his girl was on UK leave, so Tom asked when she was due back. Blank expressions all round. They knew nothing of a relationship with a female squaddie.

Tom had no better luck at the Officers' Mess. Lieutenant Farmer had driven to town last evening and stayed overnight. She planned to return in time for the disco. Sitting in his car, pondering the continuing link between those two, and trying to hit on what motive they could have for attacking two lads crazy about music, Tom was alerted by the sound of his mobile in his pocket.

'Tom Black.'

It was the Padre. 'Ah, glad I caught you. Young Tony Clegg's parents are having coffee with us and Captain Booth. They're naturally very upset after talking to the Bandmaster about their talented son, and Mr Clegg is demanding to be told what efforts are being made to apprehend the killer of their only child. I contacted Captain Rydal, but he's unable to help at the present moment. Is it possible for you to come for a short while to calm his agitation, and to give these bereaved parents some degree of assurance that everything possible is being done?'

Tom made a U-turn after saying he would be there in ten. What could he tell the Cleggs? That they had no idea who had killed their son, or why? From the outside the house was a copy of other senior officers' quarters, but Tom thought the interior bland and rather soulless. Justin Robinson greeted him warmly, then introduced Tom to Norman and Phyllis Clegg. Both looked drawn and heavy-eyed. Norman was a short, small-boned man with the ferocity of a terrier. Brushing aside Tom's murmured condolences, he launched into a sharp-voiced attack.

'Have you got him yet? Him who did for our Tony?'

Tom made allowances for grief and replied quietly. 'It only happened thirty-six hours ago, sir. We're following up every lead.'

Clegg's foxy face inched closer to Tom's. 'I read the papers, you know. Not your trashy tabloids. The classy editions. I know very well that if a murderer isn't caught within the first twenty-four hours the trail goes cold. Those are the words of high-ranking men, not your bobby on the beat, mind.' He drew in breath so sharply it pinched his nostrils. 'I want some real policemen brought in on this case.'

It was a line Tom had heard before from distraught relatives. 'We *are* real policemen, Mr Clegg.'

'I mean Scotland Yard. *Proper* detectives.'

'Your son was a soldier, the crime was committed on military property most probably by another soldier. The case therefore becomes the responsibility of Special Investigation Branch. There's an entire team working on it, I assure you.'

'With nothing to show for it!'

The Padre intervened at that point. 'Mr Clegg, why don't we all sit down and let Mr Black tell us of the measures being taken? I can add my assurances that the Branch is manned by personnel highly trained in detection procedures.' He waved a hand at the chair vacated by the overwrought father. 'Please, sir.'

Mrs Clegg was crying into a wet handkerchief. Beside her, Estelle Robinson was patting her hand and smiling. Glancing up at Tom, she said, 'Sit there!'

It sounded like an order, despite the smile. Swiftly conjuring up words that would convince Clegg SIB were hot on the trail of the killer, Tom perched on the chair and was instantly handed a cup of coffee and a plate bearing two mince pies. Without asking, the Padre's sunny wife refilled every cup from the large percolator and dispensed pies from a china bowl resembling a woven basket.

Ignoring the Christmas largesse, Tom looked steadily at Norman Clegg while giving him some idea of the exhaustive questioning they had undertaken.

'I can support that, sir,' said the Bandmaster. 'Two members of Mr Black's team travelled with the band yesterday in order to find out all they could about Tony. Who were his friends, what were his interests, what kind of lad he was.'

'I can tell him that,' came the sharp response. 'He were liked by everyone he met. His interests were music, music, music, and he were blessed with a great gift for it. What kind of lad was he? The best son anyone could wish for. Honest, loving and hard-working. Our Tony was the salt of the earth, that he was.'

Phyllis Clegg let out a wail and buried her face in the wet handkerchief. Mrs Padre patted her shoulder and smiled.

Tom allowed a moment of silence. 'Our questioning has given us the same information. Your son was popular with his colleagues; his musical talent aroused no resentment or hostile jealousy. He was a clean-living young man with no interest in drink, drugs or unsuitable women. So, sir, you can see our difficulty in trying to understand who would have a reason to attack him.'

Clegg's nostrils grew pinched again as his rage increased. 'I can tell you that. You called our Tony a soldier. Not so. He was a *musician*. You've just admitted he didn't do any of the offensive things soldiers get up to. I've seen 'em, pissed to their ears on Saturday nights, tumbling from pubs to urinate in the street while calling out obscene invitations to decent girls passing by. Many's the time the local landlords've had to call out you lot to break up fights started by men from the nearby camp. Uniformed thugs is what they are!' He pointed a shaking finger at Tom. 'You find out who was crazy with drink or drugs on Thursday and it'll be one of them. When you get him, I hope you put the bugger against a wall and shoot him.'

'No, no,' protested Estelle Robinson, still smiling consolingly. 'He will already be repenting his sin. We must find it in our hearts to understand and forgive.'

'Sanctimonious claptrap,' stormed Clegg, rising from his chair. 'I'd like to hear you say that if it was *your* son been battered to death.'

'Norm!' cried his wife through her sodden handkerchief.

The Bandmaster got to his feet, upset and embarrassed by Clegg's grief-stricken outburst to people doing their best to help him cope with his traumatic loss. 'Perhaps you'd like to collect Tony's personal things from the rehearsal rooms before returning to your hotel.'

Tom's mobile rang, giving him an excuse to step out to the hall away from the emotional tension. As he did, he noticed that the smile had finally been wiped off Estelle Robinson's face as she sat stiff as a statue beside the weeping Phyllis. Stupid woman, he thought. To quote pious nonsense at a time when these loving parents had lost all belief in God and humanity was almost an insult.

The call was from Roy Jakes with the news that Kevin had been found, unharmed, and was being returned to the hospital. 'Major Clarkson has been informed, sir. He says he'll confer with the German psychiatrist about the boy's treatment and report back.'

'That's not our concern, apart from knowing when we can question Kevin. Have his parents been told?'

'Yes, sir. Connie Bush drove there. She's just phoned in. The mother's been left on her own while he takes the girls for their usual Saturday shopping spree and lunch-time treat.'

'That fits. No concern over his missing son.'

'Connie says Mavis McRitchie seemed less than grateful for the news, just relieved the boy won't be going home.'

As Tom disconnected he grew aware of the Cleggs leaving with Christopher Booth through the side-door. Devoted, caring parents robbed of the great light of their lives, while the selfish, perverted McRitchies had their talented, unwanted son restored to them. Where is the justice in that? Tom thought grimly. Small wonder Clegg lashed out on being told to understand and forgive. Tom did not understand it, and if anyone ever harmed one of his girls he would *never* forgive. He would have to be restrained from taking physical revenge. And if that smiling fool quoted religious forbearance at him, he would have to be restrained from attacking her, as well.

The Padre came to the sitting-room door-way looking strained. Tom could see the room was now empty. Coffee cups and plates of mince pies were abandoned around the room. Estelle was probably seeking righteous solace with her Bible, Tom thought with lack of charity.

'I'm sorry about that. When we met them at the airport last evening they were calm and polite. Still in shock, of course. We invited them here to talk with Christopher because we felt a meeting in the band's headquarters might prove too upsetting.' He sighed. 'Talking about their son's musical gift broke through their numbness and...' He spread his hands. 'Well, you saw for yourself. Good, hard-working, honest souls who can't accept this terrible blow.'

Tom nodded. 'I wish I could have given them something more positive to hold on to, but we have no real leads as yet. I'm sure they're asking the same questions we're asking. Why him? What could he have done to prompt violence? Who would want to kill such a blameless lad? Nothing adds up.'

The Padre began edging towards the front door. 'You don't think it *could* have been a squaddie high on crack, or pissed out of his skull?'

Tom took the hint and moved with his host, taking his car keys from his coat pocket. 'As I said, we have no leads, but both those hypotheses would have created greater disturbance at the crime scene. Men driven by drugs or alcohol are vocally noisy and unsteady on their feet. The snow would have been churned up enough to be still visible beneath the fresh fall. And someone might have heard voices. Apart from that, all the signs point to Clegg being totally unprepared for the attack. He didn't struggle or try to run. Evidence so far suggests that he met with someone he knew, they fell out, and Clegg was hit during a sudden fit of rage.'

Robinson grew thoughtful as he opened the door. 'Why arrange to meet in a deserted spot when it was snowing?'

'You see our problem, sir?'

'I do, indeed. Thank you for coming. You and I are inured to the toils of the bereaved, hasty words forced out by unbearable inner pain. My wife has been with me in this work for only six months. She still takes things to heart. She asked me to say her goodbyes.'

'Of course,' murmured Tom, wondering why she did not follow her own advice to understand and forgive.

Back in his car Tom was suddenly seized by an urgent need to see his family, to be with the children who were so precious to him. He felt a sharp pang at the undeniable truth that they were growing up fast. All too soon they would leave home and follow their own desired course, like Kevin McRitchie and Tony Clegg. Fearful for what might lie ahead for Maggie, Gina and little Beth, Tom knew he must cherish and protect them while he still could.

Setting the car in motion, he headed for the main gate. With the emergency over

Kevin at an end, he was free to join his family for lunch at Bertrum's. There was a lump in his throat as he pictured their astonishment and pleasure when he appeared.

Ten

Only the regular top-notchers were on court at the Badminton Club that evening. A good ninety-five per cent of year-round attendees who played just for fun and exercise were at parties, dances, celebration dinners or the large Christmas market that came to colourful, vibrant life once darkness fell. The five per cent who had nothing better to do on that Saturday evening turned up to watch the matchplay.

Greg McRitchie was tipped to win the singles title, although those who did not know him well thought anxiety over his son might affect his normal canny tactics. Doubles were a different matter. Brilliant though he was, Greg was notorious for poaching shots from his partner, whose own play was adversely affected by the unorthodox juxtapositions on court.

Mavis sat with Shona and Julie in their usual places in the viewing gallery. Because there were so few spectators, and because silence was expected by the contestants, she found time dragging more than usual. It also seemed colder in the sparsely occupied upper floor of the hall as she waited for Greg's matches. It was a knockout contest, so he was frequently on one of the four courts.

Between those times Mavis went down to fetch herself some coffee, and hot chocolate for Dadda's pets. Greg was invariably in low-voiced conversation with others on the side-lines. She knew she must not go to him, but she lingered to watch him. He looked sensational in brief white shorts and a sports shirt that clung to his muscular chest. The dark hairs on his arms and legs showed starkly against the white clothes, perfectly emphasizing his masculinity. When he twist-ed to speak over his shoulder to another player, Mavis could see the significant bulge at the front of his shorts.

How thrilled she had been in those early days, when he had proudly displayed it before her at every opportunity. He had attributed siring a male child to having such a formidable reproductive organ, and as their boy had developed Greg had consis-tently checked the growth of what Kevin had named his 'tiddley'.

As Mavis feasted her eyes on the body she had once been allowed to worship, Greg applauded the winners of the doubles title as they came off the court. He then glanced up at the gallery where his daughters' adoring faces gazed down. He waved and gave them the radiant smile Mavis still found breathtaking. They waved and blew kisses, which he returned.

Back in the gallery, Mavis saw nothing of the hard-fought final played by her man. She was recalling his disgust when first Shona then Julie was born. After Kevin, Greg had been so keen to produce more sons they had made love madly and often – on the floor, on the kitchen table, in the back of the car, in a field, in her father's potting shed. He had even tried copulation on a Lilo in the pool of a Spanish villa they had rented. It had been hilarious as he tried again and again, determined not to be defeated by the unstable inflatable.

When pregnancy remained elusive he insisted that she be tested. It had been humiliating, although she had been sure she must be to blame. The crazy coupling abruptly ceased, but many months passed before she realized it had resulted only in desire for further proof of his virility. Clearance from the specialist had set Greg off again, but there was a subtle difference. The thrill, the delight could not override his obvious creative lust.

Two girls! They had slept apart for an entire year. Greg's excuse; he had a demanding job and needed his sleep undisturbed by squalling babies. Then, as the girls developed into appealing little creatures who cooed 'Dadda' and patted his cheeks with chubby hands, everything changed. Greg found a new role as the big, virile defender of these gorgeous, vulnerable toddlers and took them from Mavis as he had previously taken Kevin.

She found it difficult now to pick on exactly when Greg's interest in her had died completely, or when her own in Kevin had become a desperate bid for consolation. Oblivious to the excitement on court, Mavis thought of the Redcap who had come to tell her Kevin had been found and returned to hospital. The girl had explained sympathetically that doctors wanted to keep him under observation for a while, maybe a week or so. Mavis had rejoiced, hoped it would be longer. If she got rid of the girls as well, Greg would be hers once more. They would make love everywhere. Out on the front lawn, if he wanted to prove his virility to the neighbours. She would agree to anything he demanded, and he would see his mistake in abandoning her.

Screams brought Mavis back from the rosy prospect to discover the match was over. Shona and Julie, still shrieking with excitement, were heading for the stairs. She looked down. The top-notchers were crowding round Greg with congratulations. He was smiling that devastating smile. He had proved himself top man; a champion. His shirt stuck wetly to his back revealing his powerful shoulders and the line of his spine that she used to love to trace with her fingers. She would do it again.

As he walked to pick up his towel and drape it around his neck, two small figures in scarlet leggings and intricately knitted tunics rushed at him shrieking, 'Dadda! Dadda!' Laughing, he scooped them up with each arm and swung them round and round in exultation. Mavis waited for him to glance upward. She waited in vain.

They drove home the usual way; Shona and Julie in the front, Mavis on the back seat with the racquets, and the sweaty whites and towels that she would put to wash when they got in. Two high, admiring voices were telling him how clever he was; his baritone reminded them of how he had won vital points when his opponent believed the game was his.

'Hooray, hooray! *Wonderful* Dadda.'

When Greg entered after garaging the car, Mavis was feeding the washing machine. She heard him say, 'As a special treat you can stay up late tonight.' He laughed. 'You're too excited to sleep, anyway. Let's go up, have a shower, put on pyjamas and dressing-gowns, then come down for hot milk and teddy biscuits while we watch—' he paused tantalizingly, then announced, 'the surprise DVD I bought you this morning.'

'What? What? Tell us!' They grabbed his arms, pressing close against him.

He led them to the stairs. 'When you come down all pink and clean in your dressing-gowns. Not before.'

It set the girls rushing to their bedroom, laughing. Mavis stood in the kitchen listening to their pattering feet on the ceiling above her, mixed with Greg's heavier tread. There was more laughter and the sound of running water in the bathroom. She used to stand beneath the deluge with Greg, slippery with soap while he entered her. Afterwards, they would towel each other down, then fall into bed for a repeat performance. He was towelling *them* dry now. How long before he got in their beds afterwards?

It seemed an age before they came down. He had changed his tracksuit for a yellow sweatshirt and the very tight jeans he favoured. The two darlings, in the red dressing-gowns she had made for them, were holding his hands and smiling possessively at their trophy. They sat on the settee leaving space for Dadda, while he came to the kitchen to heat their milk and arrange teddy biscuits on a plate. He was so intent on this he did not notice Mavis standing by the washing machine. He would notice her if *they* were not here.

She picked up a sharp knife from the drawer he had left open and walked through to the sitting-room. Two aloof expressions watched her approach, and she was driven to get rid of those sneers. The knife sliced across Shona's face in both directions. Then at the arms she held up to protect it. It cut

246

into bare pink wrists and again into pink palms, until blood ran to soak into the red sleeves.

Through the curious muffled sounds in Mavis's ears broke an anguished howl. Hands pulled at her, spun her round. He looked magnificent, full of passion and mastery. He now noticed her, wanted her again! She threw herself eagerly into his arms.

The RMP Station near the main gate was undermanned on that Saturday evening. In addition to the usual weekend night patrols around notorious trouble spots in town, now augmented by the Christmas market, two men were on duty outside the Recreation Centre, with another undercover at the disco. These latter three had called in at 20:00 and 21:00. They were due to do so again on the hour.

Sergeant George Maddox was certain police presence would deter the killer from striking again. It meant the chance of catching him was removed, but it was out of the question to risk another young life to do so. The McRitchie boy had been safely recovered, so SIB might now get something from him to point them in the right direction.

He glanced at the clock. Coming up to 22:00 when his spell of duty would end. Miriam had cut up rough because he had resisted her plea to swap duties and escort her to the Golf Club dinner-dance. He had promised to be there for the last hour or so, but there had been a frigid atmosphere from the moment he had taken her a cup of tea in bed. They had been married ten years. She should be used to the demands of his job.

Ten minutes to go. As soon as the men at the Recreation Centre called in he would go home, change into a dinner jacket, then drive like hell. A glance from the window showed that the snow was holding off, thank God. It should take him no more than thirty minutes to reach the club but, as Miriam would have been making merry, he would be restricted to one drink.

The phone rang. Corporal Meacher took the call. George could hear an urgent baritone speaking without an apparent pause for breath.

'What time was this?' asked Meacher sharply. 'Right. Have you approached the house? Good. Stay indoors and keep your doors locked. We'll be there in five.' Getting to his feet, he said to George, 'Neighbour heard sounds of screaming in the McRitchie house. Says one of the little girls is standing at the window and it looks like blood on her face and hands.'

They were outside and driving fast along the perimeter road within seconds, both certain they had been protecting the wrong place tonight. The killer must have believed Kevin was back home, and had moved to finish what he had begun. George dreaded what they would find. A small girl covered in blood at the window. Where were the McRitchie parents, and the other child?

The vehicle skidded to a halt outside the row of NCOs' quarters. Lights were on in two of the block of four. In the end one two people watched from a window. The man ran out to them.

'God knows what's happening,' he said tautly. 'They came in half an hour ago. Then we heard the girls screaming, and Greg howling like a man demented. Something terrible's going on in there.'

'We'll deal with it,' said Meacher. 'Did you see anyone else go in, or leave after the screaming began?'

George was already up at the window where the child was staring blankly, her bloodied hands pressed flat against the glass as if trying to push it out. In the room behind her there was a scene of carnage. A child in a red dressing-gown lay still on the patchwork-covered settee, her features indistinguishable through the gore that marred them and formed a pool on the brightly coloured squares.

Mavis McRitchie sat on the blood-stained carpet. She was cradling her husband's head, tenderly stroking his face and hair. Greg McRitchie had a large knife sticking out of his chest.

'Dear Christ in heaven,' he breathed, then

called for an ambulance as he ran with Meacher to the rear of the house. 'The bugger's done for the whole family.'

They drew their weapons and entered cautiously through the unlocked back door. The sickly sweet smell of blood, the powerful stench of vomit and faeces and a curious odour of burning filled the place. Meacher went directly to the child on the settee, while George approached the adults, both of them treading carefully to minimize possible destruction of evidence. Experience told George that Greg McRitchie would never survive such a deadly stab wound. He had a pulse, but it was irregular and very faint. Mavis seemed unaware of another presence. She was clearly in another world. Best leave her until the paramedics arrived as she was placid and showed no obvious signs of injury.

Crossing to Meacher, George received assurance from him that the child was alive although losing a lot of blood. Leaving his corporal to give what aid he could, George crossed gently to the other little girl standing in an attitude that suggested she had been flung against the window. This one was in deep shock; rigid with it. Her skin was unbroken, so the blood on her hands and face must be from her sister. Her bowel had emptied on the floor.

At that point they heard a shot from the direction of the kitchen. Drawing their weapons again, the two Redcaps dived for cover behind the furniture, taken unawares by the proximity of an intruder they assumed had left through the unlocked back door before they arrived. Then the truth dawned on them. A saucepan left on a red-hot burner had exploded. The smell of burning was now explained.

The ambulance arrived. Leaving the paramedics to deal with the casualties, the policemen carefully searched the rest of the house. The bath and shower curtain were wet, so was the soap. No sign of blood on towels or the floor. The girls' clothes were regimentally folded at the end of the beds, shoes placed side by side. Their dressing-table was uncluttered, with two hairbrushes and combs placed neatly alongside identical trinket boxes. They had never seen a children's bedroom so immaculate. It was unnatural.

They walked through to the single bedroom. This was the absent Kevin's domain. A large board hung from the picture rail. Pinned to it were pictures of pop groups and soloists, all correctly aligned like a squad on parade. A guitar was on an upright stand in a corner. On a small chest stood a basic computer with a pile of school books beside it. The shelf above held two or three dozen CDs, standing to attention. There was no sign of DVDs, computer games, football scarves or those things usual in the 'den' of a thirteen-year-old youth. It was weird.

The master bedroom looked as if nobody used it. The dressing-table bore just a circular embroidered linen doily with a bottle of perfume placed exactly central on it. The chest of drawers had a matching pair of doilies on which were framed photographs; one of Corporal McRitchie in white shirt and shorts holding up a silver trophy, the other showing his daughters as toddlers. The duvet cover had a beautiful patchwork design similar to those worked by Amish women. There was not a crease or rumple in it.

George exchanged looks with Meacher. 'Are these people human? I've never come across anything like this before.' He inclined his head towards the stairs. 'Nothing happened up here. So why not? He set upon the family because they were there, yet he didn't come upstairs seeking his real target. There's something nasty about this. It suggests it isn't connected to those attacks on Kevin and young Tony Clegg at all.'

A shout from the paramedics sent them back to the sitting-room. 'The kiddie's our prime concern. The cuts are so deep she'll need surgery. The mother and the other kiddie are in shock. Nothing can be done for him, I'm afraid.' He looked at Meacher. 'Are you coming with us, or following on? I'll make sure they understand you'll need the knife for examination once it's removed.'

George motioned his colleague to go in the ambulance, then he began calling in a SOCO team and off-duty men to secure the site. Finally, he called SIB, who would take over this case.

'They're going to *love* this,' he muttered, looking around at the blood, vomit and faeces; the detritus of violence.

The astonishment caused by his arrival at Bertrum's turned to near suspicion from his family when Tom arrived home in plenty of time to go with them across the road to the Graumanns' open evening. Comments like, 'Have you been suspended from duty?', 'What do you want in return?' and 'Who is this stranger who keeps attaching himself to us?' all brought a mirthless, 'Ha, ha, very amusing,' from him. Only little Beth gave him a hug and said, 'It'll be even lovelier with you there.'

The happy mood suffered a setback when the girls came down dressed for the occasion. In a yellow and black plaid skirt, pale primrose stretch top and high black boots, Maggie gave Tom an unpleasant shock. Surely that jumper was far too tight, and the boots too sexy. My God, her mouth was also unnaturally pink! She looked ... He cast around for an adjective and could only come up with his father's favourite. She looked ... *fetching*!

Casting a protesting glare at Nora, he was

given a severe optical warning against making any comment save a compliment. He found it impossible to acknowledge his daughter's dawning sexual attraction, for that was what he saw. Her face was alive with awareness, her eyes sparkled with anticipation, the young breasts were moulded by the stretchy top that also clung to her slender waist. The lipstick, although only pale pink, was the final blow. Was this the end of her childhood, her innocence?

Beth drew him from his dark thoughts. 'D'you like our outfits, Dad? We got them in town after you left. Mum said we could have some new Christmas things.' As he stood silently, she prompted him, '*Do* you like them? Do we look pretty?'

'You all always look pretty.'

Nora turned her eyes to the ceiling. He had given the wrong answer. Gina confirmed it. 'No, we don't, Dad. Sometimes we look grotty. Just proves you never really look at us, because all you think of is work, work, work!'

'It isn't *important*, Gina,' cried Maggie. 'We'll be late if we don't go across now. People have been arriving for at least half an hour.'

'You attract more attention with a late entrance. I read that in a magazine,' announced Beth. 'Hans will be panting with anxiety by now, and he'll probably fall down in a faint when you appear. How romantic!'

'Let's put our coats on and *go*,' ordered Nora, ushering them to the front door.

'I don't think the sight of a boy fainting would be romantic,' muttered Gina from the depths of her coat. 'I'd consider him a wimp.'

'No, he'd be *sensitive*. Like a poet or classical composer. Someone who would *pine* for love.' Coming from her fanciful ideas, Beth asked slyly, 'D'you think Hans pines for you, Maggie?'

'I'll tell you what I'm pining for,' put in Nora firmly. 'Some hot punch and a plateful of those delicious goodies Germans produce at Christmas.'

'Me too,' said Tom, having heard more than enough girly stuff.

'All you two think of is food,' Beth accused as they all crunched over the crisp snow to the house where lights blazed a welcome to any friends who cared to call. 'Didn't you ever pine for Mum before you married her, Dad?'

Tom was saved from answering by young Hans who, seeing their approach, opened the front door and stepped outside to greet them.

'*See*, he's not wimp enough to faint at sight of Maggie. When you've grown up a bit you'll know what men are *really* like,' ten-year-old Gina told her younger sister.

The Graumanns were very hospitable and introduced the Blacks to their friends. The children present were slower to integrate, but they eventually took off to another room as more guests came. After a lengthy chat with Herr Graumann in which both men spoke in both their languages and managed to make themselves understood, Tom retired to a corner with a glass of punch and an appetizing selection of nibbles on a plate, unable to relax.

The disco would now be underway. The exterior police presence was there mainly to reassure parents. No one could enter the Recreation Centre secretly, surely would not attempt to. But Alan Rowe was on the premises as he had been last Saturday, and there would be upwards of a hundred teenage lads dancing, flirting and behaving true to general reputation. The undercover man had orders to keep Rowe and Lucy Farmer in his sight, and to concentrate on Rowe if they split up.

Tom looked at his watch. 21:15. The disco was due to end at midnight. Anything could happen in the next two and three quarter hours. Parents had been advised to collect their children or arrange for trusted friends to pick them up. Any youngsters still at the Centre fifteen minutes after the event ended would be driven home by the policemen after checking the building and locking it. Nothing should go wrong. He frowned. Even if tonight passed without incident, there was still Clegg's murder and the assault on Kevin to resolve.

'You're looking daggers at that cinnamon bun,' said Nora from his side. 'Are you still worked up over Maggie's lipstick?'

Not wanting to put a damper on her enjoyment, he shook his head. 'Like the incoming tide, her maturity can't be halted. She looks gorgeous, but there's a sadness about her metamorphosis from child to woman because it seems to have happened so suddenly, and too soon. I know, I know,' he went on wryly, 'it's because fathers hate their little girls to grow up and find other heroes. You told me. And it's true. I'm honest enough to admit it.'

'Bully for you,' she teased. 'It meant so much to her for you to come tonight.'

'That's why she's gone to another room with her blond swain and his friends?'

'I'm still here ... and it meant a lot to *me* for you to be here.' She took the little spiced bun from his plate and bit into it. 'What prompted you to join us for lunch?'

Recollection of Clegg's parents' grief smote him as it had this morning, but he just said, 'I had a sudden urge to see the four people who make my life worthwhile.'

Finishing the bun and licking crumbs from her fingers, she said, 'You're an old softie at heart, Sar'nt-Major.'

'But I'm a tiger in bed.'

'Drink any more of that punch and you'll be hard pushed to prove it,' she countered with a laugh.

He had no opportunity to prove anything but his professional efficiency that night for, fifteen minutes later, his mobile rang.

If Max had been irresistibly charmed before, he was now totally under Livya Cordwell's spell. An oasis in the desert? A river bubbling through rocky landscape? The tide flowing over a barren shore? Her sexual and intellectual impact washed away old emotional wounds and brought bright promise. Could he retain it, secure it for the future? In five days she would leave. Tonight had to be memorable enough to survive that parting.

Their table was near the large log fire, but to one side of it so the heat from it was not uncomfortable. The reflection from dancing flames caught and discreetly highlighted Livya's diamanté bracelet and long drop earrings. It also put a sheen on her cocktail-length ruby velvet dress and on her dark hair that tonight hung loose to her shoulders. Max had not seen her looking so utterly feminine before. Small wonder his father had urged her to drop formality when they were off duty.

She had accepted his compliment on her appearance with no more than a murmured thank you, but no way was he imagining the glow in her eyes or the invitation in her body language. That room on the second floor beckoned, yet worried him. This woman was so vital, so assured, so challenging.

Nights with Susan had been all he had wanted them to be. Until that final six months. He had been away a lot – the demands of his job – and had then caught a debilitating fever on their two-week holiday in Mombasa. During this time a good-looking corporal had come to her rescue when her car broke down on Salisbury Plain. Lovemaking had been spasmodic and un-satisfactory during that period, possibly because Max was not fully fit and was also embroiled in a complicated rape case.

He had not slept with a woman for three years now. Someone had once said to him that sex was like riding a bike; you never forgot how to do it. But a bicycle was a bicycle. Every woman was different, needed to be satisfied in her own fashion. He had so little time for experiment with Livya. It was tonight or never.

They had agreed not to talk shop, so their conversation over dinner was designed to discover the man and woman beneath the uniform. Livya talked at length about her mother's family and her Czech background with warmth and humour. Max said little about his childhood, instead relating several mad student escapades. They soon fell to discussing hobbies, interests and personal passions. She laughed when he confessed to having a collection of classic war films.

'Go on, tell me you see yourself making Steve McQueen's race for freedom on a motor bike.'

He grinned. 'Doesn't every red-blooded grown-up little boy? I bought a second-hand Harley Davidson when I was at uni, and raced it across local fields one day in summer.' His grin widened. 'Didn't get far. Had to keep stopping to open gates.'

'You didn't jump hedges like Steve?'

'All I had chasing me was an irate farmer. If there'd been a posse of armed Germans I'd have taken the jumps.'

'Sez you!' Her smile was excitingly intimate, so he tried to impress her more.

'I'm pretty good at digging tunnels and scattering surplus soil down my trouser leg around the compound beneath the eyes of the guards.'

While he feasted his eyes on the curve of her mouth and the creamy skin above the low neckline, she laughingly admitted that she had listened to her grandfather's tales of subversive activity during Communist occupation and fancied herself as a Resistance heroine.

'Is that why you had yourself attached to my father's department?'

She gazed at him frankly. 'It was my linguistic skills not Andrew's personal charm that led me to apply to fill the vacancy. I've accompanied him on a couple of duplicitous missions to my second homeland, it's true, but there was no danger involved.' After a pause during which her gaze seemed to be assessing his mood, she said softly, 'I'm in more danger right now, Max Rydal, I think you're well aware of that.'

With quickening heartbeat, Max said equally softly, 'Then you'll have to take the escape route to Switzerland or face what's coming with fortitude. How brave are you?'

Livya took up her beaded bag. 'Shall we skip coffee and find out?'

They kissed as soon as he closed the door behind them, but she soon broke from his embrace and walked to the centre of the room. His initial disappointment was lulled by her smile.

'I like to take it slowly and deliciously. Can't stand the tear-it-all-off-with-the-teeth-and-get-in-there-fast approach. How about you?'

He went across to touch her rich hair gently. 'I'm not usually a tooth and claw man, but don't let's make it too slow. I can't promise to hold off until dawn.'

Her arms linked around his neck. 'OK Steve McQueen, you can rev up the Harley Davidson when you need to.'

He discovered that slow and delicious was exactly the right pace for recalling old skills, but he was only half naked and she almost fully so when his mobile rang.

Eleven

The team had never before seen their boss in so black a mood as when they assembled on Sunday morning. They were all disturbed by the tragic development that had occurred when their attention was concentrated elsewhere, but he was tight-lipped with anger as he revealed that Greg McRitchie had been dead on arrival at the hospital. His daughter Shona was in intensive care, dangerously weak from loss of blood from her slashed wrists and the deep cuts to her face that would leave her permanently scarred. Julie was deeply traumatized. Mavis McRitchie was under constant supervision in a private room. Kevin had not yet been told what had happened.

'When the call came in, Sergeant Maddox assumed our killer believed Kevin had returned home and was set on finishing what he had begun at the party last week. What they saw there persuaded them the attack could be an entirely separate issue,' Max said stony-eyed. 'The family had been set upon downstairs, but there was no evidence that the killer had searched the upper floor for

Kevin, his intended victim. We can draw several conclusions from that.

'One: he demanded to know Kevin's whereabouts and, when they refused to tell him, slashed at Shona to persuade them. McRitchie ran to stop the attack on the girl and was fatally stabbed. At that point, the intruder took fright and fled.

'Two: as there were no signs of forced entry, the intruder went in by the rear door left unlocked by McRitchie after he garaged his car and came indoors. The neighbours who reported hearing screaming say they saw the whole family return from the Badminton Club around 21:30 and all was quiet until 21:50. That leaves plenty of time for the killer to enter, take stock of the situation, and await the moment when the family settled together.

'Three: there was no intruder; the attack was totally divorced from the one on Kevin last week and the murder of Tony Clegg.' His cold glance encompassed them all. 'Until either the children or their mother are able to speak about what happened, we have to draw what we believe to be the most probable conclusion from the available evidence. Mr Black will outline what we know as fact.'

Burdened by the tragic outcome of a family situation they had sensed was heading in dangerous directions, but had done little about due to the demands of another case they feared would result in another death of a young male, Tom spoke more crisply than usual to mask his feelings.

'Forensics are working flat out on this and will give us info as it develops. This we do know. The whole family had been at the Badminton Club for a knockout tournament Greg was participating in. They returned home together. The bath, the shower curtain and the soap were wet; the children were in sleepwear. Greg was dressed in jeans and sweatshirt; Mavis wore what she had been seen in at the Club. The washing machine was filled with his white shirt, shorts, underpants and several towels. The programme had been set but not started. A saucepan, presumably filled with milk but we'll get confirmation of that, was on a full-power hotplate. The pan subsequently boiled dry and exploded, putting the wind up our uniformed colleagues.'

There was a stifled snigger, but the general mood this freezing morning was subdued.

'So McRitchie and his kids had showered and changed upstairs, while the mother dealt with the laundry and the girls' bedtime drink in the kitchen,' observed Piercey. 'Only when they came back to the ground floor did the trouble start. That supports assumption two, that the intruder entered through the unlocked back door after Greg and waited for the family to assemble downstairs.'

'But why wait?' asked Connie Bush. 'He had a lone, vulnerable woman in the kitchen to threaten with a knife snatched from a drawer. Why wait for the husband to come on the scene before demanding Kevin's whereabouts?'

'Because he'd walked in only just before the family gathered in the sitting-room,' suggested Heather Johnson. 'But I don't understand why he would slice up a little girl sitting with her sister on the settee, when he had a woman in the kitchen where the knives were. Wouldn't he grab one, hold Mavis as a shield and threaten to slit her throat unless Greg told him what he wanted? That's the more usual scenario.'

Derek Beeny spoke thoughtfully. 'What if there's an entirely different angle? We've been considering a sexual link between Kevin and Clegg. Sexual invitations too often repulsed, maybe paedophilic interest in small, effeminate males. Could that focus have shifted to the girls? They're sitting in nightclothes, mother's busy in the kitchen with the washing machine, father's upstairs. The kids scream at sight of the intruder and Mavis runs at him with a knife. He wrests it from her, then hears Greg on the stairs. Frustrated yet again, the ungovernable temper we believe he has leads him to slash the girl he fancies, then do for the father. Fear drives him to run from a disaster when he imagined a simple abduction and kiddie rape.'

Tom usually appreciated inventiveness, but

not today. 'Initial report on McRitchie's body says there are no signs of self-defensive cuts to hands or arms so, as he was stabbed in the chest, we have to believe he was facing his assailant and not expecting aggression. It's unlikely a paedo would do what you suggest. He'd snatch the girl from the school playground, or entice her away from the NAAFI shop or burger bar.'

'Except that McRitchie guarded those kids too closely. They weren't allowed out without him or their mother, and friendships were virtually forbidden. Dadda had to be their all. It could have driven a paedo to break that monopoly by another man; add spice to the perversion.'

Roy Jakes glanced up from his doodling. 'I go for the third assumption; that this was a pure domestic that has no connection with the other cases.'

Max nodded. 'I also believe no one but the McRitchie family was in that house last night. But I fear it does have a connection with the other cases. Whoever attacked Kevin last week put a match to a fuse waiting to be lit. I suspect Mavis McRitchie killed her husband and attacked Shona. In what order we'll understand better when we have all the forensic evidence. When I visited Mavis it was obvious that she was going through some kind of fantasy phase. She didn't connect with who I was, and seemed obsessively focussed on pleasing her husband. Major Clarkson called on her at my request. He judged that she was simply behaving extravagantly, as women sometimes do. I had to accept his diagnosis, but I believe something happened last night to tip her over the edge.' He surveyed them all. 'Any further thoughts?'

'Two points of dissimilarity,' offered Connie Bush. 'Whoever attacked Kevin and Clegg went for adolescent, music-loving males. He's unlikely to make a play for a well-guarded female child who's surrounded by her family at home. Doesn't fit his pattern. Also, our first man killed impetuously when his victims were alone. Both times he grabbed a handy weapon and struck at the head. Knives aren't his thing. I go along with this being a domestic, divorced from the other cases.'

Tom continued that subject. 'We still have no leads on them and we need to get some fast. The police presence at the Recreation Centre last night kept any intruder from attempting a repeat of Saturday's attack. The undercover man watching Alan Rowe saw nothing to suggest he was unduly interested in adolescent males.'

'They should all have gone undercover,' murmured Piercey. 'You can't catch anyone by strutting around wearing a red cap and a gun.'

Tom scowled. 'That was done to reassure parents that we're on the case. There's a lot of aggro around because we've not yet apprehended anyone. They're unaware of the effort we're putting into it, or of the difficulty in understanding what lies behind the two attacks. We now have yet another dead-end probe. Lists of calls Kevin and Tony Clegg made on their mobiles have finally come in. The lads didn't once contact each other, or a common third party. Neither rang the number of any known drug pusher or gay club.'

'Or Alan Rowe?' asked Piercey.

'Or Alan Rowe. We must keep an eye on him, all the same. You're keen on cops going underground, Piercey, so that's your assignment today. Get to it!' As Phil Piercey shrugged on his topcoat, Tom said, 'The rest of you talk to people who were at the Badminton Club last evening, and to those living in the vicinity of the McRitchie home. Uniform did the prelims last night, but we need more in-depth investigation. Being Sunday many will be out having fun – giving no thought to the fact that we're not – but you'll have to chase up the absentees tomorrow.'

As they all got to their feet, a telephone rang. Derek Beeny answered it. After briefly listening, he waved the receiver at Max.

'The hospital, sir. Doc wants a word with you.'

Dreading to hear that Shona McRitchie had died of her injuries, Max discovered the call concerned Kevin.

'We believe the boy must soon be told the truth and have the choice to see his mother and sisters, if he wishes,' the man said, after identifying himself as the psychiatrist treating Kevin. 'From the time you have brought him back from his runaway he has shown much fondness for the young woman, Hedda. Asks always when she will come with the cat. We cannot have animals here, but it will much help if she would be here this morning when we have such bad news to tell.'

'Certainly she'll come,' Max assured him, signalling Heather to stay in the office. 'My second in command is about to set out for the hospital. He'll bring Sergeant Johnson, so you can expect her within the hour.' He could not prevent a twitch of his lips. 'She'll explain about the cat, sir.'

Before setting out to have a tough talk with Charles Clarkson, Max dealt with paperwork he had neglected during the week. Officially, he should be the man behind the desk coordinating evidence on their cases, but he was too restless and too hooked on face-to-face investigation to spend day after day in his office.

This Sunday morning he was additionally restless. In the early hours, he had gone to his room to have two hours on his bed before showering and dressing in one of his 'working' suits. He had not slept. Frustration over the ruin of his date with Livya, as well as anger at his failure to forestall tragedy, kept him wide-eyed. At seven he had rung the hotel to tell Livya he would have breakfast with her. 'Hi! Did I wake you?'

'No such luck.'

'I didn't sleep much, either,' he confessed, irrationally cheered by the thought that she had also lain awake.

'Oh, I slept, but was woken half an hour ago by a call from Flight Lieutenant Mabbs to tell me Corporal Hollins has to fly home on compassionate grounds. It means my game is now first on today's agenda.'

'I'll come straight over and have breakfast with you.'

'Too late. I'm well into room service rolls, orange juice and coffee.'

Daunted, he said, 'I'll pick you up and drive you back here, then.'

'Jeff Mabbs is doing that. I guess he's already on his way.'

'Oh.'

A softer tone. 'I'd have enjoyed the motor bike ride more, Steve.'

At seven a.m. what he had spoken of last night seemed somewhat juvenile. He had dealt with violent death and the shattering of a family in the interim, so he found himself unable to reply in the same vein.

'Does the champion's departure to the UK mean you're on the fast track to taking the trophy for the army this year?'

A short pause at his change of mood.

'Nothing in life is certain, Max. I'm not counting any chickens.'

Deeply disappointed in his hope of at least sharing breakfast and repairing the breach caused by passion so starkly interrupted last night, Max read caution in her words.

'Well ... good luck with the knights and bishops this morning. See you around.'

When the call ended he had the curious feeling that something of significance had been said. Something that should have made more impact than it had. Going over their conversation he homed in on the star player flying home on compassionate leave, but the import of it remained elusive.

He thought of it again now as he drove to Charles Clarkson's house, and came to the conclusion that the link was the prospect of McRitchie relatives flying over to take charge of the children. What a responsibility to shoulder unexpectedly!

Out of the blue came a distant memory of his grandmother speaking of her bosom friend who had had to take into her home twin babies, because her daughter and son-in-law had been seriously injured in a road accident. Grannie had asked why there always seemed to be disasters around Christmastime. Little Max had not understood that. It was a happy time. Families gathered for fun and presents. Everyone loved everyone else. How could there be disasters? Time had changed that innocent belief and, true to Grannie's words, there were often disasters during the so-called festive period. The Boxing Day Tsunami being one of the worst.

The future for the McRitchie children caught up in tragedy this Christmas time was a huge question mark; yet had it not been fraught with uncertainty before? One way or another, Kevin and his sisters had surely been on course for family disaster.

Driving past the tall, decorated tree weighted with snow, that was floodlit at night, Max's mood grew even bleaker. There had been a tree in the hotel restaurant last night, and his yuletide optimism had unexpectedly returned. Beautifully decked fir, huge log fire, happy people wherever he looked, love and laughter. The warmth, the wine, the invitation in Livya's smile and eyes banished all those barren Christmases following the death of his mother. It had not mattered that the hotel room was not large and luxurious. He had seen only her slender body as he had started to remove her clothes.

Then the intrusive ringing from his mobile. Tom had not known of his plans for the night, but multiple violence demanded his presence, no matter what. The shocking news had shattered his romantic overture instantly. Livya had understood; she knew about duty. She had empathized, done her utmost to make it easy for him, but it had been deeply galling. This one night to secure what he badly wanted, and fate had taken it from him.

The next few days, at least, would be devoted to garnering evidence to support the belief that Mavis McRitchie had attacked her family while the balance of her mind was disturbed. They must also urgently continue to seek a solution to Tony Clegg's murder before there was another.

Against all that, how could he hope to make headway with the woman who had allowed him to glimpse a revival of happiness? In truth, after this morning's conversation he was unsure how things stood between them; was unsure what she expected from him. An assured, 'Well, these things happen. Another time, perhaps?' Or would the wily chess player want him to make a determined move to keep the game in play?

Deciding on the latter, Max made a sudden left turn to drive to the church hall where Livya would be locked in intellectual battle. He really needed to see her, make her aware of that need.

He had forgotten it was Sunday. From the church across the road came the sound of lusty voices raised in an Advent hymn. All the more poignant in view of last night's tragedy, Max thought as he slid from his car. Mindful of the rule of silence, he entered more cautiously than the last time, after switching off his mobile. The scene was much as it had been before: two players concentrating on the chess board, surrounded by intent spectators. Despite Max's care, the squeak of the swing doors sounded offensive in the near reverent quietness. Heads turned.

Holding up a hand in apology, he tiptoed to join the aficionados who would understand from the position of the pieces in whose favour the game was going. The black and red figures meant nothing to Max, but they unfortunately reminded him of the ones lying alongside Tony Clegg's curled body coated with snow. That image swiftly vanished when Livya glanced up and smiled at him. It was no casual smile. It said: I hoped you'd come.

He smiled back, holding up crossed fingers, then her attention returned to the table. But he felt his inner chill begin to melt. Tapping his neighbour on the shoulder and indicating with his head that they should retire a few yards, he then asked in a whisper who was winning. A silly question, apparently, because at this level of skill a game was not won until the final clever twist.

Max left the silent hall, careful to minimize the squeak of the door as it closed behind him. After the electric lighting he found the bright glare of snow harsh on his eyes. The road was now filled with people spilling from the church, wrapped warmly against the bitter wind that was keeping the temperature only a few degrees above what it had been all night.

The Padre spotted Max and crossed to him, leaving his wife chatting to those who liked to make their piety obvious. 'I've just heard about the McRitchie family,' Justin Robinson said with urgency. 'Can I do anything for them if I go now to the hospital? What's the situation? I understand Corporal McRitchie died in the ambulance.'

'Yes, he did,' Max said, plunging back to grim reality. 'Mavis and the two girls are in deep shock, so I imagine they're mostly in need of medical help for now. The hospital priest will be able to give you a better account of their spiritual needs than I can.'

Robinson wagged his head. 'Terrible! Terrible! An entire family afflicted again. We tried our best to give comfort to the Cleggs, but the pain is too raw for them to accept sympathetic support just yet. Now this! Estelle and I have been bombarded with the concerns of our congregation. Have you *no* idea who is killing these people?'

'What happened last night is a separate issue. It's no indication that we have a deranged killer on the base. That's all I can say on the subject, I'm afraid, but please do all you can to spread reassurance. The last thing we want is a state of panic prevailing.'

'Of course, of course.' He glanced back at the church. 'My wife is very good at allaying fears. She taught psychology for some years before our marriage; understands the human mind and emotions well.' He smiled. 'The perfect partner for a Holy Joe like me.'

And someone who has unshakeable faith in the repentance of sinners, thought Max as he returned to his car and drove around the perimeter road to his intended destination.

The woman who came to the door was breathtakingly beautiful in Latin fashion. She looked questioningly at the stranger in civilian clothes. Max introduced himself, apologized for disturbing them on Sunday, and asked to speak to her husband. She invited him in with more grace of manner than her marriage partner, and led him along the hall saying Charlie was putting up the tree with the doubtful help of their children. She halted momentarily in the open doorway and silently watched the family scene with Max beside her.

Charles Clarkson was stringing lights around a tree in a corner of the large sitting-room, watched by four children surrounded by boxes and boxes of baubles. A delicious aroma of roast pork filtered from the kitchen, where Mrs Clarkson had presumably been doing her wifely duty until answering Max's ring.

The two teenage girls, along with James and Daniel, had glowing cheeks and sparkling eyes as they anticipated dressing the tree in red and gold splendour. The oldest sibling, a slim and lovely dark-haired girl of about sixteen, aired her past experience of this occupation.

'How much d'you bet me the lights won't work now they're on the tree, Dad?'

He climbed down the stepladder, saying, 'It'll be different this year.'

A cheer rose only to become a groan as the lights flashed on, then died. Mrs Clarkson stepped into the room to say, 'I knew it wouldn't be different this year, darling, so I bought a new set. It's in the cupboard under the stairs. Captain Rydal would like a word with you, Charlie. Why don't you use the office while we put the new lights on the tree?'

Clarkson's expression hardened as he spotted Max. 'Thought you'd turn up sooner or later. That affair last night, I suppose?'

The children all gazed at Max with interest. James and Daniel smiled. The adolescent girls gave him an optical once over. How different from the McRitchie home with its obsessive relationships. How attractive. How beckoning. The family Christmas of his childhood. The doctor was a man much blessed.

The wishful moment passed as they walked to the small room Clarkson used as an office, with shelves of medical books, wire trays filled with forms and information sheets, a computer, printer and Dictaphone. In short, an extension of his surgery.

Clarkson wasted no time. 'I contacted the hospital this morning to confirm that Greg was DOA. Shona is right now undergoing facial surgery. Julie is dangerously traumatized. Mavis is—'

'Riding out a flash of insanity,' Max interceded forcefully. 'You considered her behaviour nothing more than the kind of extravagance common to most women now and again.'

'That was a medical assessment, not one made by a detective looking for a solution to a baffling pair of crimes. It was the correct diagnosis *at that time*.'

Max fought to keep his temper under control. 'So what is your medical assessment of the theory that Mavis cut up her daughter and stabbed her husband?'

'That theory can only be assessed by studying forensic evidence,' Clarkson replied, steely-eyed.

Equally steely-eyed, Max said, 'I'm asking if, in your medical opinion, the woman you claimed was merely behaving extravagantly *could* have attacked her family last night.'

Clarkson studied him silently for a moment. 'This is not the same killer as the one who attacked young Clegg. That's what you're hoping to prove?'

'I'm hoping to prove this was murder while the balance of her mind was disturbed. That will take a great deal of time. All I want from you now is your opinion on that being a possibility.'

'Yes, it's a *possibility*. I'm not prepared to go

further than that.' They faced each other aggressively for several moments, then Clarkson sighed and perched on his desk in less confrontational manner. 'I should have thought you'd know this fact by now. People under stress either bottle it up and act a part, or they behave extravagantly. Maybe even eccentrically. That can continue until the cause of the stress is resolved, no matter how long it takes. Conversely, something minor suddenly makes the burden unbearable and they snap. A doctor can't foresee the future. All he can do is treat the condition he's faced with.

'For instance: a young mother with a new baby and a truculent toddler tries to cope alone while her man is in a war zone. The kids sense her distress and play up. She comes to me for help. I give her a mild sleeping-draught for the baby who keeps her awake most nights, and advise her to organize some help for one or two mornings each week until her husband gets back. A week later a saucepan of milk boils over, the toddler puts red felt-tip scribble on the wall, her husband fails to telephone at the usual time. Any of those things – or all of them together – tip the balance. The baby is wailing so she silences it with a pillow over its face. Or she simply drops it from the window.'

He looked at Max with narrowed eyes. 'A doctor has no more control over saucepans that boil over, or toddlers who scribble on the wall than you had over whoever clouted Kevin then went on to kill the bandsman.'

Thoughts of an exploding saucepan in the McRitchie kitchen kept Max silent. Had milk boiling over to sully Mavis's immaculate cooker last night been the trigger to violence?

Clarkson straightened and opened the office door. 'You'll get the truth from the children when a psychiatrist skilfully coaxes them to speak about what happened last night. The McRitchie tragedy *has* happened. Over. I'd concentrate on your unresolved case of the head-basher, because he could do it again.' He held out an arm in invitation to precede him from the room. 'How about a cup of coffee with a dash of something to keep out the cold before you go?'

It was typical of this man to change moods so swiftly. Max caught himself accepting because the pull of that family togetherness was irresistible. The coffee was served along with the inevitable mince pie, and the lights twinkled on the tree as it grew more and more splendidly gilded. Watching and enjoying the brothers' and sisters' fond rivalry in that room where family relationships were so successfully balanced, Max knew that this was what he wanted for himself. No more Christmases spent alone.

Phil Piercey had spoken to Corporal Samms, who had attended last night's disco incognito. A man of twenty-four who had a pink, chubby face that made him resemble a senior schoolboy; a tough, enthusiastic policeman who had once been refused alcohol because he was thought to be underage. He had suffered untold ribbing from his colleagues over that incident. Samms had confirmed to Piercey that Sapper Rowe had shown no undue interest in adolescent boys, much less taken one to the unlit areas of the Recreation Centre.

'He's top notch at controlling sound and lighting. Did some special effects for the song contests. Best male and female.' He had chuckled then. 'Gave the thing a bit of a boost, thank God. Some of the kids hadn't a clue. Most of 'em didn't have a voice.' As Piercey had made to leave, Samms said, 'Tell you what, though. Rowe looked more than interested in that redhead lieutenant helping Mr Fellowes pick the winners. She's a real looker, mind, but I'd say there's something going on between those two that needs looking at.'

So Piercey was doing just that on this Sunday morning. Like the rest of the team, he found it hard to accept that a good-looking soldier and a gorgeous young officer had nothing better to do on Saturdays during the run up to Christmas than help out at kids' parties. They were both possible suspects for the attack on Kevin McRitchie, which made them prime subjects for ongoing observation.

Having checked that Rowe was in his quarters, Piercey parked within sight of the accommodation block and settled to watch. He had little doubt the Sapper had plans for today.

Having munched two Mars bars and half a packet of custard creams, Piercey was thinking he might soon need to go for a pee when Rowe came from the three-storey building dressed smartly in dark jeans and a sheepskin three-quarter coat. Telling his bladder to wait a while, Piercey discreetly followed his target from the base and, surprisingly, away from town. Well, well! So where was the lad heading? Not to visit the bird his mates reckoned he had in town.

The road was reasonably busy, so there was little chance of Rowe sensing he was being tailed. Passing through a large village where children were playing in the snow while their parents stood chatting outside the church entrance, Rowe then turned right on to a narrow lane compacted with ice that looked to be leading to a forest area.

Piercey grew very interested now. Could Rowe possibly be taking him to the answer to why Kevin and Clegg had been attacked? Had the two victims been involved with Alan Rowe in drug distribution, after all? Was Rowe going to meet the boss man at some isolated forest cabin? Could this rendezvous be a meeting place for a paedophile and young victims? Piercey's interest deepened into excitement. He had been instrumental in wrapping up their last murder case back in April. Was he about to do the same again?

Because there was now no other traffic along this country lane, Piercey dropped back and only saw Rowe's car when the many bends allowed him a glimpse of his target through the trees some way ahead. The solid layer of compressed snow on the road surface demanded considerable concentration to negotiate the bends, so Piercey was taken by surprise on rounding one of them to find Rowe had pulled up outside a small inn that looked like a former hunting-lodge.

Resisting the reflex impulse to stop, Piercey drove on round the next bend and eased into a small clearing, praying he would not sink in softer snow. His prayer was answered. Climbing from behind the wheel he was engulfed by utter, utter silence and a breathless stillness that enchanted even this tough, cynical policeman. Unable to resist standing for a minute or two in this scene of natural beauty, his breath frosting in the air, his cheeks tingling, Piercey pushed to the back of his mind all thoughts of murder, domestic violence, paedophilia and drug abuse. This was pure, this was clean, this was innocent.

It did not last. He had a job to do. Coarse dark hairs with a natural kink had been found at both scenes of attack, and this man he had followed had dark curling hair. He was their strongest suspect. Grabbing his binoculars, he crunched over the frozen white layer between the trees until he had a clear view of the inn. Then he saw that one of the three other vehicles on the forecourt was owned by Lucy Farmer. Excitement mounted. She was definitely in on Rowe's criminal activity, and he had them red handed.

Finding good cover that gave him a full view of the inn's facade, he scanned it through the magnifying lenses. He spotted the pair in an upstairs room. There did not appear to be a third person there, so their contact had not yet arrived. Good. He would be able to get a good view of him and his vehicle registration when he turned up.

Even as he relished that, the entire concept collapsed before his eyes. The upper-class lieutenant and the down-to-earth soldier went into a frenzied clinch that became an equally frenzied race to pull each other's clothes off.

Twelve

They said little during the slow drive; slow because traffic heading to town was heavy. Shopping, skating, eating; all these drew crowds bent on Christmas fun. After all his years in this job, Tom still experienced that sense of disbelief that life was continuing normally all around him while he was dealing with tragedy. This morning it was especially poignant. If, as they strongly suspected, Mavis McRitchie's mind had snapped causing her to attack her family, three children were now virtually orphaned. Their grandparents would have to be informed, although they would be hospitalized for some time yet.

There were also two parents facing the turkey, tinsel and twinkling lights season with the funeral of their talented only son to arrange. Tom could not forget Norman Clegg's bitter expression as he demanded that some 'real' policemen take over the task of finding his son's killer. They still had no leads apart from two matching hairs from the scenes of the attacks on Kevin and Tony Clegg. The Cleggs' unbridled grief and the McRitchies' unconcern both weighed heavily on Tom as Heather Johnson drove towards the hospital alongside merrymaking Germans. They could do nothing yet to ease the one, and they had failed to understand the full import of the other.

He had returned home in the early hours and settled on the settee so as not to disturb Nora, but he had only half-dozed. When he had dropped off, the scene he had just witnessed became his own home with his family massacred. A desperate nightmare. Curiously, he was so hungry he had eaten an enormous breakfast with a silent Nora facing him across the table. She knew him in all his moods and made no attempt to break through his bleakness. Gratitude to her, and for his loving family, unharmed and strangers to the undercurrents that had brought tragedy last night, had led him to enclose Nora in a strong embrace and hold her for a long while before he left the house where his three daughters were still sleeping off the pleasures of the Graumanns' hospitality. He had so much to be thankful for.

He turned now to the young woman beside him at the wheel. 'Looking forward to being at home for Christmas? Will your brothers be there?'

Heather smiled. 'They'd better be, or my mother will want to know why. Keith – he's Kevin's age – is totally caught up in the restoration of an old World War Two aeroplane. Spends every free moment there, to the detriment of homework and study. Dad has a sneaking interest in it, too, so Mum has to put her foot down sometimes. I'm the only other female in the family. I disappointed her deeply by taking up what she regards as a masculine profession.' She flashed Tom a glance. 'I think she hoped I'd work as a florist, or in a perfumery. I understand. Surrounded by dirty shirts, football boots and model aircraft she longs for another woman to talk to, some pretty things amid all the male clutter.'

'I'd welcome a little male clutter,' Tom murmured reflectively.

'I guess that's what Greg McRitchie wanted, until he realized Kevin wasn't into macho pursuits and pushed the lad out of his life. What's going to happen to him now?'

'It depends on how he takes this news, most probably. He's a minor and will have to go with whichever set of grandparents will have him and his sisters when the medics declare them fit.'

Breaking through the congestion in the town centre, Heather was able to pick up speed for the final five kilometres to the hospital. Swinging on to the autobahn when the lights turned green, she said, 'If I were the welfare worker handling the case, I'd try to split them up. There's mutual dislike between those girls and Kevin. Anyone trying to cope with all three as well as grief for a son, or having to face the truth of a daughter who stabbed her husband to death and cut up her child, would be crushed by the responsibility.'

'And the kids themselves would do better in different households,' said Tom. 'We don't yet know the situations with the grandparents. If there's illness or disability, there'd be no question of putting girls of seven and eight there.'

'Or in a house where the grandfather could not be trusted with them.'

'Out of the frying-pan,' agreed Tom. 'Those poor kids have a lot to overcome before they can start being balanced human beings.'

They fell silent for a while and only spoke again on reaching the hospital. Then Tom asked if she was happy about what she had been asked to do.

She turned to him frankly. 'I'll keep in mind how I'd approach one of my brothers with devastating news, although I won't be breaking it to him. I suppose I'll be there as someone familiar whom he trusts.'

Tom smiled encouragingly. 'You'll get it right, the way you did when you brought him from RAMSCH. The Boss said you were brilliant.'

They walked to the main entrance and Heather asked, 'Do I tackle him about the attack at the party, if I get the chance?'

'Play it by ear,' he advised. 'I'm sure the

psycho will control the meeting. He knows Kevin relates to you quite strongly, so I don't imagine he'll interfere if the boy wants to get things off his chest to you. After all, he's in there for the purpose of delving to the root of his fears. Although those might be replaced by others now.'

They split up inside the building, Tom to check on the girls in intensive care and, more pertinently, on the state of Mavis McRitchie, suspected of murder. Heather took the lift, telling herself to concentrate on the vulnerable, confused boy not her own feelings.

Professor Braun came at a call from the woman at the reception desk, smiled and shook her hand before leading Heather a little way along the corridor. He waved a hand at a chair, then sat at the desk to study her with bright eyes. He was small and neat, with auburn hair that tended to stand up in tufts around his pointed face. He reminded Heather of a red squirrel.

'This is much of a tragedy at this stage,' he declared. 'He runs from his family because he feels there is no love for him there, and now they have all been hurt. There is no father any longer and the mother, she is in deep trauma. His small sisters, also. This news must be given; he must be allowed to see them to know it is the truth we tell. Also, the little girls will be hopeful to see the big brother. One who has not been hurt. One who can look after them now. It will work in two ways, you see.'

Feeling she must reveal it, Heather related what Kevin had told her. 'It might not, sir. Kevin and his sisters dislike each other intensely. Of course, you're the best judge of what he needs right now, but I doubt whether seeing him will comfort those girls or Kevin himself. Possibly do the reverse.'

She went on to tell all they knew about the relationships in that family, in the process giving an explanation of the cat Kevin wanted to see. The medical man listened gravely until Swinga Kat was mentioned. Then he smiled.

'I have such a son, Hedda. Always with the guitar. Perhaps I should bring them together in a little while. And later you can come with the Kat boys, eh? Let us now see Kevin.'

They walked through to a side-room where Kevin was watching television. His face lit up when he saw Heather and he got up eagerly.

'They told me you might come today. Have you brought Johnny, Callum or Malc?'

'It's Sunday,' she said carefully. 'They're doing family things. When term ends next week they'll be along, sure thing.'

'Thanks for coming, anyway.' He silenced the TV and sat on the bed. 'Have you managed to speak to Mr Fellowes about the discos yet?'

Heather glanced at Braun, who gave a slight nod to go ahead. 'He thinks it's a great idea and he'll put it to the committee at the next meeting,' she said, knowing the plan would go no further now.

'Awesome!' he breathed. 'I'll get busy with programming. It's important to strike the right balance. The kids want that.'

This small-framed, gentle boy had come alive in a flash. Heather found it difficult to hide her feelings as she listened to his enthusiasm, and she prayed the Professor would intervene. He did not, so she supposed he had his reasons for letting Kevin emerge from his shell before telling him facts that would put an end to his hopes.

Some minutes later, having calmed down somewhat, the boy confessed with a wry expression that he had not got into too much trouble over running away.

'They said ... well Professor Braun said,' he amended with a shy smile for the psychiatrist, 'that if I gave back all the things I took and wrote notes to everyone saying sorry, it would be OK.' His eyes appealed to Heather. 'I didn't mean any harm. I didn't know what else to do to stop them sending me home. *You* know why I couldn't do that, Heather.'

To her relief, Braun then intervened and she understood what he had been waiting for. Quietly and calmly, the psychiatrist told of an incident at his home in which his father and sister Shona had been badly hurt.

'The surgeon operated on Shona and she is

very slowly getting better. Your mother and Julie are also in this hospital suffering from shock, but they are otherwise unhurt. Kevin, I have to tell you that your father died last night.'

The boy sat as if mesmerized. Heather had seen similar unwillingness to believe tragic news several times during her career, and sat quietly leaving the German to deal with it. He also sat silently waiting for his patient to absorb what he had been told. It seemed an age to Heather before there was any reaction.

'He's really dead?'

'Yes. It's possible for you to see him, if you wish, but perfectly all right if you decide not. I can take you, whenever you ask, to see your mother and sisters. It could be that they do not know you, for now, but that will pass before long.'

Kevin's large eyes looked steadily at Braun. 'I don't want to see any of them.'

The Professor nodded. 'Later, perhaps.'

'No. I hope I never see them again.' His gaze swivelled to fasten on Heather. 'I suppose I'll be sent back to the UK. Can you fix it for me to live with Gran and Grandad Knott? They're fond of me, and he's a wicked piano player. I'll be happy there.'

On leaving the Medical Officer's harmonious household, warmed by the family affection he had witnessed and by the tot of brandy in his coffee, Max was sobered by a message on his mobile from Derek Beeny on duty at Headquarters.

'The Garrison Commander called, sir. Would like you to see him at home for a short meeting at midday.'

It was already eleven thirty. Just time to drive to the Mess, run his shaver over his chin again and spruce up a bit. Max knew why he had been summoned semi-officially. Colonel Trelawney, CO of the Royal Cumberland Rifles had become Garrison Commander four months ago when an outgoing battalion had been replaced by the mechanized regiment in which Greg McRitchie had served, and in whose Officers' Mess Max lived.

Max knew John Trelawney; had encountered him last April when an officer and a sergeant in the RCR had been murdered, and another officer disappeared in suspicious circumstances. SIB had got to the bottom of both cases, but causing the perpetrators to pay for their crimes had been less than satisfactory. It still rankled with Max, but all detectives were familiar with the maxim 'win some lose some'. This time, Trelawney would be personally concerned about Tony Clegg, an RCR bandsman, as well as the McRitchie tragedy.

There were several cars on the flagged forecourt of the large, double-fronted house when Max arrived. A tall, brown-haired boy

293

of around seventeen in well-cut black jeans and a yellow sweater over a black shirt opened the door and smiled a greeting.

'Hallo, sir, I'm Paul Trelawney. Come in. My parents are in the sitting-room with Major and Mrs Colley.'

He led the way, and Max was certain he was following a future Sandhurst cadet with a commission in the Cumberland Rifles just waiting for him. Max was surprised to learn that Garth Colley was here, a man he knew vaguely as the second in command of Greg McRitchie's regiment. Whereas the attack on Kevin had prompted no more than a telephoned enquiry, the murder of a serving soldier during a savage attack on his family in his married quarter was a very serious matter.

In the spacious sitting-room two men stood beside an electric fire with artificial glowing coals set in an ornate fireplace, drinks in hand. Their wives had settled on adjacent chairs facing them, also with drinks. On the padded window-seat was a girl of around fourteen reading a book while idly stroking a ginger cat. Another attractive family Christmas scene, thought Max, catching sight of the decorated tree in an alcove.

John Trelawney turned from his conversation to smile at Max. 'Good morning, Captain Rydal.'

Max returned his greeting in similar vein.

The Garrison Commander did not know him well enough yet to use his first name. Until a week ago 26 Section had been based elsewhere, and Max had had only two official meetings with his host last April.

The wives were introduced to Max. Both were smartly dressed and typical of their breed in that they socialized with ease and charm.

'You've just moved in to the base, I gather,' said Gaynor Trelawney.

'Seven days ago. Seems longer,' replied Max.

'Well, no wonder,' exclaimed Brenda Colley. 'But it must be easier to be on the spot now, rather than make an hour's drive from your old headquarters.'

Max nodded, thinking how well-informed she was. 'A definite advantage, although we've barely settled in yet.'

'There always seem to be disasters and sadness around Christmas,' she observed, echoing Grannie Rydal's words once more.

'By the way, the rapt maiden at the window is our daughter Megan,' said Mrs Trelawney lightly.

The girl glanced up from her book and smiled. 'Hallo. This is Marmaduke. Couldn't call a tom Marmalade – that's the breed he is so we called him the next best thing. Do you like cats?'

Being tactful, Max said, 'I prefer dogs, but Marmaduke looks a very fine animal.'

'He's a wimp,' declared Paul, busily fixing a run of small lights around the walls of the alcove behind the tree. 'Lies there having his belly tickled all day. Has no idea what a mouse is.'

John Trelawney said, 'I think that's our cue to repair to my study, gentlemen.' He looked at Max. 'Whisky, G and T, brandy?'

'Brandy dry would be fine, sir.'

'I wouldn't try the mince pies. Megan made them so they'll be full of cat fur.'

'Paul, behave!' admonished his mother, but she was smiling at Max. 'Do you have children, Captain Rydal?'

Immune by now to that question, Max merely said no.

'With Paul as an example, I expect you're glad,' commented Megan, resuming her reading.

Max followed the two senior men after accepting a cut-glass tumbler filled with his chosen drink. The study was utterly masculine in style and content. Heavy desk with hi-tech equipment and adjustable chair, bookshelves lining two walls with a third covered in regimental photographs and certificates, golf clubs in one corner and in another a fitted cabinet bearing a silver statuette of an old-time rifleman on one knee firing as if in the front rank of a square formation. Around the handsome piece were several silver cups and an engraved presentation shield. The trophies of a successful career.

Trelawney sat by his desk, the other two settled in worn leather armchairs. Despite the casual approach, Max knew there was an official bias to this get-together and prepared to answer some probing questions.

'I'd like you to give Major Colley and myself an appraisal of last night's tragedy,' John Trelawney said in calm tones. 'Early days so far as gathering evidence, of course, but was it another in an ongoing spate of violence that has already claimed the life of one of our most promising musicians?'

Max felt it would serve no purpose to prevaricate, so he put his near-certainty forward. 'During our investigation into the attack on the McRitchie boy we discovered serious behavioural undercurrents in the family, which we would have referred to Welfare when we had evidence of our suspicions.'

'Can you tell us what these undercurrents were?' asked Colley.

Max nodded. 'Corporal McRitchie ran his family like a military platoon. His fondness for his daughters was a mere step away from sexual; his total lack of interest in his son's life and welfare could be translated as abstract abuse. Mavis McRitchie was treated as no more than cook-housekeeper, which led her to seek consolation from her neglected son. If what Kevin told one of my sergeants is true, his mother's attentions had grown unwelcome and unacceptable. Both parents had made life unbearable for him at home, so Kevin absconded from the hospital in the middle of the night because he could not face going back to them.'

Major Colley looked concerned. 'McRitchie was a good soldier, an efficient and reliable NCO, a man I would have expected to rise steadily through the ranks. I knew little of what he was like at home with his family, of course.'

'None of us knows how our men conduct their private lives, until something like this brings facts to our attention,' reasoned John Trelawney. 'So what are you saying, Captain Rydal? That the Corporal's death was the result of domestic violence, unrelated to the murder of Musician Clegg?'

'We believe that's so, sir. Mavis McRitchie had been showing signs of acute stress prior to last night – Major Clarkson will testify to that – and it's my personal belief that she ran amok with a kitchen knife while the balance of her mind was disturbed.'

'And young Clegg?'

'At present, we're linking his murder with the attack on Kevin.'

'You're divorcing the assault on the boy from the violence to his family last night?' exclaimed Colley in disbelief.

'Because there are many similarities between what happened to him and Clegg, it strongly suggests an entirely separate motive behind those attacks. We do have forensic evidence which supports that belief.'

'But no suspect?' asked Trelawney.

'Not yet.'

'But the one took place at a children's party, and the other four days later in the open near the perimeter road!' Colley protested. 'Where's the similarity?'

Max visualized that small body curled beside overturned figures of a queen and a bishop, with snow settling on them all. Into his mind came his conversation with Livya this morning; his feeling that something of significance had been said. *Good luck with the knights and bishops.* Of all the chess pieces, why had she mentioned those two? Because a bishop had featured in Clegg's murder? Perhaps ... but why the knights? A red queen had been beside the dead boy, not a knight.

Max started to feel that tingling sensation that usually preceded clarity after days of impenetrable fog. He recalled Tom describing the scene in the Recreation Centre's toilets. *This pathetic young kid dressed up as a black knight.* They had been following up all the wrong assumptions. It was not music, not drugs, not paedophilia; the missing link was *chess*, and they had a large number of chess fanatics on the base right now!

By sixteen hundred hours all members of the team save Max and Tom had gone home cold, depressed and tired after their disrupted night. No advance could be made on the murder of Greg McRitchie. In-depth questioning of neighbours, and those who had been present at the Badminton Club last night, produced nothing to alter the belief that Mavis McRitchie had been pushed too far and gone berserk with the knife. Neither she nor her daughters were in a condition to be questioned, and this looked set to continue for a considerable time. The grandparents were being informed. More misery at Christmas!

Piercey had reported his discovery at the forest inn, which had raised eyebrows but brought further gloom because a sexual liaison had destroyed the promising theory of criminal collusion between the glamorous lieutenant and the Mr Fixit sapper.

During the briefing Max said nothing of his belief that chess linked Clegg's murder with the attack on Kevin, because he could not yet understand why or how. Yet his guts told him he was right, so he mentioned it to Tom as they also prepared to call it a day. He received a sceptical look in response.

'Think, Tom! Clegg was lying on an outdoor chessboard and killed with one of the giant bishops. You said Kevin was dressed as a black knight. That's another chess piece.'

Tom put down the topcoat he was about to don and propped himself against the nearest desk. 'Bit fanciful even for you, isn't it?'

'Not when you take into account that

300

there's an important chess event taking place here, and that it's a game that breeds very intense emotions.'

'I thought you knew nothing about it.'

Max covered that smoothly. 'I know enough to be aware that the level of play here requires devious minds and a very strong will to win in some of the players. I aroused murderous glares when my mobile rang in the concentrated silence of that hall.'

Tom folded his arms and asked too casually, 'You've been watching some of them?'

'What I'm saying is, that in any kind of top-level contest you'll find those who take competitiveness to extremes. They *have* to be top dog.' He waved a hand at the empty desks vacated by his team. 'Good God, we've just heard them tell us members of the Badminton Club say Greg McRitchie was a bad loser; had to be fully in the limelight.'

Tom nodded. 'In every aspect of his life. OK, suppose we have a chess nut on the base.' He grinned at the pun. 'Wouldn't he, or she because there are a couple of women doing battle with the kings and queens, wouldn't it be more profitable to attack the competition than a couple of random lads?'

'Yes, of course,' Max agreed with a sigh. 'I'm clutching at straws, but it is another link between Kevin and Clegg which is worth following up.'

'Well, we've got nothing else at the moment. Piercey has just put the dampers on

301

the slender possibility that Rowe was our man.'

'Mmm.'

'What are we going to do about that situation?'

Max got to his feet and reached for his coat. 'I'll talk to her on the q.t. We've enough on our plate without making her folly official unless we have to.'

'Stupid woman! With every unattached officer eager to take her on, why risk her career by seducing a squaddie?'

'Between you and me, I'd guess she did it for the excitement of flouting the rules. A bit of rough, as they say.'

They walked together through the darkened incident room, shivering in the damp coldness of a building that was still not adequately heated, and Tom harked back to their earlier discussion.

'When did the chess players arrive here?'

'In ones and twos during last weekend, depending on where they were flying in from.'

Tom held the door open for Max to go through. 'So some were here on Saturday when Kevin was attacked.'

'Must have been.' Max waited while Tom entered the security code. 'The commissioned ones were in the Mess in force by Monday evening.' As they crossed the crisp snow to their cars, Max swore. 'Bugger it! They were all at dinner with me when Clegg was killed.'

'The perfect alibi. So we investigate the rest tomorrow.'

Max halted by the vehicles and glanced across them at the tall tree now floodlit and sparkling, remembering the family scenes he had viewed this morning and wishing he had one of his own to return to.

He turned back to Tom. 'My guts could feel different in the morning, so let's sleep on it.'

'If you say so. They're your guts. Goodnight, sir.'

'Goodnight, Tom. Enjoy your family,' he added hollowly as he slid behind the wheel.

He parked behind the Mess, where welcoming lights spilled out to sheen the iced garden areas adjacent to the building. As he walked to the main entrance, a surprising sense of gladness to be living alongside others partially negated his melancholy mood. The foyer now contained a fir, lit and spangled with gold. Gilded bells hung at intervals on the walls decorated with holly. From the ante-room came the sound of lusty voices singing rude army jargon to the tunes of well-known carols. The subalterns rehearsing for their dubious entertainment next week. In the small annexe where coats and regimental headgear could be hung, a large bunch of mistletoe was suspended. Christmas had officially arrived.

Going up to his room, Max reflected that

this was the nearest to a family scene he would get. A rather large, rowdy family, but he could join or leave them as he wished and there would be no hurt feelings, no post-mortem on his behaviour. There was an envelope on the floor just inside his room. He snatched it up, because it bore just his first name in blue ink, and read the short message.

I'm out of the competition, beaten by a Gunner not long out of nappies! He's brilliant. How about buying me a consolation drink before dinner? In the event of duty making this impossible, a phone call at whatever time will dry my tears!

Amazing how moods could switch so swiftly, how a disastrous day could suddenly glow with promise. He made coffee and arranged his books, CDs and videos of classic war films on the shelves above the desk. If he planned to stay put for a while he should empty the last of his boxes to put in store with the rest. Maybe he could leave the search for other living quarters until the cold weather ended.

In his second-best shirt – he had worn the best one to the hotel last night – and his silver-grey suit with the jazziest tie he possessed, Max headed for the bar. How did he console a prospective lover who had failed to become champion of something he knew and cared little about? A game was just a game in his book. Nothing to get steamed-up about. Yet some of these players did, and one of them could have ... He thrust the thought away.

Livya was already drowning her sorrows in the company of the squadron leader who had sat next to her at the official dinner, and who had been knocked out yesterday, Livya had told him. Max would happily knock him out now, with a punch to the chin. She looked disturbingly attractive in a close-fitting coffee-coloured top and a cream skirt that outlined her thighs as she perched on the high stool.

'You're one ahead of me,' he greeted, tapping her lightly on the shoulder. 'Or maybe two.'

She looked round swiftly and smiled. 'A girl has to seize her opportunities. I wasn't sure you'd be free tonight.' She turned back to the good-looking pilot and slid from the stool. 'Thanks for the drink, Pete. I owe you one.'

Walking beside her to a pair of low seats by a square table, Max said, 'You've just ruined his evening.'

'He's married. Can't wait to hitch a lift home tomorrow to wifey and small son.'

Max gave a wry smile as she sat and asked for another G and T. 'You've punctured my ego. I was congratulating myself on beating the opposition.'

She laughed. 'Idiot! I don't play those kind of games. Just chess.'

'Look, sorry about the kid just out of nappies. I thought you had a straight run after the champ flew home unexpectedly.'

'Gunner Kinsey had a straight run, but I think he'd have got there anyway.'

'You don't look like a loser.'

'Oh, I never rail against being beaten by a superior player.' She looked at him enquiringly because he was making no attempt to get the drinks. 'Is something wrong?'

He smiled. 'Absolutely not. I'm just making a slow and delicious study of you before my bloody mobile rings.'

Thirteen

Tom walked downstairs leaving the usual chaos on the upper floor. Only two more mornings before the start of the school holiday. Then he and Nora would have quiet breakfasts together while the girls slumbered on. In the alcove beneath stairs hung the completed evening gown, with diamanté replacing the frill that gave it an overally look. Covered with plastic, it could easily be mistaken for a designer creation. Nora was a skilled needlewoman.

Lingering by the alcove, Tom pictured his collection of model steam engines set up in there. Something he promised he would do during the brief Christmas break. It would be good to take them from their boxes and put them back on display, but first he must put up the glass-fronted cabinet and fix suitable lighting to show them to greatest advantage.

The porridge, toast and boiled eggs were eaten, then Tom received an extravagant hug from Beth, a kiss in the direction of his right ear from Gina and a mere flutter of fingers on his head from Maggie before they departed, still chattering.

Nora poured more coffee and pushed a cup across to him. 'Haven't you anything better to do today than sit at home making eyes at your wife?'

'There isn't anything better to do than that.'

'What about last night?'

'Ah, that was in a class of its own.' He drank some coffee. 'Speaking of which, I think Max has ideas in that direction.'

'Good. Who is she?'

'Don't know for certain, but he seems surprisingly preoccupied with chess.'

'Chess!'

'There are two women involved in the inter-services championship on the go here. One's an RAF sergeant, the other's a captain in Intelligence staying in the same Mess. For a man who proclaimed when they arrived that he had no interest in board games, and couldn't understand how players could get so uptight about it, he's apparently been going to the church hall as an observer.'

'Well, well! When a man is prepared to change his attitude to influence a woman it could be serious. But she'll leave when the championship ends, and he'll be back to square one. Doesn't sound too hopeful.'

'Depends on how *she* feels, I suppose.' He drank some more of his coffee. 'He's now come up with the idea that chess features in young Clegg's murder.'

'It does,' she said, surprised by his sceptical tone. 'You found him on that outdoor board surrounded by the pieces.'

'Max now thinks that points to one of the visiting players having murdered the poor lad.'

'But aren't you linking—?'

'Yes, and we're pretty certain we're right about that, but Max has latched on to the fact that Kevin was wearing the fancy-dress outfit of a black knight. Something we haven't thought of any significance before.'

'But it could be.'

'Or it could be pure coincidence. Big snag is that the commissioned competitors were all at dinner with Max when Clegg was killed. If he's still going with that idea this morning, we have to interview the other ranks. My big beef against that is why any-one visiting us to play chess for ten days would attack a schoolboy and a young bandsman they've never met before.'

Nora leaned back in her chair and remind-ed him of a case at the start of the year. 'In the Leo Bekov affair someone who had never met him killed him by proxy. After years of discovering that people commit crimes out of desperation, on an undeniable impulse, in a sudden fit of temper, or for the weirdest of reasons, you now grow cynical? If one of the chess players *is* guilty, you'll find there's a motive.' Her eyes narrowed. 'Are you lounging around here as if you haven't a job to go to because you don't want to pursue that line?'

He deliberately poured himself yet more coffee. 'Max gets these flights of fancy whenever we reach a hiatus in an investigation.'

'And sometimes they lead somewhere.'

'And sometimes they don't.' He stopped stirring his coffee and looked at her frankly. 'To be honest, the McRitchie affair is dogging me; can't shake it off. Think, love! Mavis and Greg love each other enough to marry. A baby boy arrives and completes their happiness. Two years later the rot sets in. Greg is always out doing blokey things with the poor little sod who fails to match up, and Mavis is ignored. Five years into the marriage, when no more sons have turned up to compensate for the failure Greg has now discarded, Mavis is blamed and sent for check-ups. She then produces two girls, and expects forgiveness from him for suspecting her of being infertile. Instead of reviving his love for her, these cute little darlings become his obsession. Mavis turns to Kevin for compensation, but her affection is too intimate and makes him turn against her, too. All the lad wants is to play his music and be loved for what he is.

'Kevin's been beaten up, one kiddie has been scarred for life, the other's certain to be affected by what happened for years to come, Greg is dead and Mavis is out of her mind. All that because they each wanted something they couldn't have. Such tragedy for want of a little selfless love and understanding.'

Nora fiddled with her teaspoon thoughtfully. 'Would it have turned out differently if Kevin had been the macho son Greg wanted, I wonder?'

'I hope the kid himself never wonders that. God knows what'll become of him and those father-fixated girls.' Tom sighed. 'I'm finding it difficult to take at all seriously Max's fairy tale about vengeful chess players, with that disaster so fresh in our minds.'

'But you have no other leads on Clegg's murder, Tom.'

'No. In chess parlance, it's check mate.'

Tom drove past the base Christmas tree in anything but festive mood. At Headquarters the members of the team were collating evidence and writing their reports. The usual convivial atmosphere was lacking. Subdued morning greetings were offered as Tom walked to his office. Once there, he decided he might as well check which of the non-commissioned chess players were on-base in time for the attack on Kevin, but even as he brought up three names on screen he felt the futility of what he was doing. Why would any one of them decide to enter the Recreation Centre, and there cosh a boy dressed as a black knight? He stared at the names and service data of the three. Why then go on to batter to death another lad on an outdoor chessboard? Despite Nora's reminder of the Leo Bekov case, as a theory this was light as thistledown. Which was a pity, because it had its attractions.

His telephone rang. George Maddox was on the line. 'Sorry about this, sir. I've no alternative but to call you. Lance-Corporal Treeves' father is here in a right state. Won't accept the cause of his son's death. Says the lad was fully fit and wouldn't die just like that without any warning. He's claiming we must have beaten him up, and the medical report is a whitewash. I've assured him Treeves wasn't under arrest, simply being escorted back to base after an incident, but he's deaf to reason. Threatens to go to the papers and force an independent inquiry into the death. Would you come over and talk to him?'

Tom went out to his car reluctantly. Treeves' unfortunate demise had been overshadowed by murders and mayhem; had been tagged as case closed. He sat for a moment before starting the engine. If Treeves senior carried out his threat, the facts of his son's alleged criminal involvement in the theft of MoD property would be made public. The allegation would be based on the word of a Turkish girl claiming to be the soldier's girlfriend – something Treeves could neither affirm nor deny – but it would have to be followed up. A can of worms better left sealed would be opened up. It would involve the *Polizei*, a group of illegal Turkish immigrants, and the German couple who found the truck in their driveway. None of it would change the cause of the driver's sudden death, and his family would be further devastated.

Taking out his mobile, Tom called Major Clarkson. The Medical Officer was the best person to explain Sudden Death Syndrome to a distressed parent, although it was still something of a mystery even to the medical world. Recalling Norman Clegg's impassioned threat to put the investigation in the hands of 'real' policemen, Tom knew he had a difficult task ahead if he was to convince Treeves his son's death had occurred naturally. Grief bred aggression.

Turning the ignition key, Tom headed off along the perimeter road understanding why he had been so reluctant to come to work today.

Lucy Farmer looked at first surprised, then delighted when Max walked in to her office. Her smile was openly inviting, and he could not suppress a masculine response to her vivid attraction. It made him all the more angry over her stupidity.

'Max! I thought you had your eye on a certain chess player, but first a little chat beside the toaster at breakfast, and now a *tête à tête* in my lair,' she said teasingly. 'Coffee?'

'No, thanks. I'm here officially. I've told your staff not to disturb us.'

Her green eyes glowed with amused curiosity. 'Don't tell me I'm about to be cautioned before you put the cuffs on me.'

'You're certainly about to be cautioned, but it's no joke, Lieutenant Farmer. I'm only here because SIB has severe demands on its time, at the moment. Two murders, and two savage attacks on minors take priority over behaviour prejudicial to military discipline that should rightly be reported to the culprit's commanding officer.'

Lucy's usually mobile expression sobered, her eyes grew alert as she got to her feet. 'What are you hinting at, Captain Rydal?'

'We have firm evidence that you are conducting a sexual liaison with a member of the rank and file, namely Sapper Alan Rowe.'

'What evidence?' she challenged smartly.

'You were seen undressing each other in a bedroom at the Eichel Inn yesterday morning. You had reserved room twenty-one by phone on Saturday evening, and you paid for it with your credit card. You were also both seen at Hotel Adler in town on Thursday last, where you had booked a room for which you again paid.'

Her beauty was heightened by a faint flush. 'Haven't you anything better to do than spy on people?'

'You were both possible suspects for the attack on Kevin McRitchie. We're detectives.

We have to watch suspects. Sometimes we uncover things we're not actually investigating, and sometimes we wish we hadn't. You have everything going for you. Why, for God's sake, treat it so lightly?' he demanded with feeling.

She chose not to answer, just shrugged, which made Max even angrier. 'You appear to be the dominant influence in the liaison and, however willingly Rowe embarked on the affair, in military law you, as a commissioned officer, will be counted the guilty party. It's your responsibility to set a good example—'

'All right, cut out the moralizing,' she said. 'I know all about not abusing my rank, and not corrupting members of the rank and file. He knew what he was doing.'

'I'm sure he did, and he probably knew who would pay the greater price if it came to light.' Max paused for a moment, looking her over while he tried to understand her. 'Do you really care for him?'

'Christ, no!' she said with a dismissive wave of her hand. 'It was just a fling.'

That did it for Max. 'If I send in an official report there'll be an inquiry. You'll be suspended from duty pending the verdict, which most likely will result in an immediate posting away from Germany and a very black mark being entered on your record. It will be there throughout your years of service.

'And here's some moralizing you'll bloody well hear, whether you like it or not,' he went on. 'It costs the MoD a large sum to train an officer and it expects a reasonable return for the expenditure. You've been treating your status as a means to your own ends. Living life to the full, flirting with all your male colleagues, exploiting your right to respect from lower ranks. You deserve to be reported. If either of you were married I wouldn't hesitate, but I haven't the time to spare for immature antics like yours when I'm dealing with violent death and distressed, grieving families.' He paused to let that sink in. 'Lieutenant Farmer, unless you apply for an immediate transfer, on any grounds you care to invent, and stay away from Sapper Rowe from this moment on, I *will* make this official. Is that understood?'

Because the reigning inter-services chess champion had been called to the UK on compassionate grounds, players had been given byes that speeded progress towards the final. In addition, the Royal Artillery genius was so much one, his games ended far quicker than the usual drawn-out battles. In consequence, the final was being staged two days early.

When Livya told him at breakfast that morning, Max said he would call in to watch with her for a short while, if he could manage it. Still annoyed over Lucy Farmer's attitude, he worked non-stop on overdue paperwork stopping only for coffee and NAAFI sandwiches brought in by Connie Bush at lunchtime. During that break, he discussed with Tom reports from the Scenes of Crime team which had searched the McRitchie house and garden.

As SIB guessed, there was no evidence of an intruder being present at any time on Saturday. Mavis McRitchie had revealed to Max that her husband forbade visitors to the house for they might carry germs, and her own cleaning was so thorough the search had been completed in a very short time. All they now needed to present a case was confirmation by one or both girls of their mother's violent attack.

'And that'll be it, so far as we're concerned,' said Tom, dropping thick crusts in the waste-bin and wiping his fingers on a paper napkin. 'One of the things I dislike about this work is having to leave the job half done. We find the criminal, tie up the evidence in a neat bundle for the CO to offer a solid case, then walk away.'

Max regarded him questioningly. 'That's our remit as detectives. What else would you like to do?'

'Oh ... I don't know.' He threw the sandwich carton after his discarded crusts with more force than necessary. 'The result of any crime is a broken or altered life. Several lives, occasionally. An entire family, in this instance. Christmas is a kids' time. Kevin and his sisters will never forget this one.'

Knowing how this family man always felt about crimes concerning minors, Max turned the conversation to the threats offered by Norman Clegg and Frank Treeves.

'I'd lay my money on Clegg calming down after the initial raw grief. He might stir things up again if we don't soon get a result, so that's got to be our priority, Tom.' Seeing his steady, cynical gaze, Max added, 'Yes, yes, I know the investigation has ground to a halt, but we've got to progress it one way or another.'

'Piercey and Beeny checked out the three chess players who arrived early. When Kevin was attacked they were all in the games room playing pool. At the time of Clegg's murder they were at the church hall either playing or observing the games. Multiple witnesses in each case.'

'So my guts were completely wrong on that.'

'We've got nothing else.'

'So we'll have to go over what we have got once more. There must be something in the witness statements we've missed. Get everyone checking, then checking again.'

'If you say so, sir, but they've already done that and come up with zilch.'

Irritation bred by Lucy Farmer made Max snap. 'Then Norman Clegg will have to get his "real" policemen on the job. Maybe they will do better.'

They faced each other in silence for a moment before Tom said, 'We haven't entirely exhausted the idea of a chess link. We could be wrong in connecting Kevin's assault with Clegg's murder. That chess board outside the Recreation Centre is available to anyone on the base. I'll start the team checking who uses it regularly, where they were at the vital time, and if they had any kind of personal contact with Clegg.'

Softening his tone, Max nodded. 'Good thinking. Let's concentrate on the murder. In view of what's happened, the assault on Kevin is no longer such a priority. If we do discover a link between the two cases later on, then so be it, but we'll discount it for now. As for Frank Treeves' threat, we must hope Major Clarkson's promise to send a copy of his medical report to the Treeves' UK doctor with a request to give the man all available info on Sudden Death Syndrome will satisfy the anguished parents. Best for everyone.'

An hour later Max left his office and drove to the church hall. For the prestigious final, chairs had been arranged in two tiers to allow spectators a clear view. A considerable number were silently watching a youthful artilleryman pit his guile against an older wing commander. There was more than personal glory at stake; each wanted to win the title for his own service.

Livya was sitting at the end of the second tier. She smiled a greeting when Max tiptoed to join her, having switched off his mobile. His arrival was more successful this time. Only one head turned; that of the man sitting directly below Livya. He frowned, but soon concentrated on the play once more.

With his mouth to her ear, Max asked who was winning. Her look said it all. He mouthed the words, 'Silly question?', and she nodded.

For a little more than thirty minutes Max stood alongside the woman he wanted so much to keep in his life, but it was her nearness rather than the game that held him there. No way could he get excited over something so inactive and, not understanding the rules, the arrangement of the pieces on the board told him nothing. It came as a complete surprise, therefore, when the Gunner moved one of them and the silent watchers were galvanized into excited applause. Livya was plainly thrilled, so Max deduced the RAF had to hand over the title to the army.

He clapped politely while others were cheering and stamping their feet, as visibly excited as if they had watched a ten-round boxing match, or the Olympic butterfly stroke final. The players solemnly shook hands before the cup was presented, then the winner was surrounded by well-wishers, including Livya. Although Max found it all slightly over the top for a board game, he told himself he had better bone up on chess, because it was likely to feature very strongly in his hopes for the future.

Livya eventually crossed to him, her eyes shining with delight. 'Brilliant, brilliant! He's a star.'

'I'll take your word for it.'

They made for the door. 'There's to be a farewell drink session here later, before we all go our separate ways tomorrow.'

'Go *tomorrow*?' he exclaimed hollowly.

'The championship is over. There's no reason for us to stay.'

He was utterly dismayed. 'Isn't there?'

Seeing his expression, she said softly, 'I could leave the party after a token appearance and go somewhere with you to compensate for Saturday night. If you'd like to, that is.'

'I'd like it so much, I'll tell them you can't make it to the chess party.'

She smiled up at him. 'I'm honour bound to attend, but I'll slip away as soon as poss. Shall I book the ticket kiosk, or will you?'

Growing warm again after the brief chill of her prospective departure, Max returned her smile. 'Don't joke, ma'am. It might very well be the ticket kiosk this time.'

Thinking of Lucy Farmer's domination of a relationship, Max added firmly that he would book dinner and a room wherever he could at such short notice. As he said it, he felt the renewed pressure of having to make this one night so good she would want more.

They lingered in the fading afternoon light as people vacating the hall flowed around them. Livya then said, 'I heard that the woman and her little girls are in deep shock and unable to speak. What a tragedy! Is that why you have time to yourself right now?'

Max nodded. 'Bit of a hiatus. It'll start up again as soon as they can be questioned.'

'No home leave for Christmas?'

'Depends. What'll you do?'

'Spend a few days with my parents and various relatives in Dorset. They've a cottage beside a stream. Rather chocolate-boxy, but charming and comfortable. I actually love it there.'

'Sounds just right for a family Christmas,' he commented, thinking how much he would like to be there with her. 'Look, I must put in another hour or two on the paperwork before finishing for the day.'

'Well, I'm glad you played hookey for a while. You might not have realized it, but you witnessed an outstanding victory for a lad who's only before competed in junior league games,' she said as they walked to his car. 'Gunner Kinsey is sure to command international recognition before long, as Ian Luckett would have done, poor kid. He was another world champion in the making. Everyone said so.'

'So what stopped him?' asked Max, half his mind on making a start on phoning around to secure a room for this special night.

'Surely you remember the case. It made huge headlines in the press three years ago.'

The year Susan and our son were killed. 'I was in Cyprus for six months around that time.'

'Ah. It shocked the residents of his home village, of course, but the sleepy little place was inundated by hordes of complete strangers bringing flowers, teddies, toy rabbits, heart-shaped balloons and stuffed, hand-knitted chess pieces, all bearing messages of love and grief for a boy they'd never met or even heard of before his death. It caused Estelle Luckett to have a mental breakdown. Locals said she believed her son was being stolen by people claiming her loss as their own. Understandable, I felt. A year later, the Lucketts divorced, unable to cope with bereavement and the widespread publicity surrounding the killing.'

They halted beside Max's car and Livya said sympathetically, 'Your young bandsman's parents might suffer similarly now. Can't you just imagine what they could find outside their door; stuffed Santas, trumpet-shaped wreaths, toy snowmen and penguins, all labelled with heartfelt love and prayers from people they've never known.'

Max hardly heard her last words, because his mind had fastened on something she said earlier. 'What happened to Ian Luckett?'

She gave a slight frown at the sudden urgency of his tone. 'He was something of a prodigy. Attended a private school where he studied with pupils two years his senior. Chess was his passion; he became junior champion at eleven. A year later, he was set on by three local thugs, dragged into the woods, robbed of his mobile, a Walkman, some cash and a watch given by his parents to celebrate his chess triumph. They then clubbed him around the head with the limb off a tree and ran off. Because his skull was unusually fragile he bled to death before he was discovered by a man walking his dog.'

'Right, thank you.' Max slid behind the wheel and drove away deep in thought, unaware of Livya's puzzlement as she watched his car turn the corner at skidding speed. Her words hung in his mind. *Clubbed him around the head ... Estelle Luckett had a mental breakdown ... believed her son was being stolen by people claiming her loss as their own ... a year later the Lucketts divorced.*

On reaching Headquarters, Max walked directly to his office bent on solitude. This was the wildest theory he had ever had and he needed to rid himself of it before parading it in front of his team. Yet he felt the familiar excitement that heralded revelation.

Without removing his topcoat he sat before his computer and brought up on screen the service record of Padre Justin Robinson.

Fourteen

Ten days before Christmas. Tom stared at his computer screen registering nothing that was on it. So many soldiers were forced to spend this family time away from their loved ones: he was not one of them, yet he felt deeply depressed. The girls were geared up for a round of parties, and it even seemed possible that he would be able to take Nora to the Sergeants' Mess dinner-dance this weekend. That he could not summon up the gladness he should be feeling added to his low spirits.

He remembered the childhood belief that if he did not show enough appreciation of the good things, something nasty would happen as a punishment. God forbid that anything bad should happen to his family ... and therein lay the cause of his mood. Heavy on his mind were thoughts of the McRitchie children, Tony Clegg's bereft family and the angry bewilderment of Treeves' parents. His job involved dealing with the aftermath of unexpected death, but there was an overdose of it at the moment. He yearned for a more upbeat case – restoring a lost child to its parents, tracing an estranged partner. Bringing joy into someone's life.

He glanced at the clock on the wall. Half past six. Time to bring some joy into his own life. Time to go home. The central office was empty apart from Roy Jakes, who was on late duty. The rest of the team were out checking on who used the outdoor chess board on a regular basis. A thankless task, in Tom's view. They would most probably have realized that and gone home. He did not blame them.

He was reaching for his topcoat when he spotted Max crossing purposefully in his direction. Tom's heart sank. What bloody bee was in his bonnet now?

Max burst in and announced tersely, 'We finally have the link. It *is* chess.'

Tom said nothing, just waited with scepticism as he listened to details of the killing of Ian Luckett, three years ago.

'The tragedy caused Mrs Luckett – *Estelle* Luckett – to have a mental breakdown. She and her husband divorced a year later.' Seeing his expression, Max added urgently, 'This isn't a wild theory of mine, Tom. I've spent an hour and a half in my office collecting evidence. As I suspected, Padre Robinson married Estelle Luckett six months ago. I called Jack Fellowes. When pinned down, he wouldn't swear she was in his sight at the time Kevin was attacked at the party. As he originally stated, there was a great deal of activity in preparation for the fancy-dress parade; people in and out of the storeroom to clear away the games equipment, and children rushing around the hall. It was generally agreed that Mrs Padre did bugger-all save smile the whole time. She could have slipped upstairs on Kevin's heels, and hidden in the ladies' toilet when the Clarkson boys turned up. Her descent would have gone unnoticed in the hullabaloo those boys created by crying murder.'

Tom was beginning to see light at the end of the tunnel, but the tunnel was a long one. 'How about Clegg?'

'My call to the Padre connected with an answering machine, but I was luckier with the church organist. He gave me a concise run-down of weekly activities. On Thursday evenings, Estelle Robinson holds a discussion group for teens, main topics being sex, drugs, alcohol and family abuse. Ideal subjects for a teacher of psychology.' Max gave a grim smile. 'Those sessions end at eight, and the route from the church hall to the Padre's house runs past the Recreation Centre.'

Tom gave a long, slow whistle. 'She could have spotted Clegg maybe playing around with the chess pieces, and it set her off.'

Max nodded. 'I had a word with Major Clarkson on the subject of mental breakdowns and their aftermath. Typically, he at first declined to comment on the grounds that he's not an expert. When pushed, he said he understood that in some cases there were retrospective lapses that could induce violent behaviour. He advised me to speak to the psycho in charge of the case, and I then realized he thought we were discussing Mavis McRitchie.'

'Another nutter!' Tom muttered, growing more and more convinced this was a true breakthrough.

'I called the hospital and asked to speak to Professor Braun, but he's not there on Mondays. They wouldn't give me his private address.'

'Ah, he'd surely insist on reading the medical records concerning the breakdown before he'd be in a position to tell us anything, even if he was prepared to ignore medical ethics.'

They were both quiet for a moment or two as they absorbed this new theory, seeking flaws in it. Then Tom said thoughtfully, 'Well, I guess we might have cracked both cases, sir, but I'm buggered if I can see how we'd present a solid case to the Garrison Commander. There's not even forensic proof.'

'Dark hairs with a natural kink found at both crime scenes,' Max reminded him. 'That pointed us in the direction of Alan Rowe, but Estelle Robinson is also a brunette and her curls could be natural rather than salon-induced. We'll now give her car a good going over. The attack on Clegg was so savage, traces of his DNA could have been deposited on the car seat from her clothing. Our first task is to interview the smiling lady.'

Tom's anger smouldered. 'That woman met the Cleggs at the airport, looked after them. She gave them coffee while they talked to the Bandmaster and me, poured out their grief. Christ, she even told Norman Clegg he should understand and forgive his son's killer. And she smiled as she said it!'

'Well, it's my guess we'll find she has no recollection of mounting either of those attacks. A professional appraisal of her medical condition will probably lead to another ruling of manslaughter while the balance of her mind was disturbed.'

'I'll disturb it a hell of a sight more when we get at her,' vowed Tom, grabbing his coat and heading for the door. 'He must have known his wife is dangerously unstable, yet he raved at me to sort it because his parishioners were very alarmed. The *bastard*!'

Max followed him from the still-shambolic new building. 'People with Post Traumatic Stress Disorder, which I guess that woman is suffering from, can behave normally much of the time until something induces a flashback to which their reactions are involuntary. The Padre wasn't with his wife on either occasion, and they've been married only for six months. He probably has no idea she can behave so violently when something triggers memories of her gifted son's tragic murder. *And* its traumatic public aftermath.'

Tom faced Max across the roof of his car, his eyes blazing with anger. 'You're not *sympathizing* with her?'

Max returned the glare calmly. 'I'm professionally analysing a case we are about to bring to a resolution.'

Tom choked back words that would have overridden their tacit friendship and exceeded its permissible limits. He slipped behind the wheel tight-lipped, the image of Clegg's snow-shrouded body vivid in his memory.

They sat with their own thoughts during the short drive across the base. The tall tree was now bright with coloured lights, and there were smaller ones in many windows of the married quarters. It was a fine, cold evening with very little wind. A rash of brilliant stars echoed the artificial points of light on festive trees; frost glittered in the car's headlights. The sound of young voices raised in carols came from the Recreation Centre as they passed, and soldiers laughed and chatted as they walked together around their military home. The season of goodwill was in full swing. Life was continuing normally.

The two detectives remained silent as their boots crunched the snow-covered path leading to the Padre's house, where lights in the entrance hall and a small window to the right of the front door showed that the Robinsons were at home.

Justin answered their knock wearing a thick grey sweater over his dog collar. 'Come in, come in,' he invited, standing aside to let them in. 'I'm just indulging in a hot toddy and several of Estelle's superb mince pies. Can I offer you the same?'

Max remained in the hall beside the small nativity scene. Tom halted beside him, unable to see in the Padre's expression any knowledge of why they were there.

'It's your wife we've come to see,' Max said in official manner. 'We'd like a word with her, please.'

'She's not here, I'm afraid. Can I help?'

'Where is she, sir?' asked Tom, his anger now suppressed by the urgent demands of responsibility.

Justin gave a puzzled frown at Tom's tone. 'She's taken some members of the youth discussion group to the Christmas Market.'

'On her own?' Max demanded sharply.

'I understand they linked up with those competitors in the chess championship who wished to do some shopping before they leave tomorrow. I saw them off in one of the buses twenty minutes ago. Is there something wrong?' He received no reply, because his visitors were already starting down the path towards their car.

Tom raced along the perimeter road towards the main gate, conscious of the extreme tension of his passenger who was jabbing numbers on his mobile phone. One by one, Max contacted their team and told them to head into town. There was no doubting his apprehension. The clipped tone and the urgency of his commands told Tom his boss had real fear of a further tragedy.

Outside the base the roads were busy: late commuters returning home and the usual crowds flocking to the colourful, noisy night market. Tom had to reduce speed but overtook whenever he dared.

'It's unlikely to happen there,' he remarked quietly, keeping his eyes on the traffic ahead. 'Kevin and Clegg were on their own, isolated.'

'We don't know it'll always be that way. Can't you pass this line of dawdlers?' Max demanded tersely.

'I'm not familiar with any diversions as yet, sir.' Tom swerved back in line as a massive truck hurtled towards them, and he attempted further reasoning. 'The accent in the market is on St Niklaus, Krampas and nutcracker soldiers. No black knights or red queens there to spark a flashback.'

'For God's sake, man, she's with the chess competitors and the winner was a brilliant nineteen-year-old male reminiscent of her murdered son! *Now* will you force a way through this hold-up?'

German traffic police were controlling the flow in the vicinity of the huge parkland area covered with stalls. Max flashed his identification and they were waved through to the approach road where normal parking was presently forbidden. With much use of the horn, Tom blasted their way forward until the solid mass of pedestrians ahead refused to part. They had to abandon the car, wishing they were wearing uniform and driving an official vehicle with siren and flashing lights. Not that it would have made much difference. People filled the narrow way from hedge to hedge, leaving no room to step aside.

The dry, clear weather had brought shoppers in droves tonight. The park housing the market was extensive, so there were numerous paths between the rows of illuminated stalls, each aisle filled with a moving mass of warmly clad men, women and children. The trees in the park were hung with coloured lights or electric decorations, and festive music blasted from loudspeakers.

Having fought their way to the park entrance, Max and Tom edged into a small unoccupied triangle of ground behind one of the wrought-iron gates to plan their strategy. Above the relentless piped music they agreed to move out to the furthest aisles and work inwards towards each other, maintaining contact on their phones. As members of the team arrived they would be directed to work inwards from the other two directions, thus forming a slowly enclosing square.

'If all goes well we'll find her simply enjoying the outing, and escort her from the park
without fuss,' said Max. 'Whoever spots her
first calls the other, then any members of the
team who have arrived. They'll be directed
to home in on the nearest adjacent aisles to
block any exit, and to guard these gates that
are the only means of leaving the park.'

Tom's eyes narrowed. 'She can't make a
run for it, in the accepted sense.'

'But it'll be hellish easy for her to evade us
for hours in this mob.'

'To be honest, sir, I think your fears are
groundless. If chess is what prompts the
desire to kill, she would surely have attacked
that young gunner before now. The contest
took place in the church hall. Virtually her
home ground,' Tom pointed out.

'She never went there; didn't meet any of
the contestants,' Max countered sharply.
'Tonight is the first time, and if someone
mentions Kinsey's former success as junior
champion she's unstable, Tom, therefore
unpredictable. She's also with a group of
teenagers, some of them boys. We *have* to
find her.'

They parted, Tom turning left and Max to
the right, their phones switched on and held
to their ears. It was impossible for Tom to do
more than shuffle at the general pace as he
headed for the western bounds of the park.
He counted ten aisles before trees rose up as
a barrier several feet from high enclosing

railings. In total, at least twenty to search, not counting the crossways linking them at intervals.

Troubled by conflicting and disturbing thoughts, Tom moved purposefully between shoppers eating hot sausages, or crêpes crammed with mouthwatering fillings; past children with balloons on long strings who munched gingerbread men, toasted marshmallows or chocolate-coated fruit on skewers. His eye was caught by a father with two small girls clinging to his hands, reminding him of 'Dadda' McRitchie and his little darlings who would never come here again.

He pushed on, raking the kaleidoscope of rosy faces with a penetrating glance, ready to feign interest in the nearest stall if he should see their quarry. In the next aisle he found the press of people increasing. Local residents had eaten their meal and joined the throng. More would arrive as the evening wore on, making it even more difficult to find a specific person. A needle in a haystack!

As he edged past a static group around a stall selling nutcracker soldiers, carved wood toys and festive masks, he heard Max instructing Piercey and Beeny to search the horizontal linking lanes from east to west, and Connie Bush, who had just arrived with Roy Jakes, to start in the central aisles and work outward to meet himself and Tom. Good. Team members were starting to gather.

Turning right at the park's extremity to enter the next aisle, Tom welcomed the change from a harsh female voice hyping-up a well-known Christmas pop song to the purer sound of children singing more traditional folk tunes over the loudspeakers. The pop song had been too reminiscent of Kevin and Swinga Kat. Another child's hopes down the drain!

'Tom!' said Max's voice in his ear. 'I've caught up with Gunner Kinsey and several of the chess players. All's well. I've told them to stay where they are until we give the word.'

Tom was relieved. 'One problem out of the way. The youngsters of the discussion group are most likely to stick together. Find them and we'll have her.'

'Where are you now?'

'Third aisle. This one's very crowded. Hot punch, chestnuts, potato skins, waffles and frankfurters on sale on both sides. Static groups around each booth. Difficult to progress.'

'Keep vigilant. Food is sure to draw teens.'

'Had the same thought,' Tom replied, pressing his mobile closer to his mouth as he neared a speaker upping the decibels.

Five minutes later, as the human pattern shifted, Tom saw them buying waffles some twenty yards ahead watched by a middle-aged woman wearing a fixed smile.

'Gotcha!' he breathed, then to Max, 'I have her in sight. With the kids. All looks normal.'

A swift telephone interchange with the rest of the team ensured the guarding of those immediate exits from the aisle Tom was in. Fortunately, the seven youngsters with Estelle Robinson took time in choosing the various fillings they wanted, then stood together to embark on waffles overflowing with hot mixtures that tended to drip from the triangular containers. Tom remained at a distance, alongside a stall displaying decorated candles and blown-glass tree ornaments, but keeping watch over the heads of the shifting human stream by standing on a large wood block lying between stalls.

Fully ten minutes passed before Max appeared on the far side of the teenagers. 'I have them in sight on my left, beside a stall hung with glove puppets. Where are you, Tom?'

'Closing head-on.' So saying, Tom stepped from his perch and began to shoulder his way forward, thankful the danger had been averted.

Two girls in the group wore cute furry puppets on their hands and were causing much laughter from their friends, as Tom and Max arrived beside Estelle Robinson. She glanced up at Tom, her smile as bright as ever. Then he saw recognition dawn in her eyes.

'Good evening, ma'am,' he said.

'You're the policeman.' It sounded like an accusation. 'Why are you here? Has something happened?'

'We've come to escort you back to base. Captain Rydal has arranged for our sergeants to see the youngsters safely back to the bus that brought them here. Please come with us. We have a car waiting.'

Piercey and Beeny emerged from a nearby side aisle at that moment, and joined them just as the piped music changed again to a loud Oompah band playing German marches. The two sergeants had to shout above it as they told the boys and girls their visit had been unavoidably curtailed. They then skilfully separated them from the woman who had organized the trip, so that their attention was taken from the velvet-gloved arrest.

Max took Estelle's arm to lead her back to the park gates. Tom fell in beside her and was just able to catch his boss's words above the blast of music.

'Too much noise here. No, your husband is fine, I assure you. I'll explain when we reach the car.'

It would have been near impossible to pull her kicking and screaming through the revellers who all appeared to be flowing in the opposite direction, but she went willingly in the apparent belief that her services as a padre's wife were urgently needed. Tom thanked her unassailable conviction of her own value that made her arrest so easy, yet her calm self-assurance put a flicker of doubt in his mind. Had they got this horribly and disastrously wrong? Could this stolid, smiling, well-intentioned woman really have run amok and killed indiscriminately?

Nearing the gates, they were brought to a standstill by a surge of new arrivals pouring in from the bus stops. Tom grabbed Estelle's other arm and turned sideways to shoulder a way through that inward tide. The piped Oompah music now vied with the drums, horns and bells of street musicians outside the gates. Although Connie Bush and Jakes had been told to make for the exit by their fastest route, Tom was glad to see Heather Johnson and Staff Melly climbing from an official police Land Rover. They needed another woman in addition to a third man in the vehicle for the return journey.

It grew even more clamorous as they passed through the gates and neared the medieval-style band accompanying students collecting money for charity. The thump of drums and blasts on antique horns were deafening, so Tom loosed his hold on the bewildered woman's arm to indicate in sign language that Heather and Pete Melly should go to his car twenty-five yards behind the Land Rover.

At that moment, one of the students shaking collection boxes came towards them, arm outstretched for a contribution. On stilts, wearing a gaudy crown and dressed like a Teutonic king, he stood eight feet tall before them, rattling the money in his box as an inducement to add to it.

Tom was vaguely conscious of a curious moaning sound beneath the general din as Estelle Robinson broke from Max's hold and lunged at the carnival figure. During the next arrested moments, Tom saw her grab up a traffic cone to swing at the royal figure looming over her. The student's legs buckled and he fell backwards as Tom instinctively moved to restrain the maddened woman.

He was subliminally aware of pounding drums and vibrant brass, of frantic human activity, as she turned on him a smile that had become malicious. He saw her twirl like an athlete preparing to throw the hammer, but he was too close to avoid the blow. The base of the cone smashed into the side of his face then, as he bent forward, it hit the top of his head with the full force of a whirling dervish. The musical cacophony was silenced as the electric Christmas brightness vanished down a dark, endless tunnel.

Fifteen

Four days to go and there was no doubt it would be a white Christmas. The long-range forecast predicted a further heavy snowfall on Christmas Eve. Pretty and festive for those already snugly gathered by the family fireside, but a probable nightmare for unfortunates having to work throughout the Christian festival.

Tom gazed from the window at his girls taking turns to be dragged along on a toboggan by Hans Graumann and his visiting male cousin. Nothing for a paternal hero on his way out to worry about. Maggie was all child in green trousers, padded anorak and jazzy woollen hat, shrieking with laughter as the boys lost their footing and fell in a heap. It brought the impulse to smile, but Tom winced with pain.

A dozen stitches in his left cheek made facial movement difficult. He had been fortunate to escape serious damage to his left eye, although the dark purple swelling circling it gave him a demoniacal look, and it throbbed unpleasantly. They had discharged him from hospital yesterday on condition

341

that he remained under observation from the Medical Officer. That plain-speaking doctor had just left the house having told Nora to alert him, whatever the hour, if his patient became vague, excessively sleepy or his vision blurred. Nora had joked that her husband frequently displayed those symptoms after an hour or two in the Sergeants' Mess. Clarkson had not smiled.

Both Nora and Tom knew the dangers of severe blows to the head. Not having a thin skull, like Kevin McRitchie, the damage was nevertheless bad enough to cause concern about mental impairment. Tests had proved optimistic, but Tom was secretly worried. He had a persistent headache and felt little interest in anything. The experts told him this was quite usual, and it was early days yet. Basic calming medical spiel!

What if some of his millions of brain cells had been destroyed? At worst he could become dysfunctional; at best what his father would call 'fivepence short of a tanner' and his mother 'too slow to catch a cold'. What a prospect!

Installing him in this armchair by the window after breakfast, Nora had put on the small table the boxes containing his model steam engines, which he had had no time yet to unpack. They were still in their boxes. The painkillers Clarkson had given him were beginning to work. The headache was fading, the throbbing around his eye little more than a faint pulsebeat. His lids began to close, then they shot up in fear. He must stay alert, fight off the lethargy that heralded danger. With accelerated heartbeat, Tom stared wide-eyed from the window, defying any suggestion of blurred vision, and saw with perfect clarity Max approaching the front door.

Nora brought him directly to the room. No low-voiced medical report in the hallway that the patient should not hear. It was good to see this boss who was also a good friend. Max had twice visited the hospital, but he had then been warned not to tire or excite Tom. Well, he had been in no state to ask questions, anyway. Now he was, and would.

Nora left with a promise to bring coffee and cake in five minutes. Mince pies were never on offer from his wife. Max settled in the other armchair looking relaxed and happy, a pronounced sparkle in eyes that could look as bleak and cold as the Atlantic. 'You're looking more yourself again, Tom. I bumped into Clarkson just now. He seems satisfied with your progress.' He grinned. 'Knowing how hard it is to please him, I'd say you've nothing to worry about.'

'Only the certainty that I'll be known as Scarface by squaddies from now on,' Tom replied, already feeling more optimistic.

'Better than some epithets they've used, I'd guess. Clarkson also said it's all right to talk shop to you now.'

'Bugger Clarkson! On a need-to-know basis, I'm top of the list.'

'Good news first. Mavis McRitchie's parents are keen to have Kevin to live with them, and they've been positively vetted. Heather Johnson is going on home leave tomorrow and has offered to take him to them. Seems the grandparents live within thirty miles of her family. She's a good soul. Plans to introduce Kevin to her brothers; thinks it'll be good for him to have knowledge of a more normal family group.'

Tom nodded. 'Who says Redcaps are all dyed-in-the-wool bastards?'

'In my opinion there's hope for that boy. He still refuses to see his mother and sisters, so Welfare will have to come up with a separate plan for Shona and Julie once they're released from hospital. Professor Braun says that'll be a long haul and he feels they should be transferred to a trauma clinic in the UK. Same for Mavis, but they'd have to be kept apart. Those girls are terrified of their mother.'

'Have they spoken yet about that night?'

'No ... but they've *drawn* it. You know how child psychologists work, with dolls and pictures. There's no doubt Mavis killed Greg and slashed Shona. We'll never know what precipitated the attacks, but lack of forensic evidence showing the presence of someone else in the house at the time gives us a solid case.'

Nora came in with a tray bearing two mugs, and thick slices of cake topped with icing and halved walnuts. She shook her head in response to Max's appeal to join them.

'Duty calls,' she said with a grin. 'I've had an urgent plea to make a bridal gown for a mechanic's girlfriend. She was promised the loan of one, but she's been let down at the last minute.'

'How long do you have?'

'Three days.' Her grin widened. 'She's a very *large* bride-to-be, so the dress will be more like a satin sack. Straight up and down with lace and sequins at the neck. Won't take me long, and I'll ensure that she'll look gorgeous in his eyes.'

'She's one in a million, Tom,' Max said after Nora departed.

'I know it.' He frowned. 'Mavis could have been much the same to McRitchie, but he was too blinded by self-importance. Has Braun given any hint on her chances of recovery?'

'He says it's too soon to tell, but the courts are unlikely to give her back her girls at any time in the near future, even if she emerges from the traumatized state she's in.' He munched his cake with enjoyment, then said, 'McRitchie's body was flown home yesterday. His people want to bury him with his younger brother who was killed on his motor bike. More tragedy at Christmastime!'

Tom left his cake on the plate. Now he was hearing news of vital interest he wanted the full quota. 'Have Clegg's parents been told we know who killed him?'

'Someone from Army Welfare will call to explain once we've consolidated all the data. It'll be a few weeks yet, Tom. Medical evidence will be essential to our case, of course, but we now have DNA samples from Estelle's car that match Clegg's, and the dark hairs found at both crime scenes are indisputably hers.'

Tom stared into his coffee mug. 'It's awesome how a personality can change in an instant. She accompanied us so calmly I was beginning to doubt our reasoning, believe it or not.'

'It all added up,' Max pointed out quietly. 'I'm sorry you figured so drastically in gaining unshakeable evidence of her guilt, but none of us was ready for the sudden appearance of a king just as we were congratulating ourselves on avoiding further tragedy.' He drank some coffee. 'The Padre is badly broken up. He was apparently deeply fond of her.'

'Didn't he have *any* idea of her instability?'

'He says he knew about the tragedy with her son, and the subsequent public investigation and trial. His wife having recently died from cancer he felt great sympathy for Estelle's loss, particularly after her husband deserted her because he found the publicity was harming his standing as manager of the local bank. Robinson's ecclesiastical approach turned into mutual solace. He's taken compassionate leave and holed up somewhere. The Christmas services and any other church functions will be conducted by his deacon.'

Tom sighed. 'He's a decent sort. The men liked him, as much as they can ever like a padre, because he was one of the lads in his approach. This'll be a heavy test of his faith, I'd guess.'

'Being a military padre must be a test of faith itself. It can't be easy to equate God's goodness and mercy with the sights of a battlefield.' Max got to his feet. 'I'm taking ten days of my accumulated leave, starting tomorrow. Staff Melly will hold the fort. I think we're due a quiet spell, don't you?'

Ah, the cause of the twinkle in his eyes? 'Going home?'

Max nodded. 'They'll be praying for a white Christmas but I'll be glad to get away from one. Take care of yourself, Tom, and do as Nora tells you.'

Loath to see him go, Tom asked, 'Has anything more been heard of Frank Treeves' threat to go to the newspapers with a tale of whitewash over the sudden death of his son?'

'Oh, yes.' Max lingered behind the chair he had vacated. 'Clarkson heard from the Treeves' doctor that the medical explanation

347

has now been accepted, albeit with continuing bewilderment. I can understand that. It's not an easy situation to come to terms with.' He smiled with a hint of mischief. 'I've left the other bit of good news to the last. Klaus Krenkel called me just as I was leaving to come here. They've found our equipment in a disused barn near the border. It looks very much as if the blizzard following the theft caused them to take shelter, then the blocked country lane prevented onward movement for several days. Krenkel reckons they planned to rendezvous with someone able to cross the border easily – too risky for illegals – and the adverse weather also delayed that meeting. When it eventually takes place they'll find men waiting with restraints.'

Tom laughed very painfully. 'Bully for them! That'll save our bacon with the MoD. Next thing you'll tell me is that the heating system in our new headquarters is fully up and running.'

'Don't push your luck, Tom. Merry Christmas.'

Max drove through Dorset country lanes in pale sunshine. England really is a green and pleasant land, he silently agreed, breathing the cool, clean air as his eyes appreciated the gentle rolling curves of distant hills dotted with sheep.

The signpost at yet another crossroads showed him his destination was a mere three miles away. His excitement increased as he turned right and sped between high hedges towards the village. Kingfishers was not difficult to find. On the banks of a lazy river, the large cottage-style house was as she had described it. Chocolate-boxy in the most elegant manner. Low and rambling, with a thatched roof, it must have featured in many photographs taken back home, from New York to Los Angeles.

Right now it looked festive, with a silver and blue tree at one window and a huge holly wreath with red satin bow hanging on the white front door. Several cars were parked on the gravel forecourt bordered by rhododendrons. It was Christmas Eve. Family members must already have arrived.

Max drew up just inside the open gates and took out his mobile. Keying in the digits he had memorized all the way here, he counted the number of rings before a male voice answered. A *young* voice.

'Good morning. I'd like to speak to Livya, please.'

'Who shall I say's calling?'

'One of her army colleagues.'

'OK. She's in the kitchen covered in flour or veg peelings, like the rest of them.'

An irreverent teenager, Max decided, as he heard the now-distant voice call out, 'Liv, one of your brainy admirers on the line.'

Seconds later she was there. 'Hallo. I'm afraid my cheeky nephew didn't give me your name.'

'I didn't tell him.'

'*Max*! Where are you?'

'Come to the door.'

It opened several minutes later. She looked as wonderful as he remembered in tailored grey slacks and a deep pink cashmere sweater, but it was her obvious delight that caught his breath with relief.

'How on earth did you know where to find me?'

He approached with a grin. 'I'm a detective, ma'am.'

Only then did she register the import of his leather gear, high boots and the crash helmet in his left hand. Her eyes widened with disbelief.

'You *haven't*!'

He stood aside to reveal the hired Harley Davidson down by the gates. 'What better and faster way to come? I drew the line at jumping hedges, I'm afraid.'

Her response was all he had hoped for and told him magic Christmases were back in his life.